BROTHERHOOD OF BLADES

BROTHERHOOD OF BLADES

Linda Regan

CRÈME de la CRIME

This first world edition published 2011
in Great Britain and the USA by
Crème de la Crime, an imprint of
SEVERN HOUSE PUBLISHERS LTD of
9–15 High Street, Sutton, Surrey, England, SM1 1DF.
Trade paperback edition first published
in Great Britain and the USA 2012.

British Library Cataloguing in Publication Data

Regan, Linda, 1959-
  Brotherhood of Blades.
  1. Gangs–England–London–Fiction. 2. Police–
  England–London–Fiction. 3. Murder–Investigation–
  Fiction. 4. Suspense fiction.
  I. Title
  823.9'2-dc22

ISBN-13: 978-1-78029-009-6 (cased)
ISBN-13: 978-1-78029-509-1 (trade paper)

All Severn House titles are printed on acid-free paper.

Severn House Publishers support The Forest Stewardship Council [FSC],
the leading international forest certification organisation. All our titles that
are printed on Greenpeace-approved FSC-certified paper carry the FSC logo.

Typeset by Palimpsest Book Production Ltd.,
Falkirk, Stirlingshire, Scotland.
Printed and bound in Great Britain by
MPG Books Ltd., Bodmin, Cornwall.

For my husband Brian – the hero of my true-life book

I was inspired to write this book after a cold, dark early winter evening when a youth opened the passenger door of my car and climbed in beside me wielding a large and very sharp knife. I was taken hostage with my car and had to jump from a moving car to escape. I later found out more about the wanted youth.

I believe there is a positive to every negative in life; in this case it inspired this novel.

As ever I am eternally thankful to all the wonderful police who have given me advice and kept the police work in this novel accurate. Some of you don't want to be named, and so I have decided just to say a massive thank you to the police force in general, who against all odds do a wonderful job, and still make time to answer my endless questions on Met police procedure.

To Severn House for publishing me, and Lynne Patrick for the editing of this book, thank you, I am sincerely grateful.

I am indebted to the wonderfully generous and incredibly talented Zoë Sharp, author of the Charlie Fox series, for sharing her knowledge of guns and giving her advice freely, not to mention all the biscuits, tissues, and accessories she always has to hand when one is at a signing with her.

My super and fabulous friend Dave Headley of Goldsboro Books I thank endlessly, not only for the continued hospitality for my books and launches but for making me laugh so much and being such a special human being.

Finally this book wouldn't have been written without my husband, my true love and soul-mate, because he puts up with so much, and still believes in me.

ONE

J ason Young was nervous. He had grown up on the roughest estate in South London, and was used to carrying weapons like shanks, meat-cleavers, screwdrivers and broken bottles, even firearms. But he was unaccustomed to the taste of bile in the back of his throat.

But then he'd never had so much at stake before.

His brown fingers tapped the reassuring shape of the small knife in the pocket of his khaki combats. The big question was, would he end up using it?

He was now officially on their territory, and he knew better than anyone that rules were rules. He had grown up in the thick of this estate's escalating violence.

He flicked an angry glance towards the other side of the road, where the Brotherhood girls stood on the corner in their stiletto heels and pushed-up cleavages trying to tempt passing motorists. Most of them were addicted to smack, and offered hand-jobs to earn the tenner for their next fix. Was that what Chantelle was doing? Well, he wasn't about to let her end up like those pavement slags. Whatever it took, he was going to get her out of here.

The wind was whipping up and the rain felt like sharp pins against his face. He turned quickly off the road into the alley, the dark alley as they used to call it, in the days when he was a seven-year-old stotter working as a lookout for the Elders. His job then was to give a warning to the dealers in the alley when Feds approached, then move in quickly to hide their gear, all in return for a bag of chips to fill his empty belly.

Things changed a lot in twelve years around here. Now it was Brotherhood of Blades' territory, and he was trespassing. The Brotherhood crew were easily recognized by the BB and blade tattoo on their forearm, a sign that they had served their gang by cutting, shooting or maiming a trespasser. They knew he was out, and had sent word that they were watching out for him. So were their pit bulls, who were always ready for their next meal.

Normally he wouldn't give a monkey's fuck for their threats; he could well look after himself. But things were different now. He had a scholarship to dance school, but it was on condition that he didn't get into any more trouble. Still, he wasn't leaving until he had spoken to Chantelle, and told her about this scholarship that the probation officer had helped him to apply for. It was a chance for a new start, and he wanted her with him, to begin their life again as they had always planned – until her Aunt Haley ruined everything.

He'd reached the end of the alley and was facing the familiar Sparrow block on the Aviary, where he used to live before his gran moved to a nearby estate. Chantelle still lived here on the second floor, with that bitch of an aunt. He could see her flat from where he stood, but no lights were on.

He turned and pressed his back into the wet wooden fence in the corner of the dark alley. He would be safe enough in this corner. It was very dark, and a large bush in front of him provided camouflage. His dark fleece hood covered his head and a lot of his tea-coloured face; with luck he wouldn't be noticed. He'd watch from here, and when he saw lights on in the flat he'd risk walking up there. He'd have to take a chance that Aunt Haley wasn't there. She hated him, and the feeling was mutual. If she hadn't grassed him up to the police for the armed robbery, he and Chantelle would be far away by now, working as dancers. Happy.

The Brotherhood had homed in on Chantelle when he went down, got her into drugs and made her whore for them. She was vulnerable with no one to look out for her, and Stuart Reilly knew it. Just the thought of it made Jason want to stab the fat bastard. Stuart Reilly, Brotherhood leader. Jason took a deep breath to calm his temper. He concentrated on the music in the distance: Marley's soulful voice singing *No Woman No Cry*. He turned his head towards the sound, and noticed the bright orange low-rise flats that had been half built where the children's play area used to be. The council workers had probably started, then refused to go back after a while. Most people did; this estate had the highest crime figures in the whole of South London.

In his day the kids had dug the ground up there and built an underground refuge to hide their own nicked goods and the Elders' drugs. That was how it all started, for him.

The Elders were the older gang members, who gave the kids work as their lookouts. You didn't argue with Elders, not because they carried knives and often guns, but because they had money. If the kids were good lookouts, or stotters, they were promoted to drug couriers; that meant new trainers and flash phones as well as full bellies. If they were good at that, they were allowed to buy and sell their own drugs, and became Youngers, soon to be the next generation of Elders. That was when they started to gain respect in their own right, and respect was what mattered. With it came food, designer gear, and top-of-the-range gadgets.

They were ten or eleven by the time they became Youngers. They had carried weapons, and formed their gang: The Buzzards.

The sound of *No Woman No Cry* sounded real sweet. Then something stirred inside him, and it slowly dawned that the music was coming from the boarded-up flats. Only the estate ruling gang were allowed in those derelicts – which meant he was within a few yards of the Brotherhood crew.

If any Brotherhood recognized him, his life would be over. He'd be stabbed and left to die, or if he defended himself and got away he could get done for carrying, and then he'd lose his scholarship. This scholarship was the only chance he'd ever had and it meant everything to him. But so did Chantelle. The only friend she had on this estate was Luanne, a hooker. Around here the weak went under, and Luanne was a prime example. Well, Stuart Reilly was going to find out that Jason wasn't about to let that happen to Chantelle. He was here to take her away with him.

But he really couldn't afford trouble. His dance scholarship was everything he had ever dreamed of. Chantelle loved to dance too, and he hoped she would be over the moon when he told her.

His love of dancing had started when one of the Elders had rewarded him with a skateboard for hiding a gun during a police raid. He was thrilled with the board; no one had ever given him anything like that. He started hanging around the fried chicken joint with other kids who had skateboards, and they taught him to do tumbles and falls. He had found something he was good at.

Then they took him to their street-dancing class. Chantelle was there; that was where they met. He walked back to the estate with her every week. She was a year older than him, and her brown eyes were like Maltesers. He thought she was beautiful. They talked of their dream of dancing, maybe working on ships, sailing far away from the estate and having a proper life.

They were both virgins when they started out, and it took a couple of years before they began having sex. He had never been happier, although he still did the thieving and the drug-selling to get the money to go to dance classes, and to help his mum pay her dealer and give his gran something.

Then he was caught, red-handed.

He'd stuffed a large amount of drugs up his arse as a raid started, but one of the police sniffer-dogs sussed him, whining and growling and cornering him. He was searched by the Feds, and then taken off to the police FME where he was strip-searched. His reward was a spell in Feltham, closely followed by another when he was caught – by the same sodding dog! – hiding a stash of weapons on another block.

Feltham hardened him. After a third spell in there he upped the stakes to house burglaries, then armed robberies, and worked his way up to become the leader of the most feared gang around South London. The Buzzards.

Aunt Haley banned him from seeing her niece, but he and Chantelle still met secretly, as well as at their street-dancing class. The rest of his time was spent with the Buzzards, and doing the burglaries and robbery. He needed quick money, to get a place for him and Chantelle. And he still had to help his gran.

But then he took another tumble.

He had nicked a car for a getaway after the Buzzards did a post office, and he had his handgun in his waistband. How green was that, he thought. He was lucky it hadn't gone off. It would have blown his baby-making equipment into another century. He wouldn't think of doing anything that stupid now. He wouldn't carry a gun any more, so it wouldn't be an issue. He was given another lump for that and served a couple of years in Wandsworth. He would never admit to anyone how hard that was, or how many nights he'd cried in there, or the times he had tried to hang himself in his cell. He felt so alone. Chantelle stopped visiting, and the Buzzards were gone, either fatally stabbed, shot by rival gangs, or doing time. His mother had died from a dodgy heroin fix. He had no one.

There was the sound of a door slamming shut, and he turned his head in the direction of the derelicts to see people heading down the path. A few of them were involved in a heated shouting match with a woman. He ducked quickly down as a torch shone along the dark path; he slid under the bush, and turned part of his face up at the other side, so he could still see the pathway and the people on it, but only from their feet to their waists. He took a deep breath as one of the men drew nearer; the letters BB were clearly stitched on the side of his jeans.

Jason became still as a statue, hardly even daring to breathe as the group drew nearer the alley, still shouting and cursing at the woman, telling her she was going to be punished. His heart was beating like a trapped bird, and he calmed himself with the thought that he was lucky that they didn't have their pit bulls. Very quietly he pulled his shank from the safety of his pocket, and prayed he wouldn't have to use it.

Then a beam hit the ground just in front of his hiding place.

He watched four pairs of trainers walk, one following the next, to within three feet of him. Despite the bitter cold and biting wind his hand was sweating as he gripped his knife and they stepped towards the alley.

Then the eight trainers walked straight past the end of the alley. They hadn't noticed him, and the torchlight hadn't picked him up. They started to push one another, still embroiled in their heated argument with the brown-skinned female, whose flat black shoes he could now see.

When the woman shouted at the gang he recognized the voice. It was Chantelle's Aunt Haley.

He stood up slowly and crept up to the fence. He was

experienced at moving stealthily, not being heard: a legacy of the house burglaries. He leaned in towards the fence and strained his eyes. First he recognized Stuart 'Yo-Yo' Reilly, leader of the Brotherhood of Blades. Who wouldn't? The fat bastard was at least twenty stone. This was the toerag who had fed Chantelle drugs and put her on the game. Jason had the knife in his hand, and it took all his willpower not to jump out and stick the bastard there and then. With a huge effort, he got a grip on his volcanic temper.

The gang stopped. They were at the back of the Sparrow block, close to the edge. One of them twisted Haley's arms behind her back and pushed her head so her face hit the graffiti-clad brick wall. All four had their backs to Jason and their attention focused on Haley; he felt confident enough to lean toward the edge of the fence. He flicked a glance up at Chantelle's flat. The light was on. He cursed silently. He was trapped; he dared not chance moving.

One of the gang started smacking Haley's head into the brick wall, and she screamed.

'That's just a taster,' Jason heard Reilly tell her. 'You cross the Brotherhood, you pay.'

She was wearing a long black skirt, and her hair, usually plaited, had fallen loose and hung down her back. Jason wasn't so bothered that Haley was getting a slapping, but he was uneasy because it could be to do with Chantelle's drug-taking, maybe her debt to Reilly for the gear she was sniffing. If that was the case, Jason had to get to Chantelle before Reilly did. If Reilly hurt Chantelle, Jason was sure as hell going to use his shank on the fat, evil bastard.

But right now, he was trapped.

Jason heard the rip as someone cut Haley's skirt from her body. That confirmed that the Brotherhood carried razor-sharp knives, which could do serious damage.

Haley started fighting like a cornered wildcat. She was repaid with a heavy kick, which knocked her on to the wet concrete path.

Reilly warned her to get up and shut up. She obeyed.

Jason squeezed his lips together. He hated Haley; he held her responsible for everything that had gone wrong for him and Chantelle. If they gave Haley a slapping, or even shanked her, she probably had it coming; that was what they did to grasses on this estate. But there was more at stake here. Jason didn't want to see what was about to happen, but he knew he was unable to avoid it.

The boy holding the knife pulled his tracksuit bottoms down and his penis sprang free. Jason turned his head away. He heard another tearing sound and a desperate terrified whimper from Haley, and as he turned back her white knickers fell to the ground, leaving her skirt hanging from its waistband and her lower body fully exposed.

The boy mounted her from behind. She screamed out as he forced his penis inside her. Jason lowered his eyes again as the boy put his hand across Haley's mouth and rode her like a rodeo horse.

Jason didn't watch; he just heard the gang's cheers and Haley's muffled cries and pleas. He turned back when it became quiet. Another of the gang had covered her face with the black chiffon scarf she had around her neck, and he was knotting it behind her head. It made her face look like a monster's. She struggled to stop him, but two others held her hands to prevent her resisting. As she tried to protest, she sucked chiffon fabric into her mouth and started to choke.

The boy arched her body back and entered her from the front. Jason couldn't watch.

Within seconds he heard Stuart Reilly tell them to take the scarf off Haley's head. Jason turned back to see what they would do next.

'Get on your knees,' Reilly ordered.

She hesitated, then knelt on the path.

'Suck it,' Reilly said, releasing his large erection and pushing it into her face.

Haley instinctively turned her head away and was rewarded with a punch in the face. She toppled clumsily sideways.

Reilly pulled her up by her hair and pushed his erection into her face again. 'Take my cock in your mouth and suck it, slowly, or I'll cut your fucking eyes out.'

Jason looked away again, but was still forced to listen to the sickening sound of Yo-Yo Reilly getting a blow job. It seemed an age before the perverted bastard shouted out that he was coming.

The woman gagged.

'Say you're sorry.'

Jason turned back to see the woman slumped on all fours, vomiting and crying as she tried to do as she was bidden.

Yo-Yo gave a nod, and one of the others stepped forward, a knife gleaming in his hand. Everything seemed to dissolve into slow motion. The woman looked up, opened her mouth to plead, then screamed out as the knife entered her body. She tumbled back and hit the wall behind her, clutching her stomach. Blood soaked through her fingers and ran over her hand.

The gang scattered, leaving Jason pressed against the fence, staring at Haley who was crying out for help.

He had to make a quick decision. A lot would depend on it.

TWO

Detective Inspector Georgia Johnson tapped the end of a bundle of papers on the wide boardroom table, then turned the pile up and tapped the other end. She carefully pushed the neat bundle into the green file in front of her on the table, then clipped the two poppers to close the folder and keep the papers safe. The words SOUTH LONDON GANGS had been written in large letters across the front of the file with a black marker pen. The same pen was tucked inside the file, clipped to the edge, in case she needed it to alter it. New gangs grew up all the time in this area, and meetings were called to keep everyone up to speed with the gang-related fights, stabbings, and more recently firearm usage. It didn't matter how many of these meetings the police called; Georgia thought they went nowhere. She hated sitting around talking about postcode gangs and drug-related crime; she wanted to get out there and stop it.

But she kept her thoughts to herself. Being a DI in a busy South London station meant many meetings and much paperwork, as well as catching criminals.

Georgia was just thirty, quite young to have climbed to the position of Detective Inspector, and she looked younger than her years. She had started at the bottom as a cadet, and worked her way up through exams and experience, beating many other candidates to each post on her way up. Around here, being a woman no longer held you back in the force. Not only was she a high-ranking female police officer; she was also brown-skinned. Despite the official line on the absence of race or gender discrimination, she knew both still existed among her colleagues, but she was tough enough not to care, and clever enough to use the disadvantage to her advantage. Life had taught her that she couldn't change some things, but she could make them work for her. She never let her vulnerability be seen.

She was as ambitious as she was handsome, and had her sights firmly set on a DCI job. She came from a family of achievers and she wasn't going to let the side down.

Her work clothes were blue jeans that fitted snugly around her slim hips, a clean T-shirt, usually white, and a black leather jacket or coat. She was well educated and from a good family; there were three brothers and one other girl, and she was the youngest. The rest of her family had all gone into medicine. She was born of a white English father and a mother who was half Jamaican and half Indian. Her father, Henry Johnson, was a GP, the head doctor in a local South London practice. Her mother had been a pharmacist, and her brothers were all now consultants at various hospitals. Her sister's career was closest to her own; she had gone into forensic medicine, and worked in a laboratory near Brighton testing new formulas.

From an early age Georgia had wanted to be a physiotherapist, and had worked hard at the science subjects at school with the aim of going on to do a medical degree. But all that had changed one night when she was fifteen. She'd spent the evening with her school friend revising for their exams, and decided to ignore her parents' rule about not walking the streets alone at night. She left with the taxi fare her parents had given her in her pocket, planning to save it towards the pair of shoes she'd seen and dreamed of having. It was only nine o'clock and home was only fifteen-minute walk – if you took the short-cut, across the tree-lined common. It was dark and isolated, but she didn't mind the dark. So she set off to walk, thinking of those shoes.

She had walked briskly, unaware she was being followed, until a strong hand, reeking of stale fried food and tobacco, slid across her face and gripped her mouth. She found herself being dragged backwards, and before she knew it she was behind a large copse of trees, in dark shadow, out of sight of anyone passing on the common.

She kicked out hard as the dragging started, but lost her balance and fell to her knees. The stones and tree roots felt as if her mother's sewing machine was dropping its needle in and out of her knees and shins, and a potato peeler was at work on the rest of her legs. Dirt and grit lodged in her bleeding flesh; it smarted and stung as if a hive of bees had descended on her. On top of that was the agonizing pain as her twisted and dislocated muscles rebelled against the force, and the pressure of the stinking hand crushing her young face made her terrifyingly aware that her life could be hanging by a thread.

Everything happened so quickly. The base of the tree trunk scratched her eye; then came the shock as he ripped her white knickers off and pushed himself into her.

She'd read and talked about sex, but had no experience of it. It felt like a concrete brick being thrust inside her, and it hurt like hell. Almost as bad was the way his knees gripped her bony hips, and the grunting and spitting as he pushed at her.

Mercifully it was over quickly, but the smell of autumn earth, mouldering leaves and animal faeces affected her still. Even now, as the season changed and the first few leaves fell, the memories and the migraines started.

After he had raped her, he told her to stay where she was for at least half an hour; he would be watching, and if she moved he would know, and come back to kill her. He would also kill her, he added, if she told a soul what had happened. She was to say she fell over crossing the common.

She didn't tell: not because she believed he would kill her, but because she thought it was her own fault. She had been told never to walk home alone, and she had disobeyed. Besides, what good would it have done? They would never catch him; she hadn't seen his face, and though she would never forget his gruff, tobacco-roughened voice, unless she heard it again, she would never know her attacker.

From that evening she changed, vowing never to allow herself to be vulnerable again. She lay in bed at night, that voice reverberating around her brain. *If you move before half an hour is up, I'll see, and then I'll have to kill you.* Each night she told herself she had got through another day, and she would keep on surviving.

She hadn't known at first that she was pregnant, and would have to have to face the humiliation of a cheap abortion, which would ruin any chance of having her own child.

Her sister had given her the money. Georgia told her she owed it to someone, after a bet. They both knew it wasn't the truth, but neither ever mentioned it again. Her sister was a student at the time and had her own bank account. Georgia paid her back out of her first pay cheque from the police, and still neither of them mentioned what the loan had paid for.

Georgia never told anyone, nor did she talk about the pain and indignity of the abortion. It was devastating, but giving birth to the child of the foul-smelling monster who raped and abused her was unthinkable. And it was all her own fault for disobeying her parents. She kept the guilt to herself, not only about the termination, but also the way it left her damaged and unable to bear children. But she changed her mind about her career choice.

At fifteen she headed for a career in the police force. She was going to catch criminals and put them where they belonged – behind bars. She no longer went out after dark, but spent her evenings at home studying. She achieved excellent grades in her school exams, then went on to university, where she didn't involve herself much in student life, but left with a first class degree. She was accepted into the Met as a police cadet, and shortly afterwards transferred into CID as a trainee.

She met stiff competition in a department dominated by white males, but she could handle that; it only made her more determined. And she was doing just fine. Her experience that dark night had made her a fighter and a survivor. Now, at nearly thirty-one, she was a detective inspector with her sights set on going much further, proving that everything served as a lesson in life.

She had no steady relationship, just a string of broken ones. The ambition she harboured drove her to work too hard to keep a relationship going, and none of the men she met understood that. The result was a succession of casual encounters when she needed to de-stress; she never let anyone close.

DCI Banham had called this morning's meeting for an update on gang violence, and to share new information they had on gangs. The DCI reminded them that no matter which crew thought they were cleverest, they were going to learn different, because the biggest gang of all was the police, who also had the training. Georgia argued that everyone knew the Brotherhood were responsible for the recent police shooting, but no resident would speak out against them, so the result was that they were getting away with it. DCI Banham told her to be patient; he reminded her about the Buzzards, the last gang that thought they ran the Aviary. Someone had come forward with information on a post office hold-up and the police had rounded up the whole gang, and they were all behind bars. Banham also told her they had an informant on the estate, and it was now just a matter of time. He went on to assure them that the members of the Brotherhood responsible for the shooting of PC Elvin would be brought to court. He told them to concentrate on Stuart Reilly, street name Yo-Yo, a big twenty-stone bloke who ran the gang. Reilly was behind it all, and all the other gang members were merely his puppets. He added that he was bringing in a gang expert from the West End to help.

The Brotherhood terrorized their neighbourhood, and it was important for the residents of South London to see that street crime wouldn't be tolerated and that the police always won.

The meeting was finished. As Georgia headed over to the new coffee machine that made real Starbucks coffee, her mobile burst into a brass band chorus. Her phone was set up so that when *Onward Christian Soldiers* sounded out, it meant the call was urgent: the Hat team, the on-duty murder squad detectives, had been called out to a death, which was suspected or confirmed as murder.

Sergeant Stephanie Green pushed the front door shut with her foot. The home-delivered curry smelled delicious. The kids were out so she didn't have to prepare a meal; instead she had bought a takeaway lamb biriani in the hope that she wouldn't get called out by the Hat team and could enjoy a night in front of the television. Two teenage children and her demanding job as a sergeant in the murder division meant she rarely saw the television. Tonight's three soaps and detective drama didn't appeal, so she had pre-recorded a programme about car maintenance, which she really enjoyed, but rarely got the chance to sit and watch.

She put her curry on a tray, turned up the central heating and drew her hair from her face, securing it at the back in a ponytail with the elastic band from the curry boxes. She had a wide, Germanic face with a rosy complexion, and large, perceptive grey eyes, which needed minimal make-up – just as well, because they hardly ever got any. Her naturally fine shoulder-length fair hair was badly highlighted with thin bronze streaks, and looked as if marmalade peel was woven unevenly through it. She dressed in boyish clothes, often with trendy caps, and people in the department sometimes questioned whether her sexual preferences leaned toward the female of the species. Not for long, though; they soon heard the stories of end-of-investigation piss-ups in the pub, where she got tongues wagging by downing far too many vodka and tonics and snogging the face off any of the male detectives who were up for it. The next day she always said she didn't remember a thing. She knew the men on the team had a nickname for her: Sighs and Thighs. Sighs because of the noise she made during sex, and thighs because hers took up most of the bed. Stephanie didn't care. DI Georgia Johnson liked and trusted her, and always made sure she was on her team.

Stephanie carried the tray through to the armchair in the living room and picked up two cans of non-alcoholic beer. Things were better around here now the kids no longer needed her to taxi them around. Ben hadn't long turned fourteen, but Stephanie didn't worry so much when he went out with sixteen-year-old Lucy because she looked out for him. Ben was a typical boy, going through a rebellious teenage phase. Lucy was the opposite; she was the sensible one, and had plans to join the police force after university.

Stephanie often wished Ben had a father's influence in his life, but their father had been a waste of space when he lived with them. Nor had he done anything for them since he had left; he never even remembered birthdays or sent Christmas cards or gifts. Stephanie had to be both mother and father, and sometimes she felt exhausted.

Tonight they had gone to a party together. She hoped they would come home together, but she suspected Ben might give Lucy the slip. If he did, Lucy would use her inherited detective skills and track him down, so Stephanie could relax. Right now she had the television to herself, a large lamb biriani and two non-alcoholic beers. The diet could start on Monday. There was no one in her life to lose weight for, so why bother? She enjoyed sex, but there were lots of opportunities without a relationship – plenty of chances to socialize in the department, and indeed everywhere else in the station. She knew she had a reputation for being up for it, but she didn't care.

She realized she had let herself go. Being five foot four and eleven stone wasn't good for her job, her sex life or her health, but tonight she wasn't thinking about it. She would watch her car maintenance programme in peace and her lamb biriani was delicious. She was a happy bunny.

Then the phone rang.

Chantelle Gulati was still pretty, although the vibrant eyes that reminded Jason of chocolate Maltesers had dulled recently. Her full, pert mouth was now dry and cracked.

When she was a child it had constantly bubbled with giggles, revealing the narrow gap between her front teeth; these days, her open, child-like face rarely found reason to smile. Her body was still well-toned and muscular, albeit a little skinnier, but she no longer worked at keeping in shape; her dreams of dancing around the world on a cruise ship had faded as a craving for cocaine, and now a taste for a pipe, steadily increased, taking with it her self-respect.

Yo-Yo Reilly had been her friend at first. He had sympathized with her over Jason, confiding that his own mother was in Holloway, so he fully understood the empty pain when that special someone was out of reach. He had told her she was beautiful, that he dreamed of her, and if she ever changed her mind about Jason that he would be waiting. In the meantime he would settle for her friendship.

He gave her a present of an eighth of grass, good stuff, telling her it would help her chill and take the heat out of her day, making the burden of waiting much lighter for her. He showed her how to roll herself a nice thick joint, and even supplied the papers to do it. When she said she wasn't sure, he reminded her it was the same as alcohol but without the calories; no harm, just an escape, to dull the pain and help her sleep at nights while she waited for Jason. She liked that idea.

The joints that followed were presents too, from Yo-Yo, the friend who cared, understood and sympathized. The odd E had gone down well too. Then came the cocaine. Only occasionally, he told her, for special times. It gave her a huge high, but she could handle it. Then he'd introduced her to the joy of a pipe: a little sight of heaven, he promised – and she was hooked. That was six months ago, and now all she thought about was that little sight of heaven. These days they were no longer presents; they came at a very high price. As the need for them accelerated into desperation, her debt soared. Yo-Yo's crew, the Brotherhood, were the sole suppliers around here. No one would dare to tread their patch or undercut their rates. The reputation of the Brotherhood gang had spread across London; other gangs had tried taking them out, but had soon learned better. Anyone who dared to take them on lived, if they were lucky, to regret it. At best they bore a scar in the shape of a spider somewhere on their body; at worst they lay six feet under, a bullet lodged in their brain. No one messed with Yo-Yo Reilly or anything belonging to him. The Brotherhood were his crew, and Chantelle was now his puppet.

Her continued need for the pipe meant she now worked the streets around the estate for Yo-Yo, with her friend Luanne. At first she just screwed Yo-Yo in return for drugs, but then he brought members of the Brotherhood in for some action and she was too scared to refuse. Then he told her he was bored with her, and she had to work to earn her way. That meant going out on the streets with the other girls, and offering herself to passing motorists. When she begged him not to make her he turned nasty and gave her the first of many punches in the face. He'd split her mouth open, and worse, told her she'd get no more drugs until she showed she was grateful. He was doing her a favour, he told her, by showing her a way to make money to pay for her habit. He forced her to apologize and tell him he was right, that he was always right. Then he had made her sink to her knees and beg him to let her whore for him. Whoring was competitive, he explained, and she had to learn to use her assets to their full advantage; then he made her suck him off slowly and meaningfully. He promised to help her get work as long as she paid him a cut; but if she crossed him, he'd really hurt her.

Now she was one of the girls she used to feel sorry for in the old days, when she passed them on her way to dance classes. The days when she was happy and free, and Jason was around. She used to watch those girls as they stood at the kerb, offering their bodies to the cars that crawled the area, and her heart had gone out to them.

She should have seen it coming. Aunt Haley had warned her time and time again: *Keep away from drugs.* Drugs had been her mother's downfall, had led her to an early grave, leaving Chantelle with only strict Aunt Haley to look after her. Jason's mother had gone the same way. That was why he'd always said he'd sell, but never use; and he never had. Yet for her it had all happened before she realized. It seemed like one day she was happy, and the next she was craving a pipe and working the streets to pay for her need. Yo-Yo had assured her that that no harm would come to her because she was one of his girls, and Yo-Yo took good care of his whores – for another fat fee.

But now it had gone one stage further. Chantelle was really worried.

It was Friday night, best night of the week for trade. She would carry on as usual. What else could she do? She was dressed and ready in a red PVC mini-skirt and a black basque with red ribbon threaded through, so her brown breasts and the edge of her nipples were on display. A black leatherette bomber jacket hung over her shoulders. She checked that the tops of her lacy black hold-up stockings were visible below her hemline – always good for trade. The outfit had to be chosen for luring punters, her best friend Luanne had told her, not for comfort. Luanne was experienced; she had been whoring for Yo-Yo for a long time. She only smoked grass, but that cost too, and Luanne had a twelve-year-old sister who needed to be fed and clothed and kept out of trouble. Luanne and her sister Alysha lived on the thirteenth floor of the Sparrow block. They had no mother, only a father who only came home to sleep off his drunkenness, and was, in Luanne's words, just another liability. Luanne was a little older than Chantelle, and had also grown up on the estate. She taught Chantelle how to jump in a car; if it was blow job, which mostly they were, she could be in and out without removing anything if she dressed right. Or if you had to do the full business, and you had knickers tied at either side with ribbon, you just pulled the ribbon free and off came the lacies, straight into your pocket. Afterwards you were out of the car and into the alleyway, wipe yourself clean with the packet of baby wipes you carried in your pocket, and on went the lacies again for the next punter. And on the odd occasion while the punter was smoothing the rubber down his mostly pathetic and withering dick for an up-the-arse job, Luanne had taught her to make a mad dash for it. It filled her with such self-loathing. Mostly you were quicker than the punters and out of the car before they'd even put the rancid thing away. Some tried to catch her, but no one ever succeeded. She had the speed of a cheetah when it counted, and could outrun any of the fat bastards with their smelly cocks. The punters had to pay up front and they deserved to be ripped off. And they were hardly going to report her to the police. What would they say? *Excuse me, officer, I've just been kerb-crawling and the bitch of a whore did a runner after I paid her to let me give her one up the arse!* Yeah, right!

She stood in front of the mirror and let herself think about the time she and Jason lost their virginity to each other. They had fumbled nervously, without much tenderness at first because it was all so clumsy, but there was a connection between them, and it had grown. But that was just a memory now. She'd heard he was out, but what was the point of contacting him? She was so ashamed of what she had become, yet she knew she wouldn't be able to stop.

She stared at her disillusioned face, and picked up the cheap perfume from the ledge. She was about to spray herself with it, to stave off the stink of the men that she had to shag before the night was over, when the doorbell sounded. The perfume shot out of her hand as fear hit her heart. Was that Yo-Yo, demanding money? He held her responsible for Aunt Haley disposing of his stash. His rules were if you lost gear, you paid three times its street value, and that was one hell of a lot of fucking. She'd given him all her earnings two days back, for the debt she owed for her own stuff and the interest on it, so she didn't have any money. That meant she was going to get a beating. The last time Aunt Haley took the drugs she was hiding, and she couldn't pay what he demanded, he had beaten her first with a strap and then with his huge fists. It put her out of action for five days, and for the first two she couldn't see out of either eye.

The urgent ringing was followed by loud banging on the door.

The sound of the shower still running was doing Gran Sals's nerves in. She'd put the tracksuit through the washing machine, but there were still traces of blood on it. She'd scrubbed the marks with the floor brush too, then covered the stains with all the salt she had in the house. No one knew more about removing bloodstains than she did, what with her grandson's track record.

What if she was as nervous as this when the Feds came knocking, as she knew they would? Any crime around the area and Jason would be hauled out, whether or not the lad had been anywhere near the trouble. Tonight was different, though; he was covered in blood when he came in. Christ, that bloody Aviary estate, and that tart of a girlfriend of his! Hadn't she told him over and over to take his opportunity and get out of here? He'd never had a thing in his life, and now the boy had a chance. Over her own dead body would Haley Gulati or that slag Chantelle prevent him taking up this scholarship. She

didn't care, she'd had her life. That was the real reason she
had moved off the Aviary; everyone thought it was because
she was afraid of the Brotherhood, but she laughed out loud
at that; she wasn't afraid of any of them scumbags. She was
Sally Young, and Sally Young ran from no one. She'd moved
to get Jason away from that crime-infested estate, and give
the lad a fresh start when he came out; but he had done it
himself. With a bit of help from his social worker, he had
earned a bloody dancing scholarship. She was so proud of
him, and she would fight tooth and nail to help him make the
most of it.

Her first reaction when he came in earlier, covered in all
that blood, was that he had been stabbed. When she realized
it wasn't his blood, all she felt was relief. She checked his
clothes before washing them; there was no knife there, so
he hadn't been carrying. She asked no questions, just made
him go straight into the shower before the police came
sniffing. She'd tell them they weren't welcome in her house,
and they'd have to get a search warrant if they wanted to
come in. That would buy the boy enough time to get the hell
out of there.

Sals had a reputation for having a mouth on her. She called
a spade a spade and cared nothing for what people thought
of her; that was how she was, and at well over the half-
century mark she wasn't going to change. Besides, she had
the right to say what she thought. She paid her own way
through life, always had done. She'd never drawn the Social,
not like some of the useless, idle buggers on these estates,
and she'd never been in trouble with the police. She'd kept
her elderly parents, taking extra cleaning jobs as the bills
got bigger, and taken care of her daughter through her endless
drug addiction, as well as the illegitimate son the daughter
had brought her.

But Jason had been the pearl in the sea of heartache for
her. All her life she had worked like a slave, hardly daring
to dream of having her own stall in East Lane Market, and
not having to clean other people's stinking lavs and kitchens
for a few measly quid. And Jason had made it happen for

her. It was thanks to him that she now had her own china stall. She knew well enough he'd acquired it with his ill-gotten gains, but the boy had learned better eventually, and paid a hard price, in and out of young offenders' and prison for years.

Each time he'd gone down he had given her money to look after herself, to make sure she was OK while he served his time. Each time she had told him no, she wouldn't accept a market stall paid for by criminal activities. She only took the wad when he swore to her on his mother's spirit that all the thieving and drug-pushing and guns were a thing of the past. And now he had got that scholarship to dancing school she could finally forgive him for all the terrible things he had done. She started her oddment china stall in East Lane Market, and she had never been happier. Now it was his turn to have something.

She gulped down a large mouthful of the scalding tea she had made to calm her nerves, nearly burning the roof of her mouth. The thought passed through her mind that there could be drops of blood somewhere outside, leading to the flat. The police dogs would come sniffing, and if they found blood she'd be arrested as an accessory to whatever they came after Jason for. But she would face that if she had to. Right now Jason had to get out, and her job was to make sure he did. She'd lost his mother before the tiny skeleton of a woman had celebrated her twenty-fifth birthday. It was no wonder he'd turned bad, he'd had it rotten hard as a nipper. Anyway, what could they pin on her, even if there was blood leading to her flat? It didn't mean she'd done anything, and if she said Jason wasn't there and she hadn't seen him for days, what could they do?

The water finally stopped running, and Jason's frightened face poked out of the door. He was wearing only a towel, and his black mass of hair stood away from his head. He had a funny face, but he wasn't a bad lad, not really.

'Get a move on,' she told him. 'Those sirens never stop round here. Get dressed and get out. Make your way up west and stay there. I'll say I've not seen you.'

She pressed a wad of cash into his hands. 'This is from my stall, so it's yours really. You'll need it. I can earn it again.'

Before he had time to answer, she spoke again, her tone urgent. 'Hurry up. I'm packing for market soon and you can't be here tomorrow.'

THREE

No one on the Aviary Estate welcomed the Feds. If the residents themselves weren't connected to crime, they were frightened of Brotherhood repercussions if they were seen talking to them. In the past, police presence around this estate had started riots.

But though the residents spoke to the Feds as little as possible and asked them no questions, curiosity still ran high. As soon as the police descended on the estate, the walkways on each block quickly filled with inquisitive tenants, keen to find out who was being arrested today or if there was any information they could sell on to make a crafty few quid.

The police, in their turn, were as nervous as any other workers who had to enter this estate. But they had to be seen to be fearless; their brief was never to enter the area without full body armour and back-up vans loaded with riot-shields and gas. No one had forgotten the Brixton riots twenty years ago, and no police wanted that again. But they were all fully aware that if anything did erupt, this was the likeliest place.

Over the years officers had been involved in many a melée around here. The most recent shooting, of PC Elvin, wasn't fatal, but it had put the police firmly on their guard. It was believed that a member of the Brotherhood had shot PC Elvin in front of witnesses, but no witness had come forward, leaving the police in no doubt that the residents feared the Brotherhood more than the Feds.

The Brotherhood crew came in all hues, but skin colour aside they were all pretty similar: all violent bullies, all into pit bull dogs, and all with the same tattoo on their forearms in the shape of a knife with the letters BB across it. They wore bandanas over their faces, and identical dark sweatshirts with hoods covering their heads, so no one could ever be clear which of them was the culprit.

Only Stuart 'Yo-Yo' Reilly looked different. It was common

knowledge that Reilly gave the orders and enjoyed watching torture and violence, but he only grubbed his own hands when counting the money their criminal activities acquired.

The police officer who had been shot had lived and made a full recovery, but remembered nothing of the incident. For the moment, a Brotherhood member had got away with attempted murder yet again. But now the police were more determined than ever to bring this gang down. They wanted justice for PC Elvin, and they also wanted to win back the trust and respect that was long gone on this estate, and make it a safe place for the innocent families that lived there.

Tonight that seemed a long way off. A suspected murder had been called in. They arrived on the estate in bullet-proof vests and body armour, with sniffer dogs straining at the leash.

It was now ten-thirty on Friday evening, and kids, some as young as five or six, others perhaps fourteen, were cycling up and down, getting as near to the murder scene as they could.

DS Stephanie Green and DI Georgia Johnson were fully aware that the kids were paid by the older gang members, to keep them informed of what was going on and what the Feds were up to. These kids knew only too well how to play the innocent and get what they wanted.

The area around the back of Sparrow block had been cordoned off, and was guarded by uniformed police. A white tent had been erected to preserve the body, and a full team of forensic officers, dressed from head to toe in blue plastic overalls, fought the rain and wind as they scraped every spot of blood and picked up every loose thread of cotton, cigarette butt and dirt from a shoe-print for yards around the place where the woman had been stabbed to death.

'Stay away from that cordon,' a gangly detective shouted to a small black boy with a running nose and a bicycle too big for his short, thin, grubby legs. The kid was trying to get a closer look before the final peg was hammered into the base of the tent.

'Who's dead, mate?' the boy called.

'That's what we're trying to find out,' came the reply. 'And

I'm not your mate. You can call me Detective Constable Peacock.'

Another cyclist drew up beside the skinny kid: a black girl with chin-length plaited corn-row hair and a pretty face. 'He looks more like a penguin than a peacock,' she giggled. The pair turned their bikes and rode off in another direction.

DS Stephanie and DI Georgia Johnson knew from bitter experience that it was a bad idea to park anywhere near the estate. CID officers' private cars always finished up with scratches down their paintwork. They had parked a few streets away, and were heading for the crime scene on foot. Kids milled around them as they walked.

Georgia looked up, studying the dozen or so run-down high-rise blocks. The murder had taken place around the back of the second along the street. A new, low-rise area was being built adjacent to the high-rises, and Georgia noticed an empty derelict block next to it.

'Those derelicts are only yards away from where the murder happened,' she said to Stephanie, pointing to the cordon which stretched from the corner of the Sparrow block to the edge of the alley.

Stephanie's gaze followed Georgia's pointing finger. 'I was just thinking the same, guv. I'll send a uniform team into them to search. If anyone was hanging around in there at the time of the murder, they couldn't have missed hearing or seeing something.'

'Unless they were the ones doing it,' Georgia suggested. 'It's Brotherhood territory. It'll be their crime.' She shook her head. 'We'd bloody better get a result on this one.'

Normally this amount of police presence would have acted as an incitement: buckets of water or urine emptied from high balconies, bricks, stones, and sticks hurled down, anything to let the Feds know they weren't welcome. Some of the residents had learned that a perk of living in a high-rise was tossing anything they liked at the police on the ground; it was almost impossible for the Feds to work out which floor it came from. It had almost become a battle of wills. Officers on the ground who got soaked by flying urine often set off to run up ten flights of stairs, while others stood by the lift, thinking they could catch the offender if they tried to escape that way. But it was invariably to no avail; either the culprit scarpered up the fire escape and hid in one of the many alcoves on the roof, or they crossed the roof and went down by another route. Or, if they made it to the bottom of one of the other fire exits, they headed across the estate to the famous tunnel at the back of the new low-rise. This was a favourite with kids, who could wriggle inside the tunnel, knowing the space was too small for the Feds to get in and get them.

For now all was quiet, bar the kids riding around on bicycles, trying to suss information to sell on to the Elders. Word had gone round and residents were still leaning over their balconies to watch, but so far no one had said they had seen or heard anything.

Stephanie and Georgia were heading past the Wren block toward the Sparrow. 'Judging by this silence,' Stephanie said quietly, 'they're not as anti police presence as usual tonight.'

'Give it time,' Georgia said flatly.

Stephanie shook her head. 'I'd say they are not happy about this murder. My guess is, it's a well-liked resident.'

Georgia nodded agreement. 'Someone's mother, or wife, or sister?' she said, looking up at the sea of people leaning over the thirteen walkway railings, waiting and wondering. 'Maybe even a rival gang member's mother?'

Stephanie pointed to a couple of phone booths on the corner, by the third block. 'Where the 999 call came from?' she suggested. 'They said it was phone box.'

'Most likely,' Georgia agreed. 'If it's working.'

They had reached the Sparrow, and Stephanie asked one of the forensic team to take a look at the phone booths and see if they could lift any DNA.

'Interesting that they didn't call from a domestic phone, or withhold a number on a mobile,' Georgia said.

'Isn't it just?' Stephanie instructed trainee Detective Constable Hank Peacock to widen the police cordon to include the phone boxes. Georgia hid a smile as she saw him blush before he went off.

'Who wouldn't be carrying a mobile? And why?' Stephanie mused.

'An older resident who doesn't use one, and is afraid to give their name?' Georgia flicked her eyes in the direction of Hank Peacock, then back at Stephanie. She liked to keep up with the station gossip, and knew Stephanie's reputation for bedding the male detectives was well deserved. Stephanie grinned and shook her head. 'No way, José. He's much too young.'

They reached the phone box, and Georgia slipped on her blue forensic gloves before lifting the first receiver. 'I'm pleased to hear it,' she teased her sergeant.

She dialled a number and nodded her head. 'Withheld number on the last call,' she said. 'This is the booth the call came from.' She stepped aside to allow the two forensic officers to get in.

'Whoever called it in, they want to stay anonymous,' Trainee DC Peacock said.

Georgia exchanged amused glances with Stephanie. Talk about stating the obvious.

'I'm just surprised the phone is working,' Stephanie commented.

The uniformed officers finished cordoning the area around the two payphones. A group of youths on bicycles began to circle the area like a pack of wolves. Stephanie stepped towards them. The one in front had long skinny legs and a parka at least seven sizes too big. 'Have you been around here all night?' she asked.

'Who is it?' the kid asked. She was dressed like a boy, but when she spoke it became clear she was a girl.

'That's what we want to know,' Georgia told her. 'So can you answer the question?'

'Have you been around here all night?' Stephanie repeated.

They all shook their heads.

'OK. Did you see anybody around here earlier?' Georgia asked.

Silence.

'Do you know any women living around here, aged about forty, brown skin?' she persisted.

'Yeah. Loads,' the girl answered. 'Can I see the body?'

'No.' Stephanie pulled a notebook from the back pocket of

her jeans. 'Tell me the names of everyone you know that fits
that description.'

One of the forensic officers in the phone box called out,
'There's blood here.'

That was enough for the kids. They raced off at breakneck
speed to sell their information to the Elders, who they knew
would pay them well.

Stephanie grinned at Georgia. 'We've got DNA from all the
Brotherhood. With luck, we could have a name by the end of
the night.'

Georgia shook her head. 'You think they don't know that?'

In the tent the murdered woman was lying on her side, legs
bent as if her knees had given way. Her black skirt looked
mauve with blood; it clung to her by the waistband alone. A
pair of white knickers lay torn and in the dirt nearby. Her
white shirt was heavily stained with blood, which had pooled
around her upper body and was beginning to congeal. Blood
spatters covered her face and clung to her black hair like badly
streaked dark red dye. Both hands and one arm were thick
with dried blood; she had clearly tried to stem the flow of
blood and failed. She stank of faeces.

Phoebe Aston, the redheaded pathologist, hauled herself to
her feet, one hand cradling her distended belly. From the look
of that bump, Georgia thought, she wouldn't be seeing this
case to the end.

'She hasn't been dead long,' Phoebe said. 'And she was
obviously raped before she was stabbed.'

Georgia stared at the woman and swallowed hard. She made
her a silent promise that she would find the killer and bring
them to justice.

'The knife missed her heart,' Phoebe told her. 'But judging
by the amount of blood, a large vein was severed, and she
could have been stabbed more than once. I'll know more after
the PM.'

Georgia and Stephanie moved out of the tent to study the
pattern of bloodstains on the ground outside. Phoebe followed
them.

'Any idea what kind of a knife we're looking for?' Stephanie
asked.

'Not yet. Something else for the post-mortem.'

'The killer's clothes would have been covered in blood, too,' Stephanie said. 'Even if they came at her from behind, they couldn't avoid it.'

Georgia nodded agreement.

Stephanie looked up at the sea of faces watching from the balconies around them. 'We'll get no help from around here,' she said.

'You never know,' Georgia replied. 'We need to move quickly. Get uniform knocking on every door. Get another team searching for the weapon and any bloodstained clothes.'

'We've got a team of dogs on it,' Stephanie told her. 'That'll help.'

Georgia walked back to the white tent and stared at the victim again.

'She had oral sex too,' Phoebe told them. Her small forefinger pointed at sperm that had dried into the dark blood crusting over the side of the mouth. 'This is DNA heaven. It's everywhere. I don't think it'll take you long. Hasn't everyone around here got a record as long as your legs?'

'That's assuming it was someone around here,' Georgia answered.

'The specimens of sperm are on their way over to the lab already,' Phoebe told her. 'What age would you put her at? I'm not good with black-skinned women.'

Georgia shrugged but moved in to study the woman more closely. 'About forty, I'd say.' That fitted with the scant details they'd been given.

'Too old to be on the game,' Stephanie commented.

'Not necessarily,' Georgia said.

'Too old to make much money at it, then,' Stephanie said.

Georgia blew out a breath. 'OK. Find out if anyone around here has reported their mother or wife missing?'

Stephanie pulled her mobile from her pocket as they emerged from the tent. She stabbed in the number of the duty sergeant at the station.

The same small boy as before cycled around the trees beside the cordon, attempting to sneak a closer look. Georgia moved to block him.

'This is a no-go area,' Stephanie shouted. 'Don't you understand?'

'Someone got hurt here,' Georgia said, slipping into the good cop/bad cop routine. 'Very badly hurt. Is there anyone round here who might know who it is?'

The boy stared at her wide-eyed for a second, then quick as a flash turned the handle-bars, jolting them out of Stephanie's reach. 'Wouldn't fucking tell you if we did,' he shouted, riding off. Georgia had to jump to avoid him.

Phoebe Aston was now outside the tent but inside the cordon, squatting beside two forensic officers who were on their knees, scraping at the ground. She looked up and called to Georgia. 'Lots of footprints here,' she said. 'At least five sets, I'd say.' She slowly levered herself upright and eased her back. 'One of them is very likely her killer's. Shame about the sodding weather. It's not looking hopeful, but I'll do my best.' The rain was the steady, persistent kind.

'But why did they walk over to the phone box and phone it in?' Georgia said half to herself.

Phoebe rubbed her bump and grimaced in discomfort. 'They're all large footprints,' she said, bending over again. She straightened up gingerly and arched her back.

'When's it due?' Stephanie asked.

'Not for ages, but I'm having trouble getting up and down. Sorry, I'm not as nimble as I should be. It's bloody annoying. We'll get these tested, and get back to you ASAP. At least three or four different prints here, could be five. Need to get moving – this rain is seriously pissing us up.'

'All trainers?' Georgia asked.

'Couldn't say in this light,' Phoebe told her. 'Three, four or five different shoes, I'm nearly sure, but even that's half guess work.'

'A gang-bang,' Georgia suggested to Stephanie.

'Gang retribution or punishment then,' Stephanie said.

'Er, ma'am . . .' DC Peacock spoke hesitantly. 'I think there's something . . .'

A female uniformed constable stepped forward. 'There's a young woman, ma'am. She's hysterical, but I think she knows something. She's waiting behind the cordon by the other flats.'

'Come on,' Georgia said to Stephanie. They both followed Peacock and the constable to the edge of the Sparrow block.

When they reached the cordon, they found a pretty black teenage girl, dressed in a red PVC miniskirt and a black and red basque with a black leather jacket around her shoulders, shouting and arguing with the uniformed police, demanding to be let through.

'It's my aunt. I know it's my aunt. Let me through or I'll kick you in the . . .'

Four large officers were having trouble restraining her. Half a dozen or so other residents had gathered around, shouting at the police. 'Bastards!' Georgia heard.

Understandable, she thought as she approached the melée, especially if the girl was a relative of the victim. Georgia would have understood if the whole estate had turned out to support her, but what was more interesting was that they hadn't. Stabbings and shootings were becoming an everyday occurrence on this estate; perhaps the residents were getting too accustomed to it.

Or perhaps they truly were too afraid.

Revenge killings over drug territories were all too common. And over respect, whatever that word had grown to mean. If a person walked on a gang member's trainers, or looked the wrong way at his girlfriend, it wasn't always the offender who got hurt; more often his mother or sister was killed. That was the way things worked around here.

At the meeting Georgia had attended earlier in the day, no one had mentioned that any new gang rivalry was brewing. The meeting had been about the firearm and drug trade on the estate; top priority was to bring in the gang leader, Stuart Reilly. A gang expert was being seconded in to help. Georgia didn't know what she thought of experts, but she was keeping an open mind; if they helped her solve a case that was fine by her. What interested her most at the moment was the connection between this victim and the Brotherhood.

Stephanie went over to the girl. Georgia stayed back; Stephanie was better at handling hysterical juveniles, being a mother herself. Georgia had no maternal instincts whatever, and was happy to leave her to it.

Stephanie placed a firm hand on the girl's shoulder. 'OK, let's calm down, shall we? I'll help you if I can. What's your name?'

'I think that's my aunt that's been murdered,' the girl screamed, shrugging her shoulder aggressively to push Stephanie's hand away. 'I need to see. You have to let me. I have to know.'

A couple of other teenagers in the group started spitting at the police. Georgia walked over and faced them. 'This is the first and the last time I'm going to tell you to pack that in,' she said threateningly. 'Now move away.'

Much to her surprise, they did.

Stephanie put both hands on the girl's shoulders and turned her so they were face to face. She spoke firmly, but with compassion. 'I understand that you need to know, and I am going to help you to find out if it is your aunt. But you have to help me too. What's your name?'

'Chantelle.'

'OK, Chantelle. This is a crime scene, so I can't actually let you come any closer. But I have seen the dead woman, so I could recognize her. Can you describe your aunt? Or have you got a photo?'

'She's brown-skinned with long black hair. I haven't got a picture.' The girl had started to calm down. 'Is it her?'

Georgia sighed. *Brown-skinned with long black hair* described half the women on the estate.

Stephanie continued. 'Do you live on the estate?'

The girl pointed towards the flats. Georgia followed her direction of her finger. A few young males were leaning over the third floor balcony, watching with interest. Members of the Brotherhood, she thought; she'd bet real money that they knew who was lying under the tent. And why.

She had made a promise to the murdered woman, and she intended to keep it. She took a step towards the girl called Chantelle. 'What makes you think it's your aunt?' she asked, careful to keep her tone calm.

Chantelle darted away, but Stephanie caught her by the arm. 'It's OK,' she said, gently pulling the girl towards her. 'This is Detective Inspector Georgia Johnson; she wants to help you too. We're going to come up to your flat with you, and we need you to find a photograph of your aunt.'

'Do you have a mum?' Georgia asked her as they headed for the back stairs of the Sparrow block.

Chantelle shook her head.

'A dad?' Georgia persisted.

A laugh twisted Chantelle's face. 'Everybody has a dad,' she said. 'Don't mean you knows who he is.'

They walked up the graffitied, urine-smelling concrete stairway.

'Any brothers or sisters?' Georgia persisted, gritting her teeth in disgust as she stepped over a used nappy on one of the steps.

Chantelle shook her head.

Georgia and Stephanie exchanged glances.

'Is there anyone indoors with you?' Stephanie asked her.

'My aunt should be there. I'm supposed to be at work.'

Georgia caught Stephanie's eye again. The tops of the girl's black fishnet hold-ups were visible under the red mini-skirt, and her boobs were pushed up over the top of her ribboned bodice. It was getting on for midnight. She definitely wasn't going to the office.

They reached the third floor and Chantelle turned to walk along the walkway. Stephanie and Georgia followed. Four youths, fleece-hooded tops over their heads, approached from the opposite direction. As they passed, they asked Chantelle if she was all right. She turned her head and ignored them.

Georgia and Stephanie looked at each other. 'Who were they?' Georgia asked, as the girl stopped in front of her flat.

Chantelle said nothing until they all stood in the narrow hall. Then she shrugged and said quietly, 'Just some boys from around the estate.'

Georgia raised an eyebrow at Stephanie. It was obvious Chantelle was afraid of them.

'Were they Brotherhood members?' Georgia asked her.

Chantelle shrugged.

'Were they Brotherhood members?' Stephanie repeated.

'I'm not sure.' Chantelle avoided the sergeant's eyes. 'I'll look for a photo.' She opened one of the doors off the hallway and walked into the room.

Georgia followed, leaving Stephanie outside. This was obviously the aunt's bedroom. It was clean and tidy, and smelt of furniture polish and potpourri. A picture of a younger Chantelle in a ballet tutu hung on the wall.

Chantelle opened a drawer and rummaged for a few moments. As her hand emerged holding a photo, Stephanie called urgently, 'Guv. You'd better look at this.'

Georgia moved back into the hall. Steph was examining the door frame by the front door. She pointed to some reddish fingermarks, faint but fresh.

Stephanie pulled out her mobile to request immediate forensic assistance. Chantelle stood behind Georgia, staring at the bloodied handprint, her eyes wide with fear.

FOUR

Within minutes the walkway outside Chantelle's front door was spilling over with uniformed police and forensic officers. A cordon was set up ten yards on each side, denying access to the flats further along the floor. Uniformed police woke up angry residents, and told them the only way in and out of their homes for the time being was via a fire exit. It did nothing to help already strained relations.

Forensic officers scurried around like ants over sugar, swiftly covering every inch of the third floor walkway, looking for traces of fresh or dried blood from around the flat. They were aware of the need for speed, not only to avoid antagonizing the residents more than they had to, but also because they were working against the wind and rain.

Each little spot was meticulously scraped from the concrete floor or the grey brick walls, then carefully dropped into phials and sent post haste to the South London lab. The police exhibits officer videoed the pattern of drops of blood between the stairs and the walkway. Uniformed police were holding sniffer-dogs with noses and tails erect; the dogs ran up and down the stairway, following the scent from a fragment of the dead woman's clothing. One barked excitedly and panted over a spot of blood on the stairway. A forensic officer quickly scraped the spot into a phial, then the dogs were off again. Moments later another barked outside the white tent that covered the murdered woman. The handler praised the dog, and held another scrap of the victim's torn clothing under its nose. It set off again in search of more bloodstains, or better still, the weapon that had delivered the fatal damage.

Now the residents of the block had learned this was a murder enquiry, they receded into their flats with front doors firmly shut and bolted. They were all afraid of the consequences of talking to the law; grassing was punishable by a beating to within an inch of their lives, or worse. Haley Gulati was the proof of that.

The police remained undeterred. They knocked on every door, even using loudhailers to wake the supposedly sleeping occupants. Most of them eventually opened their doors a couple of inches, to tell the police they had heard or seen nothing. Dogs growled and snarled from inside some flats as sniffer-dogs ran up and down walkways in search of the weapon.

It was now one a.m. on Saturday. DI Georgia Johnson had told her team that their long night would continue into the next day.

The blue and white criss-crossed tape that barred access to Chantelle's flat was guarded by two uniformed officers. One kept trying to button his jacket across his rotund stomach to keep the wind out, and eventually gave up. The other was a handsome, fair-haired constable whom Georgia recognized from a Christmas do at the station. Stephanie, a little the worse for wear, had left the party draped around his neck, and kept throwing significant looks at him. Between them they afforded Georgia some welcome light relief from the grim situation.

The activity outside intensified. Georgia and Stephanie went back into Chantelle's flat, and looked again at the faint hand-print on the inside of the door.

'Are you sure no one has been in your flat this evening?' Georgia asked Chantelle for the third time.

'No, but I had a nosebleed earlier,' Chantelle said nervously.

Georgia closed her eyes. 'OK. So where's the tissue or handkerchief you used to stem the blood?'

Chantelle put a hand to her forehead. 'I'm sorry. I don't know. I really don't know. I can't think straight.'

'Spare us the theatricals,' Georgia said sharply. 'There's blood on the walkway outside too. Someone has been to this flat, and not too long ago. The blood outside is being tested as we speak. If it turns out to be your aunt's, as I suspect it will, the DNA of whoever has been here will be in it too. If you know who it is, you need to tell us now. We'll know anyway in twenty-four hours, but the sooner we know who killed your aunt, the sooner we can do something about it.'

Stephanie flicked a doubtful glance at Georgia. Twenty-four hours for forensics results these days was wishful thinking; they had both been in the murder squad long enough to know it could take up to two weeks.

She decided to play out the bluff. 'Who are you trying to protect, Chantelle?'

'No one.'

None of them spoke for a few seconds, but Georgia's eyes held Chantelle's. The girl stuffed a shaking fist in her mouth.

'Did your aunt have any enemies?' Georgia asked. 'Had she upset anyone?'

Chantelle's whole body began to shake. 'No.'

Georgia looked at the girl. Chantelle was exceptionally pretty. She had seen far too many attractive teenagers lose their looks through drug use, then turn to prostitution to pay for the habit. This girl was a new user; the needle marks on her legs were still faint.

'Chantelle, I need you to give me a full written statement,' Georgia told her. 'Normally I would let you come to the station in the morning, but as things are, I am going to take you tonight.'

'Don't take me in,' Chantelle pleaded. 'I haven't done anything.'

'You can't stay here,' Georgia said. 'This is now an official crime scene.'

Tears tumbled from the girls eyes. 'I don't want to go to the police station. Can't I stay somewhere else?'

'Is there anyone on the estate that you can stay with?' Georgia asked her. There would be police around the estate for the next few days at least, she thought, and as long as Chantelle didn't do a runner they would be able to find her. It might be more useful to leave her here.

'Luanne Akhter. She lives on this block. We were going to go out together tonight. She'll be worried.'

Chantelle gave them the flat number and Stephanie scribbled it down in her notebook. Hank Peacock was on the walkway;

she ripped out the page and gave it to him, with instructions
to go and check if Luanne was in her flat.

'Who is Luanne?' Georgia asked Chantelle.

'She's my friend. I was on my way out to meet her.'

'You were going out? At this time of night? Where to?'

Chantelle became flustered. 'C-clubbing. We were going up
the West End.'

Georgia sighed. 'Do you have other relatives?' she asked
wearily.

'Luanne's like a sister to me. She has a real sister too,
Alysha. They're like family to me.'

Georgia nodded. 'You said earlier you were going to
work.'

Chantelle hesitated. 'We were going to a couple of clubs,
to try to get work.'

'Do you not have a job?' Georgia asked.

Chantelle's dark cheeks glowed. 'I'm saving up to go to
dance college. I need lots of money for that, and the clubs
pay well. Waitressing or table dancing.'

Stephanie returned. 'She's there, ma'am. She said to come
up, that Chantelle was welcome to stay there as long as she
liked.'

Chantelle smiled with relief.

Luanne was black too, much taller than Chantelle but not
as pretty and more African looking. She had a long, oval face,
with prominent teeth and brown eyes so alert they seem to
pierce into you as she spoke. Her mauve nail extensions were
longer than the blue denim mini-skirt she wore, and her skimpy
cream chiffon bodice advertised more than a few inches of
bare brown midriff. The blouse didn't fully cover the stark
purple uplift bra under it, and purple lace spilled over the edge
of the blouse, matching the skimpy mauve shrug around her
otherwise bare shoulders. Six-inch stiletto-heeled shoes in
pearlized lilac adorned her feet, and like Chantelle's, Luanne's
black patterned hold-up stockings hardly reached the hem of
her micro-mini skirt.

It was now two a.m. Outside the rain was spitting and the
wind was harsh and biting. According to the calendar it was
early spring, but it didn't feel that way.

Luanne greeted Chantelle with a hug and took her through to the living room. Georgia and Stephanie followed.

'I hear you were going out,' Georgia said.

Luanne offered them both a seat. 'We were planning to go to a late party before I heard about this,' she answered, looking away.

'How did you hear about it?' Stephanie asked.

'My sister told me. She was out on the estate earlier, and word goes round.' Luanne fussed around Chantelle, her large hooped imitation gold earrings dangling against her long neck. They jangled against the other three pairs, which hung from different holes further up her ears. Georgia guessed she was around twenty, although her lived-in face looked as if it had seen many more years.

'This is just such a shock, and too awful,' Luanne said to the two detectives. 'Haley was like a mother to her. I'll make her some sweet tea. Do you want tea or coffee?'

'Tea, two sugars,' Stephanie said. Georgia shook her head.

Georgia was beginning to feel weary and would have loved a cup of coffee, but experience had taught her that finding a loo on a high-rise estate in the middle of the night wasn't easy, and unlike the men on the team, she minded having to relieve herself under a bush in a dark corner. The answer was simple: she abstained from liquids during the long golden hours when a murder enquiry was just under way.

When Luanne returned with the tray of drinks, her sister Alysha was with her. Georgia and Stephanie both recognized her as one of the kids who had circled the crime scene on bikes, looking for information. Alysha was wearing trendy teenage pyjamas, patterned in navy blue and pink with matching ribbons on the legs and cuffs. Her hair was neat as rows of corn; narrow plaits fell from a middle parting to hang either side of her face to chin level. She was as pretty as she was forward. She sat down next to Chantelle on the sofa and poured from a teapot. 'Why Aunt Haley? Was she targeted, or just in the wrong place at the wrong time?' she asked.

'How did you know it was Aunt Haley who was murdered?' Georgia asked.

Alysha looked Georgia directly in the eye. 'I knew someone was dead, so I went down to have a look. You saw me. Someone said Chantelle was looking for Haley and she hadn't turned up at home, so they thought it was probably her. You wouldn't tell me nothing, remember?'

'Who was the someone who said they thought it was Haley?' Georgia pushed.

Alysha shook her plaits. 'One of the kids. I don't remember who. They just said they heard it was a black woman, and then everyone said the Feds had descended on Chantelle's flat, so . . .' She shrugged.

This kid was twelve going on forty. Georgia had met her kind many times: a child who had learned to survive in the absence of parents by the rules of the estate – and that meant pleasing the gangs. It made her highly vulnerable.

'Do you have parents?' Georgia asked Luanne.

Luanne pulled her mouth into a sarcastic smile. 'We've got a dad, but he's not in.'

'He hardly ever is,' Alysha piped up. 'He's a waste of space. We look out for ourselves.'

'He works nights and sleeps days,' Luanne said quickly.

'But not always here,' Alysha laughed. Luanne nudged her, but she just smiled.

'Where does he work?' asked Stephanie.

'Nowhere special, just wherever he can get it.' This was Alysha again. She picked up a packet of sugar and started spooning it into Chantelle's tea.

'I need to take that statement from you,' Stephanie said giving Chantelle a reassuring smile. 'Won't take long, and then I think you should try and get some sleep. We'll talk some more in the morning.'

'She needs to stay here,' Georgia told Luanne. 'And I would prefer it if you didn't go out again tonight.' The fact that the girls were on the game didn't concern Georgia; the fact that it made them vulnerable concerned her a lot. A hooker had been murdered recently just outside the alley that led to the estate; she decided not to bring that subject up.

Luanne was twisting one of her hoop earrings around the hole in her ear. She took Chantelle's hand and squeezed it.

'There's no way we'd be going to a club after this,' she said.

'You'd probably catch a cold,' Georgia said with a pointed glance at the girls' skimpy clothes.

Luanne got the message. 'I don't feel the cold,' she said narrowing her eyes. 'Black-skinned girls are tougher. We have to be. You should know that.'

'What about Alysha?' Stephanie asked her. 'Who would have looked after her while you were out, if your dad hadn't come back?'

Alysha suppressed a giggle.

'She's got friends around here. She would have had a sleepover,' Luanne answered irritably.

Stephanie clicked her ballpoint and turned back to Chantelle. 'Let's get this statement done, shall we? Did you see or hear anyone coming along the walkway at any time earlier this evening?'

Luanne gave a little laugh. 'Only half the people who live in the flats. It's Friday; everyone walks up and down all the time, going out or coming home.'

'I'm asking Chantelle,' Stephanie said sharply.

Chantelle looked at Luanne then back at Stephanie. 'No one,' she said.

'What time did Haley go to work?'

Chantelle furrowed her forehead. 'She left about midday, I think.'

'Were you there?'

'Yes.'

'Did you go out after that?'

She shook her head.

'Are you sure?'

She nodded.

'Think, Chantelle. Did anyone knock on your door?'

'I can't remember anyone knocking,' she said, growing flustered again.

'So she can't help you,' Alysha butted in.

'Would you mind taking Alysha into another room?' Georgia said sharply to Luanne. 'And stay in there with her. I'd like to take Chantelle's statement in private.'

'Please let them stay with me,' Chantelle protested.

'I don't think so.'

'Just a few questions,' Stephanie said gently. 'Then they can come back.'

Luanne stood up and pushed Alysha outside the room. Georgia noticed that her shoes were smeared with mud.

'Have you been out tonight, Luanne?' she asked.

'No.' Luanne lifted her chin defiantly.

'I think you have,' Georgia said. 'Look at your shoes.'

Luanne looked down at her feet. She pushed Alysha through the door and lowered her voice. 'I was working, on the street next to the estate. I need the money.' She glared at Georgia. 'I didn't tell you because I didn't think you'd want all the gory details of the cocks I sucked earlier.'

'I'm not interested in that,' Georgia snapped. 'This is a murder enquiry.'

'Heard it all before,' Stephanie added.

'Never tasted it though, I bet.' Luanne said, looking straight at Georgia before leaving the room.

Stephanie and Georgia exchanged a look, and Stephanie turned back to Chantelle. 'Have you been out earlier too?' she asked the girl.

'No, I was in all day. And no, I don't remember anyone coming to the door.' She looked away. 'You keep asking, but no one did. If they did I would tell you.' Her forehead crumpled as if she was about to cry.

She was lying.

'When did you last see your aunt?' Georgia asked, her voice totally devoid of sympathy.

A thread of mascara began to run down Chantelle's cheek; she touched a finger to the corner of her eye to ease the sting. 'This morning. I told you. Aunt Haley went out about twelve. She said she had to get shopping on the way home, so she might be a bit late. I told her I was going out tonight, and she said I was to wait for her to come home first.'

'What time is she usually home?' Georgia asked.

Stephanie pulled a tissue from a crumpled packet in her pocket and passed it to Chantelle. She took it and dabbed the leaking mascara under her eye. 'She works at the hairdressing salon from two until six on a Friday.'

'And do you work?' Georgia asked her for the second time. 'Honestly?'

Chantelle dropped her gaze. 'I'm waiting to go to college.'

'Do you work?' Georgia persisted.

She picked at her nails. Georgia noticed they were yellowing. That confirmed what Georgia already knew: the girl was a user.

'I was working,' Chantelle told her. 'But I want to dance professionally. Street dancing, I want to do street dancing.'

'Do you go to lessons?'

She reluctantly shook her head. 'I used to. I gave it up, just for a while.' She became visibly nervous. 'I am going to start again.'

'Nice shoes,' Georgia said. 'Very fashionable. New, are they?'

Chantelle's dark eyes were vague and her skin was papery dry. Another few months of using and this girl's pretty face would look like a haggard old woman's. Georgia wanted to find out which lowlife snake was dealing to her; she believed he could be the link to her aunt's murder. She made a quick decision. A tough approach was best.

'Chantelle, you need to start talking to us,' she said. 'If you don't, you could be arrested for obstructing a murder enquiry. I think you know who came to your flat tonight. So answer me this: are you trying to protect someone? Or is it that you're afraid of someone?'

Chantelle's eyes widened and fresh tears formed in them.

'Talk to us,' Georgia said, her tone still harsh.

'If you're afraid, we can help you,' Stephanie said, slipping into the hard/soft approach she and Georgia habitually worked during teenage interviews.

Tears began to spill down Chantelle's cheeks.

'You know as well as I do that we have DNA on record for three-quarters of the people on this estate,' Georgia said. 'It won't take us long to find out.' She paused, waiting for Chantelle to speak, but the girl just looked terrified. 'You see, I think that blood is your aunt's,' she continued, 'and someone came to your flat to tell you that. Am I right?'

Chantelle was crying in earnest now, but Georgia pushed on. 'We will find out who it was, and you'll be charged with withholding vital evidence in a murder enquiry. Is that what you want?'

'Help yourself, Chantelle,' Stephanie said gently. 'You must want us to find her killer.'

Chantelle wiped her tearstained face with the back of her hand. 'Yo-Yo,' she said in a in a barely audible voice. 'He came to the flat earlier.'

'Yo-Yo?' Georgia looked at Stephanie. 'You mean Stuart Reilly?' She nearly leaped in the air. Was it going to be that straightforward? She saw in Stephanie's face that they were both thinking the same. Was this the evidence they needed to trap this bastard that CID had wanted for months? No wonder these girls were so cagey; they were terrified. Reilly was a killer.

She kept her cool. 'He's the main Elder on the estate, is that right?' she asked. She knew exactly who and what Reilly was, but she needed to hear it from Chantelle.

'He's head of the Brotherhood, the gang that rule this estate, is that right?' Stephanie pushed keeping her tone casual.

'He'll kill me for telling you,' Chantelle said in a tiny voice.

'He won't get the chance,' Stephanie quickly assured her. 'If he killed your aunt he's going to prison. He'll be locked up for a very long time.'

'Why would he want to kill your aunt?' Georgia asked her. 'Does she owe him money for drugs?'

Chantelle shook her head.

'Do you owe him money?'

Chantelle said nothing.

'Is that it, Chantelle?' Georgia pushed. 'He punished your aunt for a debt you owe?'

'Yes. No. I don't know. I work for him. I pay him that way.'

'For drugs?'

Chantelle pressed her lips together.

'Help us to help you, Chantelle,' Stephanie said to her. 'We want to protect you.'

She still didn't answer.

'Why did he come round to yours today?' Georgia asked her.

Chantelle shrugged.

'Come on, Chantelle. Help yourself here.' Stephanie was getting tough now. 'Did he come to tell you he'd killed your aunt?'

'No.' She shook her head vehemently and scrubbed at the black mascara with the tattered tissue.

Stephanie gently took it from her and handed her another clean one. Chantelle snatched it and continued to rub the mascara from her face.

'Chantelle, what did he say when he came to your flat tonight?' Georgia asked her again.

Chantelle examined the mascara on the tissue. 'He told me to go to work.' She looked up at Stephanie. 'I work the street with Luanne. That's how I pay for my stuff.'

Georgia had to remind herself again that it wasn't her job to save these girls. Her job was to get the bastards that destroyed them.

'Where does he live?' Stephanie asked. 'Stuart Reilly – Yo-Yo – where does he live?' She looked at Georgia.

Georgia managed not to smile. They certainly had Yo-Yo Reilly's DNA on record. If he was responsible for Haley's murder the case would be tied up as soon as the lab results came back. Twenty-four hours might be optimistic, but by the end of the weekend Yo-Yo Reilly would be in custody and they would be toasting another solved murder. In the meantime they had Chantelle's statement, which meant they could arrest and lock him up now. The most vicious criminal in South London was coming off the streets, and away from this crime-infested estate. And also, thanks to Stephanie, they also had Chantelle's DNA on the tissue.

'Where does he live?' Georgia repeated Stephanie's question. 'Chantelle, does Yo-Yo live on this estate?'

Chantelle didn't answer.

'We can easily find out,' Georgia told her.

'He lives on the ground floor of this block.' The voice was Luanne's. She had been listening outside the door, as Georgia had expected.

'If we tell you, are we finally going to be free of that scumbag?' she asked Georgia.

'What number?' Stephanie asked getting up from the sofa and lifting her mobile ready to call for back-up.

'He'll get us for this,' Chantelle said in a terrified tone to Luanne.

'A hundred and thirteen,' Luanne told them clearly. 'He'll be put on remand, won't he?' she asked. 'I mean, the bastard won't get bail, will he?'

Georgia shook her head. 'Not a chance. He's already got a string of offences for carrying weapons.'

'We'll need protection,' Luanne said.

Now they both looked like the frightened, vulnerable teenagers they were.

'There will be police up and down the walkways all night. You're quite safe here,' Georgia assured her. 'Just make sure you don't go out.' She handed Chantelle a card. 'If you need me, call that number. We'll be back in touch tomorrow anyway. We'll need an official statement.' She turned to Luanne. 'Do not let her out of your sight.'

'Hold up,' Luanne half-pleaded. 'We'll need long-term protection. Not just the weekend. He's a killer, and he'll get us somehow when he finds out we grassed on him. And he will find out.'

'He'll be locked up,' Georgia reminded her. 'For a very long time.'

'That won't stop him. He'll get one of the Brotherhood on to it. We can't stay here; you need to find us somewhere else to live.' She looked at Alysha and Chantelle. 'All of us.'

'The police will be around the estate for quite a while yet,' said Georgia. 'Lock yourself in, and you'll be safe. Keep your sister in too. On no account is she to go out alone. If anything frightens you call one of the police outside, then ring me.' She handed Luanne another of her personal cards.

'Everything frightens us! Blimey, where do I start?' Luanne's voice cracked and her tough front went with it. 'I can't believe I have just given him up,' she gasped. 'They'll get us. They will seriously hurt us.'

'I thought you said black-skinned girls were tough,' Georgia said with an encouraging smile. 'There are police all over the place; you'll be quite safe. And you have my mobile number.'

They let themselves out, leaving the two girls huddled together on the sofa.

'What have we done?' Georgia heard Chantelle say.

FIVE

J ason lay in bed listening to the never-ending wail of sirens. He had promised his gran he would be gone by the time she got back from the market. She had told him she would sort the blood on his sweatshirt, and he wasn't to think of anything but his new life. And she had told him over and over that she believed in him. Nothing, she told him, was to get in the way of this chance he had to start again. If he blew it, he would never get another one.

She didn't want to know any more about what had happened. That way she could tell the police that she knew nothing. If they came knocking this morning, they could knock the bloody door down, because no one would be there. That was why he had to go, and soon.

He put his hands over his eyes. He knew she was right, but if he was to go from postcode to postcode on his way to North London, he needed another shank.

If he had told Gran Sals what really happened, and that he had been to see Chantelle, she would have hollered at him as well as urging him to go. She had hated Haley so much, and Chantelle too. But he loved Chantelle, and she needed him now more than ever; he had to see her.

It had been impossible to talk to her; she was hysterical. That wasn't surprising after what had happened, but it didn't help. She was only half listening when he told her about the opportunity he had for them both, to get away from this place and dance, just as they'd always planned. 'Everything's different now, babe,' she'd said. 'You don't want me with you. I'm not worth it.'

He knew right away that that was Yo-Yo's influence. He'd tried to persuade her, begged her, even, but she was adamant. 'I can't go,' she'd said. 'Not now. Not with what's happened.'

He understood in a way. Her aunt had been killed, and she had a lot of sorting out to do. But if he hung around, he might well get arrested for Haley's murder, and that would put paid to everything. On the other hand, if he didn't wait for her Chantelle might never join him, and then he'd never forgive himself.

She said she'd come after him eventually, when things with Aunt Haley got sorted. But he didn't think she was strong enough to cope with it all alone. He thought there was a strong chance she would escape further into heroin, and not even evil old Haley was there to stop her now.

Chantelle needed someone to help her through, and if he dared not be there for her himself, Luanne was the next best thing. She was a hooker, but she was sensible, and she didn't do hard drugs. She and Chantelle had grown up together, and were best friends. He'd ask Luanne to look after Chantelle and keep in touch with him, and as soon as they'd put Haley in the ground she could help Chantelle to get to wherever he was staying. Meanwhile he would try to get Chantelle an audition at the dance school.

Chantelle had given him her new mobile number last night, and told him to call this morning. It was very early, still night time really, so he'd give it an hour or so. He'd make sure he had Luanne's number too, and get things moving.

The Feds were everywhere. If they saw him he was sure to be picked up, and in his haste he hadn't been too careful. He really needed to get out of here – but first he had to get hold of another shank to replace the one he'd dumped last night. Luanne could get him one: something small, and sharp and easy to keep hidden. Luanne could always get what you wanted.

Stephanie had rung ahead to warn the uniformed sergeant and his team on the ground that they were going to arrest Yo-Yo Reilly, and that there could be a riot.

Alongside the fleet of patrol cars, a police wagon was waiting in the grounds of the Sparrow estate, its blue light silently flashing. Georgia and Stephanie travelled the twelve flights to the bottom of the high-rise in the airless, coffin-sized lift, hemmed in by thick steel doors with a stale dog turd to keep them company.

Lights had come on all over the estate, and residents of all the high-rises were spilling from their front doors and leaning over their balconies, most in dressing gowns, to see what was going on.

Uniformed police holding alsatian dogs on leashes had surrounded all the exits around the ground floor flat where Stuart Reilly lived. Inside the flat Reilly's pit bulls snarled, spoiling for a fight.

The wind was biting, and the rain still spilled down as Georgia and Stephanie took body armour from the back of the police van. Georgia gave instructions to call for the armed response unit as back-up. The record of violence and firearms around here meant she could take no chances, and the safety of the large number of police officers on this estate was her responsibility. PC Elvin had been shot for a lot less than pulling in the most notorious criminal in South London. Reilly himself bred vicious dogs, and his Brotherhood gang ran into many dozens on this estate alone; it was quite possible they would outnumber the police.

The odd stone had already been hurled from a balcony somewhere high up on the Sparrow. It had hit the ground this time, but it hadn't gone unnoticed. The police were nervous, and very wary.

Something nagged at Georgia as she stood in full body armour, ready to arrest Reilly for the murder of Haley Gulati. The Brotherhood gang were known for torturing their victims. Reilly had earned his street name of Yo-Yo through his habit of repeatedly driving a knife in and out of his victims and watching them writhe in agony. Phoebe Aston had said it was likely the victim had been stabbed more than once, and had been raped.

But this killing didn't have Reilly's personal stamp on it. Other victims had been found with no fingers, and a couple of corpses were headless. Haley Gulati's murder didn't have the hallmarks of a trophy Brotherhood killing – and that gave Georgia a niggling doubt about Reilly.

For now she put it to the back of her mind. The Brotherhood would be involved somewhere, and locking Reilly up would take a significant load off the police. The whole of the Met wanted the bastard off the streets, and Chantelle's statement gave them enough to pull him in for at least a day or two, until the DNA testing came back. If it turned out it was one of his Brotherhood thugs committed the deed, not Reilly himself, they would find him too, and then two of them would be behind bars.

She wondered if the killing might be an initiation into the Brotherhood of Blades gang. She had been told that they had to stab someone brutally in order to become members; then they were given a permanent tattoo of a sword on their forearm. Reilly's rules again.

The whole estate would be a better place once he was locked up; and once that was sorted, she'd go after the rest of them. With luck they'd get the dogs too. That was something else he'd got away with until now: the dogs were illegal pit bulls, but no one had ever been able to prove it. This time she would; she'd call in an expert, and make sure they were taken away from him for good. Wherever they ended up they'd be better off. She'd witnessed his steel-cap boots kicking their under-bellies raw, and heard them whimper and moan in pain before attacking on his command.

As the CO19 team arrived on the estate, a volley of stones, sticks, and bricks rained down from the high balconies above them. The armed officers jumped from the van and moved in, firearms loaded and pointing, to cover Yo-Yo's door. Georgia instructed the uniformed sergeant to gather half a dozen of his most reliable officers to knock on Reilly's door. As they moved in she followed close behind with Stephanie and trainee DC Peacock. Hank was over six feet tall, skinny as a broom, with hair that stood upright from his smiling, amenable face. He had told her a few days previously that he wanted to get straight into the action. This estate, at three thirty on a freezing Saturday morning, with missiles and unthinkable liquids raining down in their direction from Sparrow block, was Hank's baptism of fire; she would be interested to see how he fared. She noticed Stephanie was watching the young DC closely, too – she hoped with a professional eye.

'Police! Open up!' Georgia shouted as the uniformed officers banged on the door. Without waiting for a response, she nodded to the officer holding the bright red battering ram, and he swiftly took the door down.

As the door caved in, more bricks and stones and a bucket of faeces pelted down. Something slimy and foul-smelling narrowly missed Stephanie and Hank Peacock and landed on the back of Georgia's head in her neatly tied ponytail. As the slippery globules dropped from her hair on to the back of her black leather coat, she fought not to cry out in disgust. The memory of that long-ago autumnal night spun inside her brain.

Stephanie handed her a large handkerchief. At the same moment Hank Peacock took off into the flat at a sprint. He had caught sight of Yo-Yo in the room at the end of the hallway, hauling himself out a window. Hank was like a whippet on speed. He leapt up on a table, grappled with Yo-Yo's fat, kicking legs and pulled him back into the room. Uniformed officers moved in to help, ducking and jumping to avoid the kicks Yo-Yo flung out in all directions. Hank wasn't about to let go; he dragged Yo-Yo's feet back to the floor, and Stephanie was ready to click handcuffs into place.

As she read him his rights the sound of the angry, barking dogs in another room almost drowned her voice. The police made a speedy exit from the flat.

Getting him into the police wagon was the next problem. It seemed as if half of the Brotherhood were now blocking their way, holding bats and chains. Georgia made an educated guess that some of them were carrying knives, and possibly even firearms.

She took a deep breath and stepped in front of Stephanie and Hank, who were walking either side of the handcuffed Yo-Yo.

'Mr Reilly is being taken in for questioning,' she told them calmly. 'Anyone who tries to hinder our enquiries will also be arrested and charged with obstruction. Please stand aside. There are more of us than of you, and we also have armed police officers in position. Please go back to your beds and let us do our job.'

Her words fell on deaf ears. More youths of all colours and sizes arrived from different parts of the estate, armed with bats, sticks, bricks and chairs. Some leaned menacingly against the police vehicles while others blocked the exit from the Aviary Estate.

Georgia stood her ground while Stephanie phoned for back-up from the riot unit.

'I'll ask you again, politely for now,' Georgia said loudly as a brick landed next to the police van. 'Step away from the vehicles and clear the exit from the estate. You are obstructing the police in their line of duty.'

No one moved. A couple of youths took a step towards her and lifted their weapons.

The uniformed police surrounding Reilly moved closer to guard their prisoner.

Hank Peacock took up a position beside Georgia.

Yo-Yo beamed from ear to ear.

The police and the estate gang stood facing each other, each waiting for the other to make a move.

The sound of sirens grew louder, and a fleet of police vans sped into the estate only to be blocked by a horde of angry youths. The siren's scream stopped, replaced by an urgent growl from a loudspeaker, and a warning to move back or take the consequences.

Some of the youths gathered to form a barrier. The police vans' riot grills dropped over the windscreens. The vans slowed, but kept moving, sirens shrieking.

Then a brick flew out of the crowd.

The vans halted and the doors flew open. Police clad in face shields and body armour jumped out, ready to face the threatening mob. Some of the crowd dropped their bats and sticks and hurried off, realizing they were probably going to lose and get arrested.

Others held their ground.

Stephanie, Georgia, and Hank Peacock were now flanked by a dozen uniformed police. A handcuffed Reilly stood in the middle of the group, wearing only boxer shorts and a dressing gown, socks and trainers on his feet. They attempted to hustle him through the crowd and into the van, but each time they tried, they were pushed back by armed youths.

A tall youth holding a jar threw its contents at Georgia. She realized it was urine, and ducked to prevent the putrid liquid from hitting her face. In that instant the same youth pulled a blade and danced in front of her, waving the knife and urging her to take it from him.

Another man seemed to come from nowhere. Quick as a fox, he knocked the knife out of the youth's hand, sending it clattering to the ground. Hank Peacock moved quickly to lift and bag it. Stephanie and three uniformed police moved in to arrest the youth, and Stephanie managed to knee him hard in the balls as they struggled with him.

'Move back,' the newly arrived police shouted as some of the mob surged forward. Sticks and stones were still flying, but most of the mob retreated as more sirens screamed into the estate. The police outnumbered the crowd by quite a margin now; not only would Yo-Yo Reilly's supporters fail to prevent his arrest, they would end up being arrested with him.

The man who had jumped in and knocked the knife out of the youth's hand watched the crowd retreating. 'I think I came at a good moment,' he said to Georgia, managing a brief smile.

'Thank you,' Georgia said without looking round. She felt desperately uncomfortable, and horribly aware of the smell of whatever had landed in her hair. 'I don't think we've met?'

'David Dawes. Detective Inspector. I've just been seconded to this enquiry.' He didn't look at Georgia, but kept his eyes pinned on the last of the youths as a uniformed sergeant warned them to stay back.

None of them moved. DI Dawes took a step nearer to them and shouted above the din. 'Move back, now. If anyone makes any attempt to prevent us leaving with this prisoner, we will arrest you, all of you if necessary, and you will be charged with obstruction.' He nodded to the uniforms flanking Yo-Yo, to indicate that they should get him into the prisoner's van as quickly as possible. This time no one tried to stop them.

Once Yo-Yo was in the van, Hank Peacock pushed the other handcuffed youth in beside him and the van was locked. The driver took off toward the station without further delay. As it sped out of the estate, more bricks and chairs were hurled down from high up on the estate. But as it disappeared, the crowds started to disperse.

Georgia was angry and upset. She didn't want anyone else to see the effect that the faeces in her hair were having on her. The memory of Clapham Common all those years ago was back with her. She needed to be on her own, preferably at home and in the shower. She made her way quickly towards Stephanie's car.

Stephanie caught up with her and clicked open the car door as DI Dawes came up behind them.

'Probably not a good place to get acquainted,' he said flashing his ID card. 'I'll see you at the station. I'm on attachment with you, for this case.'

Stephanie was beaming at him. 'Drop me home first,' Georgia said to her. 'I need to shower and wash my hair before I go back to the station.'

Stephanie drove in silence, much to Georgia's relief. Stephanie was oblivious to Georgia's history, but though she joked about most things, in the five years they had worked closely together she had learned that Georgia's cleanliness phobia wasn't a subject for hilarity. Only occasionally, when they paused at traffic lights, did she lift her eyebrows, wrinkle her nose and twinkle in Georgia's direction.

Georgia stared out of the window and said not a word.

As Sally Young set up her stall her mind was turning nineteen to the dozen. It seemed only yesterday that her teenage daughter Wendy had broken the news that she was pregnant. Wendy was a crack addict, so poor Jason was born to suck a drugtaker's milk, then left to fend for himself while Sally worked long hours at cleaning jobs to bring in money to keep a roof over the three of them.

It was years later, after Wendy died, that she found out that the boy had often been left hungry. She never forgave herself for not noticing. It was no wonder he turned to stealing.

If she had of known of his love of dancing earlier, she would have done something about it: paid for his dance lessons by working another shift, or whatever it took. That might have saved him from the thieving and drug trading and ultimately from the prison sentences. But it was no good wishing, she herself; she had to deal with what was, not what might been.

blew into her hands to keep warm as she piled plates

on the hard, frosty ground. She'd let her daughter down too, she thought sadly. If she'd been any kind of mother to her, Wendy might still be alive and Jason wouldn't have ended up the way he did. He was a good boy deep down. He had been the one to come through for her; after all, he'd given her the money to fulfil her dream and set this stall up.

She stood back and admired the wobbling plates, then moved them in case they toppled. Breakages ate into her profits, and she needed to save as much money as she could now. It was payback time; she would look out for Jason as he had for her. She hated Haley Gulati anyway, always had done, and wasn't a bit sorry she was dead. The stuck-up cow thought Jason wasn't good enough for her niece. She should have known her darling Chantelle was nothing but a cheap little slapper, not a patch on Jason. He had a scholarship and he was going to make something of himself, and he'd never need to steal again. Chantelle was on a bad road.

This crockery was a good little business, and she'd use it to make sure he had the things he needed until he was sorted and on his own two feet. He was a clever lad and he'd have a training soon. She would take a cleaning job, too, if need be, to help him. She was used to hard work; as a child she had to miss school to cook and clean for her alcoholic mother. Then she'd met Frankie, and got pregnant herself at fifteen. Frankie soon disappeared, and she found herself with Wendy to feed and no bloody help from anyone. But it was all worth it; she adored her new daughter, and happily worked four cleaning shifts a day to feed her as well as keep her mother in gin.

As Wendy grew up, Sally's mother fell ill, so after a long day's work she had to spend her evenings bathing and caring for her. Looking back, she knew she hadn't given her daughter the attention a child needed, but she was always so busy.

Shortly after her mother passed away, Wendy announced that she was pregnant, and gave birth a few months later to a beautiful, healthy, brown-skinned baby. They named him Jason after his father, who they never saw again. It was, Wendy told her, just a fling.

While Wendy supposedly looked after Jason, Sally w

cleaning again. It was years later that she learned Wendy spent the housekeeping as well as her benefit money on drugs, and left Jason neglected.

By the time Wendy died of an overdose Jason had grown into an angry twelve-year-old who had learned to stand on his own two feet and was well versed in the ways of crime, thanks to the gangs that ran riot on the notorious Aviary Estate.

Sally herself had never crossed swords with the law, and she wasn't afraid of the youths that had formed gangs on the estate either, even when they carried guns or knives. If they kept out of her way, they got along just fine, but if they hung around outside her door they'd get an earful from her sharp tongue. She was born on that estate and it had always been her home. She had only moved down the road to help Jason get a clean start when he came out of prison, not for an easier life for herself as the gossips were saying. She wasn't afraid of them, she wasn't afraid of no one. She earned her own living and kept herself to herself and wasn't about to change.

It was about nine o'clock last night when Jason had staggered up the stairs in that terrible state. Earlier that day he had talked about his future. He had learned a hard lesson in prison, he said, and now he intended to stay away from crime and be a dancer. She wasn't a fool; she knew that no matter how she warned him not to go back to the estate to see that slag Chantelle, he would still go. Love was love, and Jason thought he loved Chantelle. Sally knew she was bad and would drag him back down the wrong road, but it was no use arguing with Jason. He was strong-willed; when he was a child she had often been afraid of him. Even at the tender age of eight he was capable of terrifying violence. She remembered a particular incident when he'd gone half mad at her for something or nothing, picked up a sharp carving knife and stabbed it into her new kitchen stools, one after the other, and after she'd saved so hard to buy the bloody things. She loved those stools; the seats had been covered to match the floral blinds in her kitchen. She had kept them, meaning to have them re-covered when she'd saved up enough money, but she never had; they were still slashed and stabbed now, as a reminder to herself never to push Jason too far.

She'd have to hope he'd forget Chantelle when he got into his new dancing life. She wasn't going to risk him turning on her by telling him what the slapper was up to every night, on the street in front of the estate. Sally had seen the little tart with her own eyes, flagging down motorists and offering them sexual favours. Jason would have to find out for himself. And she hoped he would.

And as for that Haley! The woman really provoked her, banging on at her to keep Jason away from her niece because he wasn't good enough for her. Well, the truth was he was too bloody good by a mile.

So when Jason came home, and stood shaking inside the door, with blood all over his hands and clothes and in his hair, her first thought was that someone had tried to take him out, and after all that had happened to her precious family, she was now going to lose her only grandson to someone who wanted to get even for something in the past. Oh, the relief when he'd assured her that he wasn't hurt, but had to get out of those clothes! He told her something terrible had happened and he didn't know what to do.

They had both sat in her kitchen on the stools with the slashes across their floral plastic coverings, and Jason told her that Haley Gulati was dead and lying at the bottom of her block of flats with knife wounds in her chest.

Sals had picked up the phone to dial 999. But he had stopped her; he had taken care of everything, he said, but now he needed to get away. She had asked no more questions; she just got on with helping him, as she always had.

SIX

The flat was quiet and empty as DI David Dawes unlocked his front door and let himself in. He stood in the hall for a moment and took a couple of deep breaths.

In the short time that she was there, Philly had turned his neat home into bedlam. He was forever shouting at her to tidy her stuff from under his feet and turn her music down. Now he missed the mess, almost as much as he missed her.

He knew it would take time, but it had been well over a year now, and the numbness still suffocated him. Every time something reminded him of her, he silently promised her that he would find the dealer that sold her the heroin that killed her and make the bastard pay. Now that goal was within his grasp.

He walked into the bathroom, turned the tap on and held his cupped hands under the cold tap. A vigorous cold splash followed by a brisk rub with a clean towel made him feel more awake; the long hours police work demanded were no joke. He hung the towel tidily on the rail and looked around. Here, too, he found he missed the mess: bottles without tops, their contents leaking over the glass shelf.

Some of her clothes still hung in the wardrobe. He'd thought about taking them to a charity shop but couldn't quite bring himself to pack them up; knowing that something of hers was still there was a comfort. It was only a pair of jeans, and a few party tops he had bought for her, knowing better than to give her money. He had enjoyed choosing them, and she had loved them, but never got round to wearing them.

He still had her teddy too, in a drawer in the back bedroom: the pink Care Bear she'd had since childhood and she took everywhere. The tearstained, grubby toy was hardly even pink now, but he had been her prize possession and no one was going to take it away from him.

His father had told him to get a grip and clear her stuff out, but he didn't listen. Perhaps if his father had shown more feelings before and not maintained his stiff upper lip, maybe, just maybe . . . But Dawes was tired of maybes. Things were as they were, and that meant nothing but a few cans of beer on top of the fridge to welcome him home.

He switched on the CD player and, as Willy Nelson's soulful voice began to croon *Without Her,* he flopped on to the sofa and popped a can of lager.

He didn't feel especially tired, even though he had been working flat out for nearly twenty hours. Hearing about the murder down on the Aviary, then learning that he was being seconded to the case because of his knowledge of South London gangs, had set his adrenalin pumping. Finally all his research on South London gangs was paying off. They'd had a hard night tonight but the police had won out, and they had that bastard Reilly in custody. Dawes was almost sure he was the one who had dealt that fateful heroin to Philly.

The lager felt cold and sharp as it slid down his throat. He couldn't wait to get Reilly in interview. He knew Reilly ran the drug trade down on that estate, but he needed to find out exactly how long that had been the case. More than that: he wanted to know if the Aviary had been exclusively Buzzard territory before Reilly's Brotherhood moved in, or if other dealers had used the territory too. He was pretty sure Reilly was his target, but he had to find out for sure, and now Reilly was securely locked away Dawes was confident the residents would start talking. He had been told there was an informant down on the estate already.

This was also a crucial time for police/resident relations. If they could persuade some key people that the police could be trusted, there was a good chance they might get a grip on the violence which was teetering out of control. DI Georgia Johnson had said she was confident that they would tie up the case against Reilly over the weekend; it was all but in the bag. They even had a witness; all they needed was confirmation of the DNA evidence to put it to bed.

Dawes hadn't said a word, but he didn't share her confidence.

Stuart Reilly had a very smart brief. No one had made any charge stick thanks to him; he was more bent than the two hundred-odd South London gangs put together. Georgia Johnson had taken on a lot, and she would learn it wouldn't be as easy as she thought.

But once Dawes knew for sure it was Reilly who had sold the heroin that killed his sister, that bastard was going nowhere. Reilly might have spread terror across the Aviary estate by cutting fingers off his enemies or marking them with spider scars, but if he had sold Philly that fatal dose, it would be the end of the road for him. Dawes would do whatever it took.

Dawes wasn't entirely convinced that Yo-Yo Reilly had murdered tonight's victim himself. He was certain he was behind the killing; he was behind all the crime on the estate. But if he hadn't actually done the deed, the case was far from open and shut. If Reilly had stabbed her, the victim would have had twenty or thirty wounds, not three or four; the spider scar was his trademark. But Dawes wanted him in custody; he wanted it more than the rest of the Met put together. If DI Johnson thought Reilly was guilty of the murder, Dawes would say nothing, at least for the moment. His task was to bring in the person that murdered Haley Gulati, whoever that was. He would, too; he was a good detective and he'd do his job. But for now it was enough that he had Reilly in custody; he wasn't going to miss the chance of a crack at him.

As soon as the front door closed behind her Georgia Johnson peeled all her clothes off and dropped them on the mat. She hurried into the bathroom and straight into the shower. After covering her skin and hair with almost a whole bottle of body wash, she scrubbed herself under the near-scalding water for ten full minutes until she was sure all the excreta that clung to her had been removed. She repeated the process before stepping out of the shower and wrapping her body in a large fluffy black towelling robe and her hair in a matching towel.

Wearing heavy-duty rubber gloves, she picked up the

foul-smelling clothes from the doormat and dumped them in a black bin liner, which she put by the back door for the bin men. She then returned to the bathroom to wash her hands again, over and over under more scalding water.

Suddenly hungry, she headed for the kitchen and poured soup from a can into a saucepan. While it was heating, she went back into the bathroom and carefully scrubbed under her nails with a brush, then as an indulgence, she smothered herself in expensive body lotion. She flicked the towel off her shoulder-length black hair and plaited it.

After she had drunk her soup, she turned on her electric blanket, set the alarm clock and slipped into bed. Within minutes she was out for the count.

Sally Young wiped each piece of china carefully before laying it back on her wooden trestle table. These were the best pieces; most of her stock was in cardboard boxes and wooden crates, which stood on the ground next to the table so that prospective customers could root through it.

Her striped woollen mittens came halfway up her fingers, leaving the exposed half to grow stiff and cold, but it was easier to grip the crockery without fear of dropping it. That was one downside of this trade: her merchandise broke easily and she had to pay for her own losses; she wasn't making enough to afford an insurance policy yet. She needed to be even more careful now she wanted to help Jason through dance school; cracks and chips ate into her profit.

Pilfering was a problem too; she needed eyes in the back of her head and an extra pair on her shoulders, and still expensive items like casserole dishes disappeared as if the bloody fairies had arrived.

She had to make this stall work. She was used to the humping and cleaning; it was the selling she found the hardest. Selling was new to her. The other stallholders seemed able to sell any old junk. Hers wasn't junk, just oddments. Everyone needed odd pieces of crockery, milk jugs, and plates and dishes to make up broken sets. That was why she bought plenty of plain white, you couldn't go wrong with that. All she needed was to learn to convey that to customers, then she'd be on a roll.

She was too honest to try to sell someone something they didn't want, but the other traders told her it wasn't dishonest; some folk didn't know they needed it until they'd bought it. She was learning all this.

She loved it down at East Lane, and was starting to make friends for the first time in her life, joining in the banter with other street traders, sharing stories and chat while they warmed their frozen joints in the café over a bacon roll and a mug of tea, even standing in for another trader while he or she took a break. Making friends had never come easy to Sals; she hadn't time, and she had always been a loner.

Cleaning offices had been quite different. No one spoke to the cleaners, mostly no one even saw them; they came in when the offices were closed, and mainly worked alone. That had never bothered her, but now she liked hearing, 'Morning, Sals,' and 'How's it going today?' or 'Watch my stall, would you, Sals, I've got to 'ave a pee.'

This morning as she dusted and displayed her wares, her mind was elsewhere. Jason was all she had, and she was so proud of him. Getting that scholarship can't have been easy; it showed he must have talent. But now she was worried for him. He was still silly enough to be in love with that Chantelle, and she wanted him to move on. And as for that Haley, interfering stuck-up madam, always telling her Jason was a bad boy, and running to the police; she got what she deserved. Sals didn't like it when the kids broke the law, but she'd never shop them to the Feds. It was only a matter of time before someone did Haley in. Sals just hoped Jason wouldn't jeopardize his big chance over all this. She knew he could lose control of that temper of his, and although he had sworn all that was in the past, she still worried for him.

It was seven thirty in the morning, and the light was just coming up over the market stalls. With a jolt, Sals caught sight of Dwayne Ripley, a so-called lieutenant in the Brotherhood, sauntering up the lane, a fag between his fingers. What was he doing here? She had never seen him around the market before. He looked around before dropping his cigarette butt and treading it into the ground with his heavy boot. Dwayne was feared on the Aviary estate. Sals thought he was a brainless bully, but she knew he spelt trouble.

She had no intention of showing she was afraid of him. She folded her arms and stared as he approached the stall.

'What do you want?' she snapped.

He lifted his grey fleece hood over his head, sniffed loudly and wiped his hand on his tracksuit trousers. It was a wonder they didn't fall down, Sals thought; the crotch nearly reached his knees. Tufts of greasy hair poked out under his hood, and his skin was as pocked as ever with acne. Sals wanted to tell him that washing his hair occasionally might help with the spots, but stopped herself. Instead she snapped, 'If you've something to say, spit it out. I'm busy.'

Dwayne returned her stare. Slowly his mouth moved into a half-smile, then one of his boots flew up and caught the edge of the trestle table. Sals' precious stock of crockery wobbled precariously. As her hand instinctively flew out to steady it, his boot landed on her fingers. She pulled her hand away with a yelp. The table wobbled again and some of the pieces slid backwards and crashed to the ground behind her.

Nearby traders watched in horror, but no one moved in to help.

Sals fought angry tears and fell to her knees, crawling around to salvage whatever she could.

She missed the approach of Winston Mitchell, whose street-name was Scrap. He held two heavy gilt and leather leads in one hand, and pulled at the throats of two flat-headed, slavering pit bull terriers.

She caught sight of the dogs just too late to get out of their way. They both pounced, and one sank its teeth into her upper arm. She was wearing two woollen jumpers and a thermal vest, with a jacket over the top to keep out the early morning damp, but the animal's teeth penetrated the layers until it found flesh. Sals screamed in agony.

Some of the other traders moved towards her, but before they could reach her Dwayne landed a boot in her face and the second dog's teeth were ripping at her half-gloved fingers. Blood dripped to the ground and Sals screamed again.

'I'm calling the police,' one of the traders said, stabbing numbers into his mobile phone.

'Better call an ambulance too,' another shouted.

'I think you need a new table,' was the last thing she heard Winston Mitchell say before he sped off, taking the dogs with him.

'Bastard!' she yelled after him. 'Lousy, fucking bastard!'

Dwayne leaned across the table till his face nearly touched hers. 'Next time it'll be your head.' As he pulled away, he landed another punch in her eye, and she felt a warm globule of spittle slide down the side of her face.

He moved in again, and she smelled heavy smoke on his breath. 'Tell your grandson we know he's around. We're looking forward to welcoming him to our territory.'

Then he was gone.

Some of the other traders started to pack her broken china into boxes, while another, ignoring her protests, lifted her into his van and drove her to Casualty.

Jason had scoured the floor with bleach until he was satisfied that no sign of Haley's blood remained on Sals' kitchen tiles. The washing machine was churning again, and he was confident that this final wash would remove the last traces of blood from his tracksuit. Gran Sals had suggested taking all his clothes with her in a black bin liner when she loaded her little van to go to market, but Jason had stopped her. The police were about, he told her, and their dogs had the scent of Haley. They only lived a hundred yards from the Aviary estate; the dogs would pick the scent up, and both Sally and Jason would be arrested. Jason had been in enough trouble in his life; he knew well enough how to clean up after himself. All his clothes, underwear and all, had gone through the washing machine twice, with bleach as well as soap powder. At least, that was the idea; as he emptied the water he'd used to scrub the floor, he spotted his bloodstained sweatshirt still lying on the floor. How could he have forgotten to put it in last time? He screwed it into a ball and stuffed it behind the machine. As soon as this cycle was finished, he'd see to it.

He hadn't expected his gran to be so understanding. She'd said she wasn't going to let anything get in the way of his chance; nothing else mattered except his scholarship and his new life. She'd even given him money and told him to get the hell out here. If only it was that simple!

Sals had helped clean him up, and given him one of her dark tracksuits to wear instead of his own. He looked a sight in it, but he'd worn worse inside, and right now all that mattered was staying out of trouble. Apart from being with Chantelle of course. Last night, when he'd knocked at her place, she'd been surprised to see him but pleased all the same, at least till he told her about Haley. As soon as he laid eyes on her he knew she was on the game and doing drugs; that would have been why she stopped visiting him in Wandsworth. Somehow that wasn't quite as bad as if she'd stopped loving him, but his heart had nearly broken in a million pieces when he saw faint track marks on the inside of her leg. It was his fault, his and Haley's, that she had turned to drugs.

Aunt Haley had taken the place of Chantelle's mother. She'd given Chantelle a home since her real mother died, sent her to dance classes, brought her up to be a good girl. He understood how Chantelle felt about her aunt; she had a lot to be grateful for. But Haley wasn't what she appeared; what Chantelle didn't know was that her aunt didn't really want the best for her.

When he'd rung her this morning he was pleased to find she was staying at Luanne's. Luanne was strong, and seemed happy to look after her for the time being. Chantelle warned him to get off the estate and go as far away as possible; she had told the Feds it was Yo-Yo who had been at her flat, but they could be on his tail soon as well, so he had no time to hang around. Luanne had agreed to get him another shank to keep him safe on his way up west.

The knock on the door made him jump. Chantelle's voice came through the letterbox. 'Jason. Open the door, quick, before anyone sees us.'

He opened the door and Luanne and Chantelle both stepped quickly inside. Chantelle's eyes were swollen; the sight of it brought a lump to his throat, and he put his arm around her.

'I'm so sorry about Aunt Haley,' he said holding her close. If she was so unhappy now, she must never know what had really happened to her aunt. 'What did Haley do to Yo-Yo?' he asked Chantelle. 'Why did he have her killed?'

Chantelle said nothing, but looked at Luanne.

'He's supplying you, ain't he?' Jason asked. 'Did she find your gear, and threaten to tell the Feds?'

Chantelle hesitated. 'Worse than that,' she said. 'Yo-Yo hid a lot of gear at mine. She found it, and handed it to the police.'

Jason scratched his untidy mass of dark curls and leaned against the wall. 'Jesus. You ain't safe either. He'll have you punished. You should come with me right now. I need to look after you.'

'Don't do this,' Luanne argued. 'We're scared enough already.'

'Then both of you come with me.'

Luanne shook her head. 'I have Alysha to think of.'

Jason sucked air through his teeth. 'Bring Alysha too. We'll all start fresh. It's not safe for you here. You're all in his debt big time.'

Luanne shook her head again. 'I can't, Jason. How can I leave that useless lump of a father of mine? We'll be OK, all of us together. Alysha and I will take care of Chantelle for you. By the time everything's sorted with Haley, you'll be up west and you'll be set up. Chantelle will join you then.'

Jason's eyes pierced into Luanne's. 'I'm relying on you. Don't let her out of your sight.'

'I'll look after her.'

'They won't release the body for a while,' he told Chantelle. 'You know it takes time when it's murder. If you change your mind, or anyone frightens you, ring me and I'll be there.' He turned back to Luanne. 'Did you get me a shank?'

Chantelle opened her bag and took out a supermarket carrier. 'There's some money in there too.'

'I've got money.'

'Take it. You can use it to set us up somewhere when I join you.'

Jason pulled the wad Sals had given him from his pocket and waved it at her. 'I said I've got money. You need this more than I do.' He took the knife and pushed the cash back into her hand.

'Do you really need a shank?' Chantelle asked. 'If you're caught carrying you'll go straight back inside.'

He smiled. She did still care, then. He balanced the knife in his hand. Good size, easy to conceal. Luanne had chosen well. 'The Feds don't understand. They don't have to cross gang territory. I'm not looking for trouble, it's just that I'm a mixed race boy, and I can't walk from postcode to postcode without protection. This shank is a good size.'

'It's Alysha's,' Luanne told him. 'She's Michael's Younger. He gets her all sorts.'

'You be careful,' Chantelle said, close to tears again.

He reached for her and held her close to him. 'I love you,' he whispered.

Over her shoulder he saw Luanne smile and wrinkle her nose. Chantelle buried her face in his shoulder. 'I'm not worth it.'

'Yes. Yes, you are.' He dropped his arms and took her face in his hands. 'It breaks my heart to hear what's happened, but I still love you. I'll never stop loving you. I'm going to sort everything. But you have to get yourself off that shit, you hear me? I'm back now.' He let go of her and slumped against the wall. 'Is that why you never came near me this last two years?'

Chantelle pressed her lips together to stop herself crying. It didn't work.

'Jason, don't . . .' Luanne put out a hand and touched his arm.

He swung around angrily. 'I need to know,' he shouted. 'Chantelle, I need to know why you never came to me.'

'Keep your voice down, for fuck's sake,' Luanne urged.

He took Chantelle in his arms again and forced himself to speak gently. 'Don't cry. OK. It's OK. I'm gonna sort it. As long as you still love me, nothing else matters. I'll sort this.'

Chantelle didn't answer.

'I'm going to help you. Just tell me you want us to have a life together. All I need is to know you love me and want to be with me.'

'I love you,' she whispered. 'But you deserve better.'

He shook his head. 'No. You're my girl. I don't want no one else.'

Chantelle looked away.

'Are you still my girl?'

She looked at him. Her forehead crumpled and her lips quivered. Those large chocolate eyes had filled his thoughts while he was away.

She nodded.

'OK,' he whispered, stroking her hair. 'We can do this. You don't need drugs now. I'm here. You have to go cold turkey. It's the only way. You can do it, baby. I'll help you.'

She nodded again.

'We're gonna get there. You and me.' He smiled sadly and dug into his pocket for the money Sals had given him out. He divided it roughly in two, and handed her half. 'If any of the Brotherhood get on your case, give them this. I'll get you more. You do not go back on the streets, you hear me? You're my girl. No one touches you.'

'You ain't top dog round here no more, Jason Young,' Luanne interrupted. 'You can't upset the Brotherhood like that. You'll make it even harder for her. The Brotherhood run things now. They've already killed Haley cos she crossed them. They're planning to kill you too, and then they'll kill her. Is that what you want?'

Jason threw Luanne an angry look, then twitched his head sideways to tell her to get lost. She opened the door and stalked outside, slamming it behind her.

'I'm sorry, Jase,' Chantelle said weakly. 'I just wanted stuff to stop me missing you.'

'I know, baby, and I'm sorry I had to leave you alone all that time. But I'm back now, and I love you. If you love me too, that's all that matters.' His voice softened. 'You're not safe here. You've got to let me take care of you. If you've given Yo-Yo up to the Feds, you need to get away. Come with me.'

'I can't leave till my aunt's stuff is sorted. If I go they'll come after us for the money I owe for the stuff Haley gave to the Feds. If I pay Yo-Yo, they'll leave us alone.'

'I'll get you money to pay Yo-Yo.'

'No. I'll sort it. Then I'll follow you.'

'How?'

'He won't hurt me if I keep making money for him.'

Jason took a sharp breath. At that moment he wanted nothing more than to kill Yo-Yo Reilly for touching his girl. He said nothing, but made a silent promise to himself. When he spoke again he made an effort to keep his voice even. 'Baby, if you think whoring for him will keep you alive, you ain't got nothing up here.' He stabbed at his temple, fighting his temper down.

Chantelle didn't reply.

'You really ain't safe, baby, you gotta believe it. He's doing you to get at me.'

She stared at him dumbly. Her eyes looked bigger and sadder than he'd ever seen them. 'Are you not listening to me?'

She gave herself a little shake. 'I will come and join you. But I can look out for myself.'

'I don't think you can, not against Yo-Yo. Come with me, let me care for you. Please.'

She didn't answer.

He gave her shoulders a little shake. 'Do you still want to dance?'

She nodded.

'It's our dream, right? I'm going to make our dream happen.' He kissed the red cocaine scars at the edges of her nose. 'We said we'd dance and now we've got the chance. Let's get out of here and start again.'

'Yes, I will, but not today. Please, Jason! Don't ask me again.'

He dropped his hands to his sides. He'd been shot and stabbed, spent years locked in institutions and been hungry on the streets. The pain that he felt at that moment was worse than all of those put together. He bent to fix Alysha's knife inside his sock, using the time to regain control over his temper.

'OK.' He stood up and put his hands on her shoulders. 'Stay. Do what you have to do. But keep my number with you all the time.'

He tried to read her face, but those beautiful, gold-flecked eyes couldn't look back at him.

SEVEN

It was seven o'clock on Saturday morning and Georgia Johnson was on tenterhooks. She had slept for less than an hour before getting up and making her way into the shower for the second time that morning. She allowed the hot water to stream over her taut body as she scrubbed it all over with soap again and again.

She dressed quickly in a freshly laundered white T-shirt, black sweatshirt and expensive ice-blue jeans, then pulled comfortable white socks over her feet and slipped them into pristine black trainers. As she grabbed her short black leather jacket, her heart sank. Her keys were still in the pocket of the coat she'd thrown out last night. She would have to go through the process of putting on the thick, black elbow-length plastic gloves and tipping up the bin liner containing the ruined clothing. Then she'd have to push her hand inside the coat pocket to retrieve the keys. She took a deep breath and headed for the door.

When she came back into the flat she dumped the gloves in the pail, stripped off her jacket and sweatshirt and ran her hands and arms under hot running water before lathering them with soap. The rinsing water was so hot it turned her skin bright pink, and the towel seemed to scour off a couple of layers.

Before she left the flat she smeared Vaseline over her mouth and dropped two eye drops in each eye, then flicked a mascara wand over her dark lashes and blinked herself awake.

When she arrived at the station, the forensics on the blood spatters on Haley Gulati's door and hallway hadn't come back. That was only to be expected. It could take at least forty-eight hours to get those results; the problem was they couldn't hold Reilly all that time without charging him or getting an extension. Applying for an extension would mean committing to paper the first-hand evidence Chantelle Gulati had given regarding the visit Reilly had paid her after her aunt's murder. Georgia didn't want to jeopardize Chantelle's safety by making that information public. Reilly was one of the most powerful gang leaders in South London; he had ways of putting Chantelle's life in grave danger, even from a police cell.

Right now they were closer to nailing Reilly than ever before. Previously he'd always slipped through their fingers; well, not this time, Georgia vowed. But first she had to get his statement, and also make sure he was refused bail. Even if he claimed he knew nothing about the murdered woman, the forensics would prove different; it might take a few days, but that test would put Reilly's DNA in Haley's blood on Chantelle's door. Then she had the bastard for first degree murder, and no bent solicitor would get him off. But she needed time, and right now without naming Chantelle she had no sound evidence to hold him. She could charge him for breeding illegal pit bulls; that could mean a custodial sentence, but it wasn't cut and dried. First they had to prove the pit bulls were pit bulls, and when they'd tried it before his crook of a solicitor had found someone to swear they were crossbreeds and therefore perfectly legal.

She tapped her papers into a neat pile. She had never needed quick DNA results more than today. Every police officer in London would raise a glass when Reilly was behind bars; she wanted the honour of putting him there, and soon. The sight of the victim had set the bee loose in her bonnet. She wanted justice.

Reilly had already made the phone call he was allowed, and brought in Alan Oakwood, solicitor to the lowest of the low in the criminal world, specializing in the rich drug barons around South London.

Oakwood was there when Georgia walked into the custody area, bending every ear that would listen: his client was innocent, they had nothing to hold him; even his dogs, which the police had wrongfully seized and locked in a pound, weren't pit bull terriers at all, but crossbreeds. Once that was proved, he would insist that the dogs and his client be released immediately.

'Change the record,' Georgia said to Oakwood as she walked past. She called the custody sergeant aside. On no account, she told him, was he to listen to Oakwood's drivel, or release anyone without her say-so. The sergeant told her the youth who had waved the knife at her had been released, with Oakwood's help of course, and bailed to appear in court charged with carrying an offensive weapon with intent to harm a police officer.

Georgia was less than happy about that, but she had bigger fish to fry. She had to find a way of persuading the Lambeth lab to get those tests done at speed, then Alan Oakwood could shout his hairy head off about the pit bulls. Once Reilly was banged up, Georgia was confident crime in South London would calm down for a while. Of course a new gang would appear, or one of Reilly's crew would move up to the role of chief Elder, but Georgia would face that when it happened. It was unlikely anyone else would be as big a threat as Reilly.

But they could only ignore Oakwood for thirty-six hours; after that he would be within his legal rights to demand Yo-Yo's release. The guys in the lab at Lambeth were doing their best, but couldn't work miracles. DNA testing took time, especially when there were two sets to look for: first Haley's blood, then Reilly's perspiration and skin cells in the blood.

Time was something Georgia Johnson was short of at this minute, and she hadn't a lot of patience either. She had a sister who worked as a microbiologist, but unfortunately not in Lambeth.

A thought struck her. At yesterday's meeting, when they were told DI David Dawes was coming in because he was well up on gang crime, someone had also mentioned that he was from an influential family. She didn't recall what kind of influence they had, but maybe he knew someone who could pull strings and move her tests to the front of the queue.

She left the custody area and made her way to the incident room. Stephanie Green was sitting at her desk dunking short-bread biscuits in a plastic cup of vending machine tea. There were wet brown stains on the reports she was reading.

Georgia refrained from commenting. 'Have you got any background on DI Dawes?' she asked.

'Like what?' Stephanie dropped the remains of a wilting biscuit into her tea.

'Like personal details?'

Stephanie scooped the biscuity mess from the cup with her fingers and shovelled it into her mouth. 'Word is he's been sent over from the West End. He's an expert on London gangs, studies them all, and he'll be an asset to this case.' She ran her tongue over the back of her teeth to retrieve the last few crumbs of shortbread and raised her eyebrows at Georgia. 'Apparently he has a good reputation, and a good pedigree.'

'Pedigree, eh?' Georgia used a manicured nail to bend a loose hair back into her ponytail. 'Any more on that?'

'Unlike you to take a personal interest in a new DI, ma'am.' Stephanie tossed the last of the tea down her throat, and squashed the plastic cup and aimed it at the bin. Her eyes twinkled at Georgia. 'Like the look of him, do you?'

Georgia gave her a look that spoke volumes. 'I heard he has friends in high places. I'm hoping he might have a contact in forensics. I need to get this DNA pushed through.'

'Well, I wouldn't mind.'

'You have a one-track mind,' Georgia said sharply. 'You can fuck each other's brains out for all I care. I just need to get these DNA results. We can't afford to let Stuart Reilly out this time. And I heard Dawes has influential friends.'

A voice spoke from behind her. 'I'll see what I can do for you, but I make no promises.' David Dawes. Georgia closed her eyes. How long had he been standing there? Had he heard the entire conversation? She caught Stephanie Green's eye.

'I don't know anyone personally in forensics, I'm afraid,' he said. 'But I know a few other people that might help. I'll try and pull a favour. At least, I'll do my best,' he added.

Stephanie's complexion had reddened and mottled all the way from her chin to her hairline. She bowed her head and bit into another biscuit. Georgia was glad that blushing didn't register on Caribbean skin, but she certainly felt the heat. She turned to face Dawes. 'I'm so sorry, that must have sounded crass,' she said. 'I'm just frustrated – pulling my hair out to get this arrest. I don't want Reilly let out in case he disappears, and I really believe the DNA results will get us the conviction.'

'No offence taken,' he said with a grin. He pulled his mobile from his pocket. 'I'll make a call. It's private, I'll do it outside.'

Alan Oakwood was red hot at his job. His outward appearance was of a 1960s hippy who had lived his whole life on a diet of vegetarian food and herb tea, but it belied his true personality. The multi-coloured paisley shirt, single small gold earring and silver bangles around one wrist served only to make him look what he was: a man in the wrong job. All the other solicitors who visited the station came suited and booted. Oakwood's relaxed look fooled no one, least of all Georgia Johnson. This man was callous, deceitful and highly intelligent – a dangerous mix when it came to keeping crooks out of prison. His pale, flyaway grey hair was long and thin, matching his physique. Tiny pebble-lensed glasses, not unlike the late John Lennon's, covered grey eyes that were small, cold and heartless, and what he lacked in weight he made up for in verbal dexterity. He had a brain sharper than any knife belonging to the low life he represented, and he savoured every opportunity to get one over on the police.

He knew his clients were far from innocent, but he cared only for the fees that they earned him. Georgia frequently said he belonged in prison with them, and she'd like to put him there, or failing that, knock his know-all brain against a wall. Right now she wasn't about to let him see he had the upper hand, that she had nothing to hold Reilly on, at least until the DNA results came through. When they did, Stuart 'Yo-Yo' Reilly would no longer be running the Aviary estate or threatening innocent citizens.

The truth was, Georgia doubted Reilly had actually murdered Haley Gulati; three stab wounds to the heart simply wasn't his style. But he was behind it, she was sure of that, and the last nail in his coffin was that he had boasted to the victim's niece.

What she needed to find out was why he'd had Haley killed. Reilly was known for wreaking revenge on the relatives of someone who crossed or owed him; Georgia had seen that

Chantelle was a user, so putting two and two together she had her answer. She needed to talk to Chantelle again, but not until the girl was calmer. Meanwhile she was going to have a crack at getting Reilly to give up the lowlife who did the stabbing; that would take another of his gang off the street.

She pulled out a chair, settled herself beside Stephanie Green, and switched the recording machine to ON.

Reilly had been given a white forensic suit to wear while his clothes were taken for testing. He looked like an oversized snowman.

'Where were you between the hours of ten p.m. and two a.m. last night?' Stephanie asked him. Alan Oakwood noisily clicked the catches of his briefcase, drowning out her voice. She repeated the question.

Oakley let out a sigh of irritation and, without looking up from his briefcase, he replied in a flat, condescending tone. 'My client has already told you that. He has witnesses.'

Georgia leaned across the table until her forehead nearly touched Oakwood's nose. He pulled his head back, ostrich-like, and met her eyes.

'Detective Sergeant Green is asking your client to tell her again,' she said. 'So, for the tape, will you please answer the question, Mr Reilly?'

Reilly leaned back in his chair and laced his fingers behind his head. 'I was having a fuck,' he said, widening his ugly mouth into a grin and displaying a gold tooth at the side of his mouth.

Reilly and Oakwood looked like Laurel and Hardy sitting side by side. Reilly was heavily overweight, his brief was built like a string bean. It was clear he was shrewd enough not to indulge in the class A drugs he dealt. None of the big dealers ever did, Georgia thought angrily; they didn't give a toss that a high percentage of the kids they lured into the habit lost their lives to it. In Georgia's book, dealers were only one rung below rapists, and Reilly was probably both.

She stared at him. His dark hair fell over his forehead, shining with grease, badly in need of a wash. He was twenty-seven-years-old and weighed nearly as many stones.

'Her name?' Stephanie asked crisply.

Yo-Yo shook his head and shrugged. 'Never asked,' he said, letting out a loud fart.

'Unfortunate,' Stephanie said. 'We have a witness who says you had a falling out with Haley Gulati, and stabbed her in the heart.'

Reilly shrugged again. 'They're lying. I was having a shag.' He looked at Oakwood, who was wiping his pebble glasses with a white handkerchief. 'Shame I didn't ask her name,' he said to Oakwood. 'She was a good fuck as it happens.' He turned back to face Georgia and Stephanie, jiggling his crotch.

'What did it cost you?' Georgia snapped. She longed to fling herself across the desk and smack him hard in the face. Patience, she told herself; when she had him for first degree murder, she'd wipe that disgusting grin off his disgusting face.

Just for a moment, she succeeded anyway. The smile disappeared, and his eyes grew small and dark. 'I've never paid for it,' he answered coldly.

'It's your charm they fall for, is it?' Stephanie goaded. 'Not the free drugs, then. Or your ill-gotten riches.'

'You don't have to answer that,' Oakwood chipped in.

'Do you have a contact for her?' Georgia again. 'This shag whose name you don't recall?'

'My client has already told you . . .'

'That he doesn't know her name.' Georgia cut Oakwood off in mid-sentence. 'But not where he picked her up, or what she looked like. See, we have a problem, Mr Reilly. You say you were having a shag, but can't provide a witness, and we think you killed Haley Gulati, and do have a witness.'

'You haven't charged my client,' Oakwood pointed out in a clipped upper-class tone. 'So do you have proof to back up this accusation? If not, you know as well as I do that this conversation is going nowhere. I suggest that what you have is merely circumstantial.' He pinned his eyes on her. 'So bring out your evidence, or else I insist you release my client.'

'Housing dangerous dogs is an imprisonable offence,' Stephanie said. 'We've called in a dog expert. If it turns out that your dogs are pure pit bulls, we will confiscate them, and charge you with owning illegal dogs, too.'

Georgia didn't look at Oakwood. Stephanie's remark would have told him they were playing for time.

Oakwood raised a disdainful hand. 'My client's dogs are not pure-bred pit bulls, and your expert will tell you as much.' The side of his mouth bent into a tiny smile. 'So I am going to insist . . .'

Georgia cut him off mid-sentence again. 'Interview terminated at eleven oh seven p.m.' She clicked the recording machine to OFF and left the room.

David Dawes was waiting outside Georgia's office when she arrived back from the interview suite. She opened the door and beckoned him in.

The room smelled of lavender furniture polish. A large, healthy pot plant, drops of fresh water still clinging to its leaves, stood upright in the corner. Three cans of Red Bull were stacked in the shape of a triangle on a shelf by the newly-painted wall; next to them stood a china cup and saucer and a packet of artificial sweeteners. Everything on her desk was in tidy piles.

'I phoned a friend, then I phoned Lambeth,' Dawes said. 'I told them the Aviary material was top priority. They're on it.'

Georgia opened her mouth to thank him, but he lifted his hand. 'But there's blood, and sweat in the blood – that's two lots of testing.' He grimaced apologetically. 'That takes twice as long.'

'But at least they're on it.' She sat down in her chair and waved him into the one opposite, then put her elbows on the table. They exchanged appraising looks.

Georgia had arrived where she was by being completely upfront; she had a reputation for speaking her mind, and was liked and respected by her team for it. Dawes was new to the squad, and on this showing he would be a big asset.

'I was told you had friends in high places,' she said.

He waited a beat, then replied, 'I do my job as best I can. I'm not superman.'

'I never said you were.' She kept her gaze fixed on him. 'How come the interest in gang crime?'

His jaw tensed. Something had hit a nerve. 'It's personal, but I'm glad I'm on this case.'

Georgia took a breath. 'If I have to apply for an extension to keep Reilly here, I'll have to tell his brief about my witness statement. That will put my witness at risk.' She rubbed her forehead. 'Even from inside, he can do damage. I can't let him out. We have to keep him locked up.'

'Then we charge him under the dangerous dogs act. He can go down for that.'

'I want him for murder.' She banged her fist on the table. 'We've got a chance to get him for murder. No one has ever given evidence on that estate, and now someone has. I want him behind bars for life.'

Dawes nodded. 'We all do, believe me we all do. And with a little patience we will. Has the witness got protection?'

'We're sorting out a family liaison officer at the lunchtime meeting.'

'Good. Let's charge Reilly with harbouring dangerous dogs. That will keep him locked up while we pull the murder charge together.'

'Supposing he gets bail? That solicitor of his is a slippery bastard.'

'Oh, I think we can swing it,' Dawes assured her. 'No one is above the law. Do you remember the Buzzards? The gang headed by Jason Young?'

'Vaguely,' Georgia said. 'A bit before my time.'

'They were dangerous, and very clever, but we got the leader. Jason Young, his name was. He went down for armed robbery, and the gang folded like a pack of cards. Some of the others are serving time too, and the ones left behind got shot or stabbed. Everyone knows Reilly was behind that, but it was never proved. Still, we got the Buzzards.'

There was a knock on the door and Stephanie Green came in holding a piece of paper. Her rosy face looked serious.

'DNA results,' she said.

Georgia flicked a glance at Dawes. 'Already?'

'And?' Dawes asked anxiously.

'Not from the blood on Chantelle's door,' Stephanie said apologetically. 'Sorry. This is from the semen on the dead woman. Forensics have picked up four different DNA samples – two in her vagina, one on her face, and one on her body.'

Georgia lowered her eyes. Her heart went out to the woman lying in the mortuary. She had probably prayed for death. Georgia hoped she hadn't felt too much pain. She had trained herself to keep her feelings and memories hidden, but sometimes it wasn't easy.

'Go on,' she said crisply.

'Michael Delahaye, street name Mince, and Dwayne Ripley, street name Boot, match the two in the deceased's vagina. The one on her body is Jason Young's. He's a former gang leader around there.'

Georgia looked at David Dawes. 'But I thought . . .'

'He's out,' Dawes told her. He looked at Stephanie again. 'What about the fourth one?'

Stephanie smiled. 'That's the best bit. The sperm on her face is Stuart Reilly's.'

Georgia resisted the urge to punch the air and shout, 'Result!', but her grin was as broad as Stephanie's.

'Shall I bring the other two in?' Stephanie asked.

'Delahaye and Ripley are Brotherhood Elders or lieutenants,' Dawes told her. 'Vicious bastards. But Jason Young . . .' He tapped the table with his fingers. 'He's their enemy. He was in Wandsworth till last week. And he's more of a firearms man than knives. He went down for armed robbery.'

'Only one way to find out,' Georgia said.

'Delahaye and Ripley have got previous for carrying blades,' Dawes said. He looked at Georgia thoughtfully. 'This doesn't add up. If Young is involved, we can be pretty certain Reilly isn't. They would never work together. And Yo-Yo leaves spider scars as his trademark. Haley Gulati was stabbed three times, and one cut went straight through into her heart. Are we sure this is Reilly's work?'

'Someone knew exactly where to aim,' Stephanie pointed out. 'What about Dwayne Ripley?'

'Could have been some kind of initiation for someone new to the gang?' said Georgia.

'Looks like it's not as straightforward as we thought,' Dawes observed.

Georgia turned to Stephanie. 'Better warn the duty sergeant we'll be needing a lot of back-up. We're going back to the Aviary Estate to bring those three in.'

Jason should have been feeling pleased with himself. He was out of prison, and had a chance to live his dream; and Chantelle had said she wanted to be with him. But wandering along the street right at this moment, it didn't feel like it was going good for him. Things were going to be OK now that Chantelle had fingered Reilly, and he had his dance scholarship – so why did he feel so uncomfortable? He could look out for himself, and he had a shank to protect himself, if necessary. Was that it? He wanted to go straight, and he didn't want to carry, but it was like life just wouldn't let him. Carrying with previous meant a custodial; if he got stopped and searched he was right back in the slammer. They said estate kids never got to do right, and it was true. But he wanted to prove them wrong.

He walked toward the bridge and stopped to look at the view of London, all spread out in front of him.

This was going to be where it all began again for him and Chantelle. After college they would get an act together and be paid to dance, hip-hop and street stuff, just the two of them. Wouldn't that be cool? Memories of making love together came back to him. It had been a long time since they'd done that. Her warm skin against his, and the cute *umph* sounds she made to let him know the touching felt good and he was turning her on. He smiled, remembering one night they were doing it in Aunt Haley's front room; he tried to hush Chantelle's loud *umphs* as he brought her to orgasm. He kept *ssh*ing and *aah*ing in delight, and trying to keep quiet himself too, and it sent them both into a fit of giggles. Then Chantelle got the hiccups, and that was what woke Haley, not the *umph*ing. Haley came in and caught them, stark naked and him with an erection like a bloody erect water fountain. Haley went ballistic, beat him about his head with a stale French loaf and threw him out. It was worth it, though.

The smile quickly left his face as the thought of Chantelle sucking off strangers for the price of a gram of coke hit home.

He'd kill Reilly, and any other bastard that touched her. No matter what she said back there, he knew he couldn't leave her for long; she was getting a habit and that could make you do bad things. He would get everything sorted real quick: work all night if he had to, to pay their way. He'd get her off the shit, and give her back her life.

She was born to dance, just like he was. Omar, his social worker, who had helped him so much, and encouraged him to apply for his scholarship, had told him to believe that you could take control of your own destiny. He had, and now he had to help Chantelle to take control of hers. If she carried on down the path she was on, she would be dead within two years. That was the way it worked when the stuff took you over.

He wasn't letting that happen to his girl.

EIGHT

Chantelle stood in front of the mirror in Luanne's grubby front room. Her nose itched, and she rubbed it with the back of her hand.

Jason thought this dance scholarship was going to change everything, but it wasn't going to happen for him, she knew that. Away from the estate, he'd be mixing with kids who had parents who'd cared for them, kids who hadn't spent their lives on the street or in young offenders', and he wouldn't be able to cope. He'd be back on the Aviary in no time, and things would go back to how they were – he'd start stealing and dealing again, and he'd get caught and go down for another stretch.

That was how you lived around here: stealing, dealing, and whoring. Guns and knives were the tools of the trade. Nothing changed, except Yo-Yo ran things around here now, not Jason.

She rubbed her nose again, and smeared dark red lipstick on her mouth. She noticed her leg wouldn't keep still.

Luanne and Alysha were on the sofa watching the TV. Luanne looked up.

'Don't stress, babe. Yo-Yo won't do nothing to you,' she assured her. 'It'll take a good few days before they get those DNA results and find out it wasn't Yo-Yo, and Jason will call for you before that. It'll be OK. Try and chill. D'you want a joint?'

Chantelle shook her head. 'I need a hit.'

She pulled the money Jason had given her out of her cleavage. She could get a rock for a tenner. She'd promised Jason she wouldn't, but this was an emergency; the Feds had told her she'd have to go and identify Aunt Haley's body later today, and she'd need something to get her through that. She'd give the drugs up after all this calmed down.

'I'm going to get a rock,' she said to Alysha, 'Will you come with me and look out for the Feds?'

Alysha was dressed in embroidered jeans and a black satin puffa jacket. Her corn-rows were newly plaited, and she was wearing some of Chantelle's dark red lipstick. She was twelve, but could have passed for sixteen. She jumped up from the sofa. 'You bet.'

'Are you mad?' Luanne shrieked. 'The boys won't give you any stuff – the Feds will be watching every move you make.'

Chantelle pulled her phone from her bag.

Luanne put out her hand. 'Don't use that,' she warned. 'When the police start asking questions, they might check our call history.'

'I could go,' Alysha suggested. 'The Feds won't notice me. I'll find Mince and tell him to get Boot to bring you a rock.'

'Good girl.' Chantelle handed her the money.

'You've got a big crush on that Michael the Mince,' Luanne teased. 'You wanna watch out. You're only twelve.'

'Nearly thirteen.' Alysha pocketed the money.

'Yeah, yeah, whatever,' Luanne retorted. 'Hey, get some chips too. If the Feds are around when you come back, you can say you went out to get chips. They were on our case this morning. We told them Chantelle felt faint, and we were going to get some fresh air. We had to talk them out of coming with us, and then had to race to get the shank to Jason and back double quick.'

Alysha held her hand out for money to pay for the chips. Chantelle gave her another fiver.

'Just don't hang about, are you hearing me?' Luanne warned.

Alysha headed for the door. 'Yeah, yeah, whatever.'

It wasn't long before she was back, bearing the chips and a message that the hit would be delivered as soon as the coast was clear. She and Luanne sat down to eat the chips. Chantelle couldn't face food. She rubbed her nose a few times and sniffed.

Then the doorbell rang.

Jason stood in the queue in a fried chicken bar. He'd never been able to resist the smell of Kentucky fried. As a hungry kid he used to hang around outside, watching for people who dumped their cartons leaving half the meal behind. He'd collect the discarded cartons, and take them back to the cave to share with the other kids: cold chips, sometimes even a bit of meat left on the bones.

As time went by and he and his gang got braver, they went into the Kentucky bar in twos and threes, and when a customer's supper was placed on the counter, one of them would distract him by asking the time or something trivial, and another would grab the food and make a dash for it. They were fast runners and no one ever caught them.

From there they went to breaking into the fried chicken joints through the toilet windows, sneaking into the kitchen when the coast was clear, grabbing what they could, and escaping by the same route.

Later, when he was a Younger, working with guns and drugs and earning his own money, he would go in on the way back from his beloved dance lessons, decked out in new trainers and his own headphones and sounds, and pay for his chicken and chips. That made him feel proud of how far he'd come.

There was money in his pocket now, but he'd have to go careful. Gran Sals had given him five hundred, and he had given half to Chantelle. It was only Saturday, and he wouldn't be able to get into the dance school till Monday. He couldn't blow cash on somewhere to sleep; he'd have to sleep rough for the next couple of nights. That was when things could get dodgy, sleeping on some other gang's territory. He really hoped he wouldn't have to use the shank.

Another problem was that he'd stink by the time he turned up for the first day of dance classes. The woman that ran the joint had found him somewhere to stay, with a family near the school. He had the address. Maybe he could check that out, ask if it was OK to move in a couple of days early; that way he could get a shower before the first class.

He was optimistic, but nervous. A lot of the estate kids dreamed of being rap stars or athletes, but he had a real chance. One day he and Chantelle would look back, when they were far away and earning their own money, and maybe even had babies of their own.

It was his turn at the counter. He just ordered the chicken, figured he needed the protein at the moment, though there might come a time when he'd have to live on chips. He paid, and took his plastic tray to a seat near the window. There were trees down this road: a real treat. He loved to study their shapes, some of them like dancers' arms, bending and moving in the wind. He really missed seeing trees during his time in Wandsworth.

A group of boys were hanging out outside, three black and a couple of white. He turned his back to the window. He wasn't courting trouble; he was going to avoid it at all costs. He bit into his chicken and thought about the last twenty-four hours. How had all this shit happened?

He had hated Haley. She called him a bad boy and told him to stay away. How bad was it to love someone? And what was all that finding Jesus stuff that Haley was into? Where was she when Chantelle was being lured into drugs? On her knees in some church, he had no doubt. Chantelle must have felt so alone and desperate.

He wiped his mouth with a serviette. He needed a shave; fat chance of that for a few days. He picked up his tray, dumped his rubbish and left the shop. A couple of guys weighed him up, but he ignored them. His next problem was how far to walk today, and which was the safest street to sleep in tonight.

Alysha jumped up at the sound of the door. 'I'll go,' she said, swallowing down a mouthful of chips and wiping her mouth with the back of her hand. 'Mince said he'd bring your stuff.'

'She's got it bad,' Chantelle said, following her.

Winston 'Scrap' Mitchell, Dwayne 'Boot' Ripley and Michael 'Mince' Delahaye, the three lieutenants of the Brotherhood gang, stood framed in the doorway. All three had their sweatshirt hoods up over their heads. It was a bitterly cold morning. Some washing pinned to a rope further down the walkway stood to attention as the biting wind fought to free it from the line.

There were no Feds around. Boot stepped quickly inside the flat, closely followed by the others, and kicked the door shut behind them.

'Someone's got a mouth on her,' he said, taking a step towards Chantelle.

'I ain't said nothing,' she protested, trying to see what he was holding behind his back. It was a cricket bat.

She flicked a glance at Alysha. The kid was by the door and might get a chance to slip out and get help. Alysha was streetwise, and got the message. She'd opened the door and she was about to dash out when Mince Delahaye grabbed her. Mince's jeans were so low-slung they might have slipped off his bony hips at any second.

Chantelle pushed him. 'Let go of her!'

'And there's us thinking you liked Yo-Yo, and were grateful for the stuff he got you.' Mince stepped back and kept hold of Alysha, leaving space for Scrap Mitchell to move in behind Boot. Chantelle had to take a pace backwards.

Boot leaned forward till his face nearly touched hers. 'Cat got your tongue?' he asked menacingly.

Luanne was standing in the hall in seconds. She grabbed Mince and tried to pull him away from Alysha. 'Leave her alone.'

Mince released Alysha and grabbed Luanne's arm. 'What?' he spat at her. 'You want your arm broken, do you?'

Alysha grabbed the opportunity and was out the door and running in a flash.

'Get the Feds,' Chantelle screamed desperately after her, then tugged at Mince's sweatshirt. 'Leave Luanne out of this, she ain't done nothing, she . . .'

The head-butt seemed to come out of nowhere, and sent her flying backwards. Her head hit the wall beside the door, and before she registered any pain blood spurted from her nose.

After that it all happened quickly. The bat waved in front of her eyes, and as she opened her mouth to scream a firm hand gripped her face and squeezed her cheekbones. She felt a crack, and her whole head seemed to explode in pain. Then something bounced off the top of her head. It wasn't till she saw more blood shoot out that she realized the cricket bat had cracked open the top of her skull. Her back thumped against the wall and her head fell against her shoulder as her body slid downwards. Blood spurted in all directions. She tried to speak, but a strange sound echoed inside her brain. A boot ploughed into her face as she stared at the carpet, and a distant voice said, 'See? Yo-Yo don't like being set-up by his cunts.'

She tasted blood sliding down her throat and prayed to pass out. Just before she did, she felt her ribs and back rock from side to side and was vaguely aware of being kicked, but her strength had left her and she couldn't even roll into a protective ball. Her arm seemed to bend toward her face, then there was excruciating pain and a sound like a twig snapping. As she slipped from consciousness her last thought was that if Jason had stayed with her, he would never have danced again.

The next thing she saw was a blurred version of Luanne sitting on the floor beside her. She made out a bloodstained towel and a phone, and Luanne screaming for help and an ambulance. Chantelle hoped she was dying. She didn't want to live, not the way she'd look after this.

It was a good moment for Georgia and Stephanie. They shut Alan Oakwood's lowlife legal mouth good and proper when they told him his client's DNA had been identified in the sperm in the dead woman's mouth, giving them ample grounds to hold Reilly for further questioning.

David Dawes wasn't too pleased to be given the job of bringing in Dwayne Ripley and Michael Delahaye; he wanted a go at interviewing Reilly. But Georgia wasn't having it. She had decided to make it clear from day one that she was running the investigation. She told him she and Stephanie would bring in Jason Young; Dawes said nothing, but she could tell by his face that he wanted a go at Jason Young too.

He gave Georgia and Stephanie his notes on Young's history with the Buzzards, and told them again that he found it almost impossible to believe Young's DNA was on the victim as well as Reilly's. They were confirmed enemies, and wouldn't work together if their lives depended on it.

Georgia read the notes as they drove along to pick up Young at his gran's flat. Most of the Buzzards were serving time for armed robbery; that much she already knew. What stopped her in her tracks was the way Jason Young and his gang were caught. There had been a tip-off from an informant, and that informant was Haley Gulati. And now Young was newly out of prison, and Haley Gulati had been murdered.

The pieces of jigsaw were beginning to drop into place. Faced with DNA evidence, Reilly's excuse was that it was Haley he'd had sex with earlier, with her consent. There was no arguing that one, Haley couldn't disagree, it was Reilly's word against no one's. No court would put him away for that. Forensics had confirmed that Young's DNA was on the woman, but not his sperm. It was now looking likely that it was Jason Young who had stabbed Haley, after the Brotherhood had gang-raped her.

So they had strong evidence, and this new information from Dawes gave them a motive. Jason Young was now their chief suspect. She needed to get him quickly, or the slippery bastard would do a runner.

The manner of this woman's death had got under Georgia's skin. She'd seen many black women murdered, but it was the gang-rape that really preyed on her.

Stephanie's chirpy voice broke into her thoughts. 'I wonder why Dawes is so interested in South London gangs?' There was a pause, then Steph said, 'Are you OK, ma'am?'

Georgia blinked herself back into the present. 'Yes, course. And you only have to call me ma'am in front of the others, you know that.' She blew out a breath. 'I'm thinking about Haley Gulati,' she said. 'She was the informant that got Young sent down for armed robbery, so now we have a motive for both sets of DNA. It's starting to look like the Brotherhood raped her first, and then Young murdered her. Dawes is adamant that they wouldn't work together on anything, though.'

'Could be coincidence,' Stephanie offered. 'Both were after her and both got to her on the same night. It does happen.'

'Chase up the footprints around the murder from forensics. Let's see if we can place any of these lowlifes at the actual scene.'

'Will do.' Stephanie stuck her hand in her pocket and pulled out a Twix bar. The lights changed and she drove off, one hand on the wheel, the other ripping at the wrapper.

'If only we could find the weapon,' Georgia said. 'That would tell us a lot more.'

'A bit like finding a needle in a haystack on that estate,' Stephanie said through a mouthful of chocolate. 'Peacock's in charge of that. So far they've turned up eleven knives, and a treasure trove of other weapons around and about, but none of them match the cuts.'

Georgia looked down at the notes Dawes had given her. Anything to avoid watching Stephanie with chocolate all over her chin. There was one sure way to stop her eating that rubbish, Georgia thought mischievously.

'I'll bet you a tenner that you bed Dawes during this enquiry.'

Stephanie laughed raucously and licked chocolate from her fingers. 'By the end of the enquiry? We've got a suspect, we've found a motive, all we need is a confession. It could be in the bag before the end of the day.'

'We need proof,' Georgia offered.

'Not if we get a confession.' A grin split her face. 'Why are you asking me to try and seduce Dawes? Not that I'd say no given a chance.'

Georgia smiled. 'Go for it,' she said, 'I want all the gossip on him.'

Her mobile rang. It was DCI Banham, and he had break-through news.

'We're on our way to pick him up,' she said into the phone. She hissed to Stephanie, 'The blood from the door at the Gulatis' is Haley's, and the DNA from the perspiration is . . . Jason Young's!'

But the DCI hadn't finished. She stiffened. 'No, sir. *No!* You can't let him out!'

Stephanie threw her eyes northward and sighed.

Georgia listened powerlessly as DCI Banham told her they had no grounds for holding Reilly. He admitted having sex with a woman whose name he didn't remember. He said it was consensual sex, and there was nothing to prove otherwise. Banham depressed her even further; the dangerous dog charge hadn't held up. A canine expert had been called in, and confirmed that Yo-Yo's dogs were crossbred. There were no charges to answer to, and Reilly's solicitor had insisted he was released. Reilly was out and free again, and the police could do nothing about it.

Georgia clicked her phone off and repeated the news to Stephanie.

'With a bit of luck they'll kill each other,' Stephanie said. 'They're both the lowest of lowlife.'

They drove in silence for a few minutes, then Stephanie said, 'You're on.'

'On what?'

'Your bet. A tenner. I'm going to give it a go. The case is definitely not cut and dried.'

Georgia smiled, nodded and gave a thumbs-up. This would be interesting. Dawes had got the DNA pushed through very quickly. She wanted to know more about him, or all about him, and she certainly wasn't going to seduce him to find out. Thankfully, Stephanie wanted to.

Dawes walked into the Aviary estate alone. At least a dozen uniformed police moved in behind him as he headed toward the Sparrow block.

He was afraid of none of the lowlife on the estate. The dealer that had sold the fatal hit of heroin to his sister came from this hellhole, and he was going to find him and make him pay. He spent his spare time studying every available piece of information about gang members for that very purpose. A lot of the squad up west called him a sad trainspotter but he didn't give a damn; he was on a mission.

Over here on attachment, he had a chance to get another lowlife off the street, but more importantly to get closer to the pond-scum who sold his fifteen-year-old sister that heroin. If he could save other vulnerable young girls from being seduced by drugs, that was a bonus.

He felt partly responsible when his parents' marriage broke up. Philly went to live with their father; he was extremely high up in the Met, and very strict on Philly, and she became very unhappy. David had let her come to live with him, given her the spare room, but his job, like his father's, meant he wasn't home enough, and he didn't really know how to look after a teenager. He allowed her too much freedom, and she made friends with the wrong people.

How he wished a law would be passed allowing drug barons

to be done for first degree murder. He knew no one who didn't agree that they were worse than the worst kind of killers; they knowingly sold poison that sucked the life out of their vulnerable prey.

He didn't present much of a threat as he walked towards the Sparrow block, where he knew Boot and Mince hung out. He wasn't particularly tall, broad or muscular; but anyone who thought they could take him on would find they had made a mistake. He had learned a lot growing up in a family of police officers: first how to look out for himself, and more recently to use what he had to full advantage. He wasn't big but he was quick, and after intensive training at the new Gravesend police centre, he wasn't afraid to take on youths who flashed knives. He was angry too, and determined to win his private battle.

Trainee DC Hank Peacock stood on the corner. Peacock looked far too young for his twenty-three years, another reason he'd be an asset to the squad working on gang crime. Hank could pass for late teens, and his low-slung combat jeans and trendy trainers blended in well. He leaned against the edge of the building, smoking a cigarette and taking in the surroundings.

Dawes nodded to him, and noticed Winston Mitchell walking toward them holding two Rottweilers on short chains. Both animals looked angry and uncomfortable, and clearly ready to attack at a given order from their master.

Dawes knew Scrap Mitchell's face from the pictures he had of the Brotherhood lieutenants. He was easy to spot; he was half-oriental, with heavily peroxide hair gelled to stand upright. He looked like a porcupine that had fallen in a pail of bleach. His bare forearms were tattooed with the initials BB twisted around knives.

'Where are your mates, Scrap?' Dawes asked, keeping a safe distance from the dogs.

'I'm holding them,' Scrap said, pulling his mouth into a wide grin and revealing the stud in his tongue. He tugged on the chains, and the dogs took it as a signal to stand by to attack; they flattened their ears simultaneously and stood stock still, waiting for the command.

Uniformed police moved in, some holding stun-guns.

Dawes didn't take the bait. 'Your other mates. Michael Delahaye and Dwayne Ripley.'

'No idea.'

Dawes and Scrap Mitchell held each other's gaze and the dogs growled. Mitchell smiled sarcastically, and Dawes resisted the urge to lean over and punch him between the eyes.

'Go and lock your dogs away. I need you to come to the station and answer a few questions,' he said flatly. He had no grounds to arrest Mitchell; his DNA wasn't on the murdered woman. He was there to bring in Boot and Mince, but he knew if Scrap agreed to come, the other two wouldn't be far behind.

'What about?' Mitchell raised his eyebrows. 'You ain't got nothing on me.'

'You're right,' Dawes answered. 'You're not under arrest.'

'Confiscate the dogs,' Hank Peacock said.

Dawes clenched his teeth. He was playing Scrap, to get him to lead the way to Dwayne Ripley and Michael Delahaye. This young trainee DC had just blown it by riling the boy.

'Mind your own fucking business,' Mitchell snapped at Peacock.

Peacock flashed his warrant card. 'I've been watching you for the last hour. Those dogs are dangerous.'

'They ain't touched you,' Mitchell shouted. 'You can't fucking take my dogs unless they do something. You back off.'

Dawes interrupted. 'I'd like you to come to the station of your own accord, and answer a few questions,' he said. 'You haven't done anything, so it won't take long. It's just procedure.'

'What for?'

'The youths we want to question about last night's murder were wearing sweatshirts with BB on the back. I notice you've got the same tattoo on your forearms. We'd like you to give us a DNA sample, so we can eliminate you.'

'And we'll overlook the charge of the dogs being a public nuisance,' Peacock added.

Dawes took a sharp breath. Peacock had a lot to learn. He ignored him, and looked at Scrap, waiting for an answer.

Peacock spoke again. 'We're only interested in finding out who killed Haley Gulati. If you didn't, keep the boss happy and give us the DNA.'

Scrap ignored him and looked at Dawes. 'Which boss is that?'

'DI Johnson.'

'The one with her nose on top of her head?' Scrap asked. Now he did look at Peacock. 'Rumour has it she takes it up the arse.'

Peacock took a step towards Scrap, and jumped back as the one of the dogs growled. Dawes thought Peacock actually was going to hit the lad, but at that moment two ambulances screeched into the estate.

NINE

The address Stephanie had been given for Jason Young was his grandmother's third floor flat. She and Georgia stood outside, blowing on icy fingers to warm them. Someone was moving around inside, but Stephanie had to bang a second time before the door finally opened.

When Sally Young's face peeped out, Georgia was appalled to the see a worm of dark red coagulated blood clinging to red, puffy skin over one eyebrow. The woman's eyelid was half shut, and the sliver of grey eye it revealed was blood-shot. Her mouth was swollen and distorted, as if a trout-pout job had gone very wrong indeed.

Georgia's first thought was that Jason Young had set about his grandmother. Then she noticed teeth marks in the fingers that clung to the door frame. More likely the Brotherhood had learned that Jason was out of prison, and Sally had born the brunt of their displeasure.

'It's your grandson we're after,' Stephanie said.

'He ain't here,' Sally replied. She sounded completely exhausted.

'Where is he?' Georgia asked.

'I don't know,' came the weary answer.

'What happened to your face?' Georgia put out a hand, but Sally pulled away.

'Look, I've had a bad morning, right? I'm on my way to Casualty. I need a tetanus.' She paused. 'I don't know where the boy is. All I do know is 'e ain't 'ere.'

She tried to push the door closed, but Georgia blocked it with her foot.

'What happened to your face?' she asked her again.

'Someone don't like my grandson, and took it out on me.'

'Do you want to make it official?'

'No. I just want to get down to Casualty and get myself a tetanus jab, and then forget this ever happened.' She tried to close the door again, but Georgia's foot still prevented her.

'Mind if we take a look around inside?' Stephanie asked.

'Got a warrant, have ya?'

'We can get one.'

Sally shrugged and stood aside. 'Make it quick. I've got one hell of an 'ead on me.'

Georgia took the lounge and Stephanie the kitchen. Sally followed Georgia, watching her check behind the settee, lift the cushions and open the drawers in the cheap teak-effect sideboard.

'He ain't here, I've already told you . . .'

'Guv.' Stephanie stood in the doorway. 'I assume this isn't yours,' she said to Sally, holding out a bloodstained grey sweatshirt. 'I found it behind the washing machine.'

Sally put a hand over her bad eye. 'It is mine,' she said defiantly. 'It's my blood. From the injuries what I got this morning.' Her voice rose. 'Look, you can bloody see I've been set on. It's mine, and it's my blood.'

Stephanie pulled a large evidence bag from her pocket and dropped the sweatshirt inside. 'We'll need forensic confirmation of that,' she told her.

'What are you doing? Setting him up? Is that what this is?'

Georgia spoke patiently. 'Mrs Young, we need to speak to your grandson in connection with a brutal murder that took place last night on the Aviary estate. We have evidence that puts him at the scene of the crime. If you know where he is, you need to tell us. Our forensic lab will confirm whose blood is on that sweatshirt in a few hours.'

Forty-eight, if they were lucky. But Sally Young needn't know that. 'If it turns out it isn't your blood, or indeed your sweatshirt, I'm sure I don't have to remind you that obstructing a murder enquiry is a very serious offence. I suggest you tell us what you know, for your own sake as well as your grandson's.'

'Look, 'e's not guilty, all right?' Sally's voice cracked with emotion. 'My Jason served 'is time, and 'e's turned over a new leaf. It's that fat bastard Stuart Reilly what you wanna be questioning. My Jason's turned good. Why can't you just let him be?'

'Why has he gone on the run, then?' Georgia asked flatly.

'He ain't.'

'You just said you don't know where he is.'

'He's gone up west. He's got a dancing scholarship, but I don't know where.'

Georgia and Stephanie exchanged looks.

'Been knocking you about, has he?' Stephanie asked.

Sally shook her head, wincing with pain.

'He's got form for violence, you know that as well as we do,' Stephanie pushed. 'Don't make trouble for yourself by covering for him.'

'My Jase'd never 'urt me,' Sally declared. 'And 'e's killed nobody. It's them bleedin' no good Brotherhood scum.' Tears filled her eyes. 'They're looking for 'im too. But he's done his time, he's . . .'

'Where is he, Sally?' Georgia's patience was wearing thin.

'I told yer, I don't know. Time you went now. I wanna get myself to Casualty.'

'Where's your phone?' Stephanie asked.

Sally looked at her. 'Kitchen table, in me bag. Ain't you got one of your own?'

Stephanie went back to the kitchen; Sally and Georgia followed. Stephanie found the phone and scrolled the recent call history. The letter J came up four times.

Stephanie pressed the Call button and handed Sally the phone. 'Ask him where he is.'

Sally shook her head sadly, but took the phone. Jason's voicemail picked up and told the caller to leave a message.

Stephanie took out her notebook and wrote down Jason's phone number.

'We will find him,' Georgia said to Sally. 'If he hasn't done anything, you need to help him prove it.'

''E ain't,' Sally said again.

She was nothing if not loyal, Georgia thought. 'I'm going to get one our drivers to take you to Casualty to get you looked over,' she said. 'Then I need you to come to the station to give us a statement.'

Sally looked horrified. 'I ain't going nowhere in no cop's car.'

'We'll need a statement from you about your grandson's

movements last night,' Georgia told her. 'And I'd prefer you were checked over and got your tetanus jab first. It'll be an unmarked car; no one around here will know. But I have to insist.'

'Oh, they'll know.' Sally shrugged. 'Can we go out the back way then?'

Stephanie went down to arrange Sally Young's ride, and a few minutes later Georgia shut the car door and tapped the roof to send it off to the hospital.

'TIU will have a trace on Jason's phone within the hour,' Stephanie told her as the car drove off.

'Good. We'll get Sally Young to give us his comings and goings last night.'

'I don't think she'll tell us much,' Stephanie said. 'If I've read her right, she'll protect him with her life. Then again, she has no previous. I don't know if she'd lie to keep him out of trouble.'

'Better get the sweatshirt to forensics ASAP,' Georgia told her as they made their way back to Steph's car. 'See if the blood is Sally's or Haley Gulati's.'

'You don't think Sally Young killed her?'

'No. What I do think is that with luck we'll have Jason Young back behind bars within a day.'

'Hardly worth letting him out,' Stephanie sneered.

Hank Peacock and David Dawes rushed up thirteen flights of stairs, leaving the lift for the paramedics. They arrived to find Chantelle being strapped to a stretcher. Her eyelids fluttered as she drifted in and out of consciousness. Two uniformed police officers escorted the paramedics.

David Dawes flashed his warrant card at the paramedics and leaned over the stretcher. 'Chantelle, tell me who did this,' he urged gently, his mouth close to her ear. 'Was it Jason Young?'

The larger of the two paramedics intervened. 'I'm sorry, sir, I realize you've got a job to do, but this is an emergency and I'm going to have to ask you stay back. You're welcome to follow us to the hospital.'

Dawes stood up and nodded assent. It was clear Chantelle

was in no fit state to tell them anything. He turned to the uniformed officers. 'Did anyone see what happened?'

The paramedic spoke again. 'We were told three women have been attacked. The one that called us has an arm injury, but she ran off to look for the third.'

Dawes's concern turned to anger. 'Weren't you told to keep an eye on these women?' he growled at the uniforms on the walkway.

'Sir, we're all working flat out. We were told to go looking for the knife,' a young female constable with glasses answered. 'We were a couple of floors down, at the other end of the building. We came running when we heard screaming. The other girl ran straight into us. She was holding her arm and shouting that they had been attacked, and she asked us to help her friend. She had to find her sister, she said.'

'Who attacked them?' Dawes asked.

'She didn't say, and we didn't see anyone approaching or leaving. We came as soon as we heard the screaming.' The young officer was clearly upset. 'The girl said she needed to go to the hospital, but she had to find her sister first, in case she got hurt again. We called it in, and back-up was here within seconds, but no one on the estate admits to seeing the attackers.'

Dawes punched Georgia's number into his mobile. He updated her, and told her he was still looking for Boot Ripley and Mince Delahaye. 'I'll send a couple of uniforms to the hospital to be there when Chantelle comes round,' he said. 'Oh, and I've asked Scrap Mitchell to come to the station and give a DNA sample, but I'm not holding my breath.'

Georgia told him about Reilly's release. 'Looks like Chantelle lied to get Reilly arrested. This attack is more than likely retribution.

'It's looking more and more as if it was Jason Young who stabbed Haley Gulati,' she went on. 'We're running a trace on his mobile phone, and his description's been circulated.'

Dawes leaned against the graffiti-covered brick wall of the flats. 'Reilly will be going after Jason Young too,' he reminded her.

'His gang has already had a go at Sally Young. She looks

as if she's gone ten rounds with Joe Calzaghe.'

He sighed gloomily. 'Maybe we should leave them to kill each other, and save ourselves the bother.'

'I'd rather get a proper result,' came the curt reply.

He answered with a flat, 'Of course,' wondering how Georgia would feel if someone she loved had died at the hands of a money-grabbing drug baron. Would she still want to stay within the law and bring them to court, only to watch a bent solicitor get them off?

Jason had found a spare patch of pavement under the south side of Waterloo Bridge. He hoped it didn't belong to one of the vagrants who lived down here. He didn't want to start any trouble, but he did need a safe place to sleep. Soon the post-code gangs would be out; Saturday evening they always patrolled their territories. He could look after himself, but didn't want to take on a full tribe of them.

He hadn't slept last night and was feeling pretty shattered, so he wanted to get a few hours' sleep this afternoon, then walk on through the night. He'd be safer that way, especially if there were gangs about. Tomorrow he would be a day nearer to being with Chantelle. He planned to knock at the stage school. He would have to hope the woman who owned the gaff was around on a Sunday. He liked her; she had helped him before, filled in the application form for him when he told her he couldn't write properly. He'd been well embarrassed, but she'd said that with talent like his, writing wasn't important. He might ask if there was somewhere he could have a wash too; he was going to ask the family he was to stay with if he could come a bit earlier, and he didn't want to stink and put them off.

His phone trilled and Luanne's name came up on the display. 'Hey, babe . . .'

But after a few seconds he was trembling as if an electric current had run through his whole body. Chantelle was in a bad way, Luanne told him, but an ambulance had come and she was in good hands. She was going to the hospital herself as soon as she found Alysha, who had run off when the Brotherhood attacked them.

Luanne cried as she told him what had happened. She had

tried to pull Boot Ripley away from Chantelle, but Mince
Delahaye had twisted her arm up her back so hard she thought
it might be broken, then punched her in the face. That was
when she told Alysha to leg it.

Jason was shaking with fury. 'How bad is Chantelle?'

'She's taken a hard beating.'

'Boot and Mince, you say? I'm coming back.'

'Jason, no! It's not safe. The estate is swarming with Feds,
and they're looking for you.'

'I need a gun. Can you get me a gun?'

There was a pause. 'I don't think that's wise, man. There's
Feds everywhere. If you get caught . . .'

Jason gritted his teeth. 'This is Chantelle we're talking about.
And they've hurt you, and Alysha. I ain't having that. Help
me out here, Luanne. Get me a gun. I'll be there in less than
an hour.'

There was a beat.

'Luanne?'

He heard her sigh. 'OK. But I ain't happy about it, and it
may take a while. The Feds are everywhere.'

'Where shall we meet? Where's safe?'

Another pause. 'In the shed at the end of your gran's estate.
It's not on Brotherhood turf, and there are less Feds around
there. If I can get you a gun, I'll leave it in the shed, wrapped
in newspaper. Or in the rubbish dump there.'

'Make sure to get poppers to go with it.'

'Are you going to the hospital first?'

'Yes, I'm on my way now. Then I'm sorting this.'

'Be careful. The place will be surrounded with Feds, and
they're looking for you. I have to find Alysha, and I have to
get myself there. My arm hurts like hell. I'll try and call you
again.'

'They'll pay for this, I promise.'

'Yeah. I was afraid you'd say that.'

TEN

'There's exits everywhere,' the bespectacled female constable told David Dawes. 'Three fire escapes, a stairway to the upper floor, another up to the roof, and then there's the lift. They could have used any of them to get off the estate. None of us saw anybody running.'

'I'll bet none of the residents will have seen anything either,' the other uniformed officer added, a slight edge of hysteria creeping into his voice.

Dawes said nothing. He didn't trust himself not to lose his temper. He knew it wasn't their fault; the station was short of manpower, and they'd been doing as they were told and searching for the weapon that killed Haley Gulati. At the end of the day it was CID, not uniform, who were to blame; they should have known the girls could be in danger.

Hank Peacock was still loitering on the walkway. 'Get a forensic team up here,' Dawes told him.

'I'm very sorry, guv,' the WPC continued. 'We were told to search . . .'

Dawes cut her off in mid-sentence. 'Luanne Akhter and her sister Alysha are hurt and frightened. They won't have gone far. See if you can find them.'

He turned his back on her and leaned over the balcony, peering down at the routes in and out of the estate. He felt both guilty and angry. Those vulnerable young witnesses shouldn't have been left unprotected after they had been brave enough to speak out. This would do further harm to the fragile relationship the police already had with the terrified residents.

He spotted a van below with the RSPCA's logo on its side. A huge man came out of the flats and walked towards it. It was impossible to mistake Yo-Yo Reilly. No one else around here was that big. Even from thirteen floors up, Dawes was aware Reilly was looking up at him.

There was no doubt in Dawes's mind that Reilly was responsible for what had happened here.

Two dogs jumped out of the RSPCA animal welfare van, and the uniformed dog warden holding their chains handed them over to Reilly. According to Georgia Johnson, a so-called dog expert had declared they weren't pure-bred pit bulls, so now Reilly had them back. The dog expert, Georgia had told him, was Michael O'Flannery. He was known to the police as Manic Mickey; he had a heroin habit and Reilly was his supplier. Something else the police knew but couldn't prove. Reilly had got Mickey hooked on smack, then put him on the payroll; Mickey looked out for him, and kept his dangerous dogs legal. There was a tattoo of a knife on the inside of his middle finger, a sign of an associate member the Brotherhood.

Mickey himself had been a breeder of pit bulls, but had gone out of business when the ban came in. He was a qualified vet, which earned him some respect in the animal world, and was acknowledged as an expert on pit bulls. Reilly could afford to be cocky and confident when his dogs were confiscated; Mickey would make sure he got them back. Other pit bull experts around London had been bought by Reilly, too: something else the police knew about, but hadn't enough proof to expose.

Now the savage dogs were back in Reilly's care. Both the RSPCA and the police knew 'care' was a joke; Reilly mistreated them and often left them hungry. If not much else was happening, the Brotherhood would kick their dogs until their underbellies were torn and bleeding, then let them take their pain, misery and hunger out on each other – all for a bit of a laugh. If a dog lost an ear or an eye, it wasn't the end of the world; Manic Mickey would patch it up or put it down.

Dawes was angry. Not only had the fat bastard escaped a murder charge; he had his dogs back, and since he was in police custody at the time he also had a perfect alibi for his whereabouts when the girls were being beaten up. Just as well he couldn't see Reilly's face from up here, Dawes thought; the toerag would be beaming with pride at having got one over on the police yet again. Well, not for long, if Dawes had anything to do with it.

He watched Reilly prod the dog with a long stick. The dog cowered and snarled, and the RSPCA officer seemed to be issuing a warning. Reilly's body language was easy to read; he pointed the officer towards his van, obviously telling him where to stuff his advice.

Whatever had passed between them, the animal welfare officer chose to ignore the finger Reilly poked up at him. He climbed quickly into the van alongside his colleague, and the van accelerated out of the estate.

The dog stood obediently beside Reilly until the van had disappeared. Then Reilly drew his boot back and kicked the animal until it lay on its stomach and yelped in agony.

Dawes turned away, sickened.

'Reilly's been released,' he told Hank Peacock. 'He's down there, and his dogs have just been brought back. I'd bet serious money that word about these women got to him while he was in custody.'

Peacock looked dubious. 'But he only had one call, and that was to his solicitor.'

'There you are then.' No one that naïve should be in CID Dawes thought.

'You mean . . . Reilly got a message out through the solicitor?'

Dawes pursed his lips. 'Bet your life.'

'Now one's in hospital unconscious, one's run away terrified and the other's out looking for her. And when we find them they'll be too scared to say a word.'

Give the boy a gold star. 'You got it.'

'Do you think the girls know their attackers?'

'Don't you?'

Hank nodded slowly. 'The top dogs run this land, and I'm beginning to think that that's not us.'

Dawes suddenly felt sorry for the lad. Everyone started out like that, full of faith and ideals. 'Don't get disheartened, mate. You're only a trainee. Think of it this way: there are some big gangs in London, but we're the biggest. This is just history repeating itself.'

'How do you mean, sir?'

'A few years ago, before Reilly took over the patch, the so-called top gang around here was the Buzzards. Jason Young was cock of the walk then. We got Jason eventually, and as for the Buzzards, some are dead – gunshots, stabbings, over-doses, the usual. Young's out again, but not for long – we've got evidence now to put him away again for murder.' Dawes took a deep breath. 'And Reilly's day isn't far off either, mark my words.'

The bloodied sweatshirt had gone to forensics, and Georgia and Stephanie were back in Georgia's office, grabbing a late lunch and reading Jason Young's prison reports. A large cardboard Starbucks cup stood on Georgia's shiny desk; a chocolate bar broken into little pieces lay on a serviette, and a paper plate served to catch any drips from her cappuccino.

She forced herself to ignore the tomato pips spilling out of Stephanie's sandwich on to the warm, newly faxed papers. Stephanie must have read her thoughts; she flicked a couple of pips off the papers on to the floor. Georgia said nothing, aware that the irritation was two-way; her neatness irritated Stephanie as much as Stephanie's mess exasperated her. But over the past five years they had bonded, and helped each other out of many a scrape. Be glad it's only a sandwich, she chided herself. Last time they had lunched together in Georgia's office, Stephanie had brought saveloy, chips and a gherkin. The smell had clung for days, impervious to air freshener.

All the same, Stephanie was the only member of the squad whose company Georgia ever sought out; she liked and trusted her, even though they were chalk and cheese.

Stephanie usually made the morning meetings by the skin of her teeth, face devoid of make-up, hair uncombed. Mornings were bound to be fraught for a single mum; and, as Steph had explained, given the long hours they worked when they had a case like this one, giving her kids breakfast before school in the morning might be the only time she saw them all day.

Georgia would probably have felt the same, if she'd been

lucky enough to have kids. She had freedom instead, she told herself. She could be in the office as early as she chose, usually long before the morning meeting. Stephanie, on the other hand, sat there holding a cup of hot chocolate with marshmallows floating on top in one hand and a pen in the other to make catch-up notes; but Georgia never doubted that her brain was fully engaged and she'd taken everything in. Stephanie was as sharp as a butcher's knife, and her memory could challenge an elephant's. What Georgia admired most about her was her openness and honesty. Her reputation for never refusing sex went before her; rumour had that she had slept with half of the Met. But she stayed friends with all her conquests, and could be relied on to call in a favour when it was needed. She seemed to know someone in every department, whereas Georgia never let any man get close to her. Stephanie often tried to persuade her to go for a night of lust; good for the stress count, she assured her with a warm, infectious laugh.

When Stephanie lifted her head from the prison report, she looked as if she had stepped out of a sauna. Steam from her mug of scalding black coffee had dampened her face, her nose shone, and strands of her fine, marmalade-streaked hair stuck to her rosy cheeks.

'Interesting,' she said, pulling a stray hair out of her mouth.

'What does it say?'

'He was sent to Wandsworth, but others in his gang served their sentences in Rochester. He was victimized in Wandsworth, but never fought back.'

'That's surprising, given his history of violence.' Georgia popped a square of chocolate in her mouth.

'Maybe that's why he killed Haley Gulati – he'd bottled up the violence all that time.' She read aloud from the report. 'He became withdrawn and depressed toward the end of his sentence. He was befriended by his probation officer, who is now helping him pursue a career in dancing. By his release he had secured a scholarship with a leading stage school in central London.'

Georgia sipped from the paper cup and wiped a trace of

froth from her mouth with the serviette. 'My bet is he played
the system. He intendcd to kill Haley Gulati all along, and
used the stage school application as a way of getting an early
release.'

Stephanie screwed up the paper sandwich bag into a ball
and wiped her hands on her jeans.

'What bothers me,' Georgia said, 'is that our new friend DI
Dawes doesn't think it's likely that Young stabbed Haley. He
feels sure he would have shot her.' She paused before adding,
'And Dawes is supposed to be the expert on South London
gangs.'

'We've got Jason Young's DNA all over the victim, and in
her blood on the wall of the Gulatis' flat,' Stephanie pointed
out. 'And he's got strong motive. That's enough for me, expert
or not.' She aimed the screwed-up sandwich bag at the waste
bin, threw it and missed. 'Forensics on the blood on the
sweatshirt is just icing on the cake. Just as well – it's going
to be another twenty-four hours at least.'

'Shame you haven't got a *friend* in forensics,' Georgia teased
her.

'I'll keep looking,' Stephanie laughed. 'You know, if we
found the murder weapon it would help. Reilly's Brotherhood
all use similar blades; if the one that killed Gulati is
different . . .'

'Yeah, well, we'll just have to wait for that. Any luck with
the trace on Young's mobile?'

Stephanie balanced her coffee on the papers and dug in her
vast shoulder bag for her phone. 'I haven't got a friend in
forensics, but I have got one in TIU, luckily for you,' she said
with a cheeky smile.

Georgia looked doubtfully at the precarious coffee cup. She
moved it off the papers on to the desk, then, catching Georgia's
eye, she slid it on to a used brown envelope. 'You wait till
you've got kids,' she grinned, rubbing at the coffee ring on
the desk and making it worse.

Georgia grinned back. Stephanie had everything, she
thought, except a top for her pen and a button on her jacket.
And she wasn't to know that having a child wasn't an option
for Georgia. She smoothed her hands over her perfectly

gelled hair, checking that the clip was secure, and fought the urge to un-stick the loose strand that now clung to the top of Stephanie's mouth as she waited for someone to answer her call.

'Will you be able to cope with an affair with Dawes?' she teased her.

'You bet! He's got sensitive hands.'

'How did you work that out?'

Someone picked up the phone so Stephanie didn't answer. A few seconds went by, then Stephanie raised her head. 'They've got a trace. He's somewhere around the shopping centre at the Elephant and Castle. They don't know the exact location, but they think he's in a vehicle, on the move.'

'Get Hank Peacock to ring Oyster, and say a prayer he's using one,' Georgia told her, tossing her coffee cup in the bin. 'He could be on his way back to the estate. That means someone has tipped him off about Chantelle. Alert all patrol cars to keep a lookout. We've circulated a description, haven't we?'

'Done.' Stephanie aimed her empty coffee cup at the waste bin. It missed. Georgia stooped to pick it up. 'It's probably Sally Young. Or does he have any other known associates on that estate?'

Casualty was busy and Sally was anxious. She hated hospitals, had spent far too many days and nights in them. She wouldn't be here if it wasn't for those bastard dogs, she thought angrily. A few cuts she could deal with, but not a disease from those flea-bitten creatures.

It was time someone stood up to those yobs that thought they ran the estate. She decided she would tell the police everything she knew; she could even tell them who shot that young cop. After this morning Yo-Yo Reilly's mob deserved all they got. She'd let the police know what really went on down the Aviary, and when she did maybe they'd stay away from her Jason. That boy was going to get the chance he deserved.

She walked outside for a fag, and the first people she saw hanging about were Dwayne Ripley and Michael Delahaye. She took out her phone and pretended to dial a number, then spoke into the phone as if someone had answered.

When she clicked off Dwayne and Michael walked up to her. Dwayne spat on the ground next to her. 'Your face looks rough,' he said. 'Walk into a door, did you, Sals?'

'My Jason is coming back to sort you lot,' she said, determined not to show she was scared. 'We ain't afraid of your bullying. I'm having a tetanus cos of your dogs attacking me, and if you don't pay me for what you broke on my stall this morning, I'm going to the Feds to make this official.'

'Christ, I'm so scared. I think I've pissed me pants, innit.' That was Delahaye.

Sals sniffed loudly. 'I've got friends where I got me stall, and they all witnessed what you done. You'd better pay my breakages or I'll go to the law.'

Dwayne looked at Michael. 'Better get her money then,' he said.

Michael nodded. 'Yeah, better get her paid up, innit.'

'Just put notes through me door, and extra for the pain,' she told him. 'I'll say nothing this time, but try it again and I'll go to the Feds and get you all locked up.'

'You'll get paid,' Dwayne said flatly.

She nodded, dropped her Silk Cut and ground it under her sensible flat walking shoes, then limped back into the hospital.

It didn't take long. They patched her up, gave her two stitches over her eye and a large dressing to cover them, then injected her with anti-tetanus. She had to admit she felt a bit better, but that was more to do with what had happened outside than with the injection. She could take a couple of days off now they were paying for the breakages. It was cold out in the wind, so it would be nice to watch some daytime telly and keep warm. In a day or two she'd buy new stock and get back to the market. She wouldn't in a million years have let Jason know what had gone on; he'd have come back and given that Dwayne Ripley what for, and that would hardly help him rebuild his life. But she'd sorted it herself now.

The police car was waiting for her when she came out. She was grateful; she had to admit she wasn't as young as she used to be, and her legs were feeling a bit wobbly. She told the driver she was going to give the police a statement about Jason, but first, she said, she had to go back and get the clothes he had worn last night, so she could bring them to the station. She actually had no intention of getting those clothes; she'd dump them later, and bring some other clothes of his, then there would be no way he could be implicated in Haley's murder.

With luck those lowlifes would have left the money in her door when she got back. She'd go to the station and make her statement, tell about them as well as Jason, then once the Feds picked up Ripley, Delahaye and the whole bloody lot of them and threw them all in jail, she could buy her stock and live in peace.

The police car pulled into the estate. Sally asked them to wait by the entrance; it wouldn't do her any good to be seen in a Feds' car. Haley Gulati had lost her life through talking to the Feds. Sally needed to be more careful.

Jason stepped off the bus and walked stealthily around the perimeter of the Aviary estate. No point going to look for Alysha, he reckoned; she was a smart kid, too smart to hide around the estate, the Brotherhood knew all the Youngers' hiding places. Besides, as Luanne had warned, there were Fed cars everywhere. He had to be quick, do the business he'd come to do, then see Chantelle.

He walked toward the Romney where the gun would be waiting for him. Luanne wouldn't let him down, he was sure of that.

He turned quickly into the small slip road which joined the two roads, one on to the Aviary, the other on to the Romney. As he crossed into Romney territory he stopped in his tracks. Coming toward him were Dwayne the Boot and Michael the Mince. Dwayne held a pit bull terrier on the end of a thick leather and gilt lead. He kicked the dog in the balls when he saw Young, making it snarl. Jason was terrified of dogs, but he had kept his fear under wraps since he was a kid. Right now fear was the last thing on his mind; he was too busy working out what to do next. He reckoned he might be able to take the dog out with his knife, but the odds weren't in his favour. He needed the gun and it was now only just yards away.

He had a bottle in his leg pocket. He could knock the neck off it in a second, and there'd be eyes and skin on the ground in another. But there were two of them as well as the dog. Another few minutes and the gun and the poppers would be in his hands, then the job would take seconds. But at the moment he was in a no-win situation. If he took them on they'd let the dog loose and he'd be savaged.

At that moment he was so angry he couldn't have cared less about dancing, or even living. What he did care about was that they didn't get away with what they had done to Chantelle and Luanne and Alysha. He knew he had to play for time.

'I ain't on your territory,' he said flatly as they approached. 'This is Romney territory. I live here. I ain't trespassing. So let me pass, OK?'

Boot looked at Mince and they both pretended to laugh. Boot scratched his arse. 'This is your postcode now is it?' Boot said, kicking the dog again. The dog snarled and lifted its lips, revealing froth and sharp teeth.

A few years ago Jason would have lost it, but prison had taught him a thing or two. Being neither black nor white, he'd been picked on by both sides, and he'd learned to choose his battles carefully. If he went down here, his chance to even out what they'd done to the girls would disappear forever. The gun was only minutes from his grasp; once he had it he would blow their brains to hell. He kept his cool, and played a smart game.

'I don't run nothing no more,' he said evenly. 'And I don't run nowhere, neither. I ain't on your territory. You let me be.'

Boot and Mince stared at him. Neither said a word.

'I ain't spoiling for a fight,' he carried on. 'If you see me on your soil, that's when I'll put my hands up. Till then back off. Let me go see me gran.'

'I hear she's not too well, innit?' Mince said. He looked at Boot and they both laughed.

'Well, ain't that a shame?' Boot kicked the dog in the balls for a third time, and it tried to leap at Jason. He jumped back and Mince burst out laughing again.

'Stay off our patch,' Boot warned him.

Jason bowed his head in a limp salute. It took all his willpower not to pull the knife and slice the bastard there and then.

'Can I pass?' he asked.

For a single second they all held eye contact, then Boot and Mince pulled at the dog and walked on by.

Jason gave himself a few seconds to let the tension flow out of his body, then he made his way into the alleyway leading to the Romney. He punched Luanne's number into his mobile. She picked up. She was waiting at the hospital, and couldn't talk for long.

'Have you seen Alysha?' she asked.

'I'm looking. I'll call you when I hear something. How's Chantelle?'

There was silence for a few seconds, and something cold clutched at Jason's chest. Then Luanne said, 'She's with the doctors. There are Feds all over. Jason, you'd better not come here. I think they're looking for you. They're going to fit you up for Haley's murder.'

Somehow that wasn't important. All that mattered was that Chantelle was still alive. He asked Luanne about the gun. It was waiting where they'd agreed, she said: in a bag in the bin by the shed, and she'd put poppers in the shed.

'You want to hurry up and get the hell out of there,' she told him. 'Don't worry about Chantelle; I'll look out for her. Call me if you find Alysha, yeah? And keep her away from the shooting.' She didn't need to mention Yo-Yo and the rest of the Brotherhood; they both knew what she was talking about.

He clicked his phone shut and kicked a lamppost, nearly breaking his toe. Why didn't he take Chantelle with him last night when he had a chance? He couldn't even go and see her now. He pulled himself together; too much to do to waste time on might-have-beens. He'd lose his scholarship, and any chance of a life away from here, but nothing, *nothing* meant more to him than Chantelle.

It was true what they said, he thought wryly; estate boys never got away. They died from drugs or guns, or rotted in prison. Right now he was too angry to care.

A police car drew up at the edge of the estate. He moved back, pulled his cap down and his hood up and pressed his body against the broad tree trunk at the end of the alley.

He stayed there a couple of minutes, keeping perfectly still. When he looked up the car was parked, and the two Feds sat talking to each other. Neither of them was looking in his direction. He seized his chance and sauntered casually towards the shed.

Georgia and Stephanie had joined Dawes and Peacock at Luanne's flat on the thirteenth floor of the Aviary. Uniformed officers were out in force, knocking on doors and asking neighbours for a description of anyone they'd seen earlier. No one had seen anything. All they had gathered so far was a lot of abuse.

Forensic officers were busy scraping scattered particles of dried blood and skin that were stuck to the door and hallway. Hairs and bloodstained mud from inside and outside the flat went into labelled phials, which were pocketed in evidence bags ready for the lab.

'This is my fault,' Stephanie said. 'I told uniform to search for the weapon that killed Haley Gulati. That left the girls vulnerable.'

Georgia felt just as responsible. 'If we find the weapon, it will help us send Jason Young back to prison,' she pointed out.

'There are more weapons to look for now.' Dawes was tight-lipped with anger. 'I saw the damage. It looked as if Chantelle had been attacked with a bat or a hammer. Her head was broken open.'

Georgia and Stephanie exchanged a glance, but before Dawes could make them feel any worse, Stephanie's phone bleeped into life. As she pulled it from her pocket, sweet papers and a chewed biro top came with it.

'TIU,' she mouthed to Georgia. 'They've picked up another signal.' She gave a thumbs-up. 'Yesss! Jason Young's just used his phone again. He's moved from the Elephant. He's around here!'

ELEVEN

Sally's legs felt as if they were made of lead as she trudged slowly up the three flights of stairs. It had been a long night and an even longer morning, and her head was thumping like a set of bongo drums. She wanted nothing more than to put her feet up and have a nice cup of tea. Still, she consoled herself, after this all died down she could take a few days off the market without having to worry; at least they were paying up for what they'd done to her crockery. She'd still go to the station and tell on the Brotherhood though. It would distract the police's attention from Jason, and give him time to get well away. She only hoped the blood on that sweatshirt was too faint to point the finger. She wasn't going to let that gang of bullying crooks get one over her; she was going to stand up to them and get them locked away. And when she'd done that, the police would drive her home, she'd make a whole pot of tea, drink the lot, then go to bed for that hard-earned rest.

As she reached her front door and put her key in the lock a shot rang through the air. Sally heard it at the same moment as the explosion inside her head. Her forehead hit her door and white stars gently bobbed around the edge of her vision. Then her body slid heavily to the floor, and she watched those same stars diminish and fade to black. She couldn't see the blood pumping from the hole in her neck and she didn't hear her elderly Jamaican neighbour call her name. Everything went dark and still.

The uniformed police officers waiting in the car below jumped out as they heard the shot. One dashed up the stairs two at a time while the other radioed for back-up and an ambulance. 'Papa Yankee Seven,' he shouted, following his friend toward the stairs. 'Urgent help required. Gunshots on the Romney Estate, block three.'

The call came through the radios of the uniformed officers outside Luanne's flat.

'That's Sally Young's block,' Georgia said urgently.

By the time Stephanie and Georgia had driven round the corner to the Romney estate, uniformed officers and at least a dozen residents were swarming around Sally's flat.

Georgia pushed her way through, yelling at a uniformed sergeant, 'Cordon off the whole of this floor. This is a crime scene. Clear it!'

The elderly Jamaican neighbour who had run out to help Sally was on his knees beside her, crying.

'Move away,' Georgia shouted to him. 'Clear the area, now.'

'I can't clear,' he said. 'I live here. Sals is my neighbour.'

Georgia dropped to her haunches beside him. 'Did you see anything?' she asked noticing his skin was grey with shock.

He looked nervously at her and shook his head.

Stephanie stripped off her duffle coat and jumper and laid them on the ground, then pulled off her coffee-stained T-shirt and used it to try to stem the flow of blood. 'She's alive,' she told Georgia.

Sirens signalled the ambulance's arrival.

'Tell me exactly what you saw?' Georgia asked the neighbour gently.

A look of terror spread across his face, as if she had asked him to jump over the balcony. He backed away and retreated behind his own front door. Just before he closed it in Georgia's face, he whispered, 'Nothing. I saw nothing man.'

Georgia sighed. 'Are forensics on their way?' she asked Stephanie.

Stephanie nodded.

Two paramedics laden with blankets, oxygen and medi-kits puffed up the stairs. Stephanie jumped up out of their way. After a brief examination they strapped Sally to the stretcher and carried her carefully to the waiting ambulance.

Uniformed officers secured blue and white cordons across both ends of the walkways. Hank Peacock and David Dawes arrived. Peacock turned scarlet at the sight of Stephanie's ample bosom barely covered by a scarlet double DD cup bra. Two kids, neither of them more than eight or nine, followed them and stood wide-eyed, trying to see what was going on.

'Time to go home,' Dawes told them.

'Whatcha doing?' one shouted.

'Trying to help a lady who's been hurt,' Peacock answered. 'Did you see anyone down there?'

'Wouldn't tell you if we did,' one of the children said. 'Unless you give us a fiver.'

'Then we still won't say nothing,' the other one added. 'Cos we'll get more to keep our mouths shut.'

Dawes suddenly lost his temper. 'Bugger off, both of you, before I throw you in a cell.'

Stephanie caught Georgia's eye. This was a DI from one of the toughest stations in London, seconded to them because his knowledge of South London estate gangs could win him a trophy on *Mastermind* – and he was letting two estate kids get to him. Something had ruffled his feathers. Georgia knew the signs; there was a personal issue here, something she needed to know more about if he was to stay on her team. But that was for later. Now she chose to pretend she hadn't noticed.

Stephanie was struggling to put her jumper back on and move the kids on. She ignored their jibes about her red bra and called to the uniformed officers to keep the public away. 'This is crime scene,' she shouted. 'Let's keep it clear.'

David Dawes seemed not to have noticed that Stephanie was half-undressed. There was a flash of M & S lacy knickers as she unzipped her jeans to tuck in her jumper, but he didn't seem to clock that either.

'We'll take a drive around the estate,' Georgia said. 'When you've finished getting your clothes back on, that is.'

The place was crawling with Feds. Jason needed to be careful, though he knew the Romney estate better than any of them. He moved slowly until he got to the shed, then opened the door and crawled in on all fours. There was a large waste bin in the corner; he shuffled across the floor and sat behind it, holding the gun tightly. He had to bide his time now until it was safe to come out. He knew all the shed's hidden corners; if he heard anyone approaching, he could be in the roof space in a couple of seconds, and no one who looked inside would see him.

His plan was to wait until it all calmed down out there, then back to the Aviary to finish his business. After that he didn't care a toss what happened to him. The bastards who did Chantelle over deserved to pay; and they would; that was the law of the street.

It could all have been so different if Chantelle had left with him last night. They could be having an adventure together by now, sleeping under the bridge. His mind briefly replayed their tender lovemaking: the way she gazed into his eyes as he touched her; the gentle way she moved with him, almost as if they were dancing; the way she told him over and over that she loved him and always would. No one else had ever told him they loved him.

Life was a bitch. He blinked away tears, and told himself to concentrate on what had to be done. He needed to find Alysha. She was a clever kid, sharp and resourceful; no doubt she was hiding out somewhere until this was over. When it was, she would have Luanne, and they'd take care of each other. Luanne was going to look after Chantelle too, while Jason was in hiding, but it would all be settled one day, and then maybe they could all move on together, like a family. Chantelle had to be OK.

He stared down at the gun. It was only yesterday that he had turned his back on all this, but some things couldn't be ignored. A lot of his Buzzard pack had been shot standing up for people they cared about. That was what a pack did. Those girls were his pack now, and he would look after them. You had to help each other to survive, and you made your own family.

The door creaked slowly open and he nearly jumped out of his skin. He rose to his feet and leaned against the pillar by the empty bin, flicking a glance at the beamed roof space. He could be up there in two seconds, and the doorway would be right in his line of fire. If this was one of those Brotherhood bastards, he could get ready to take his last breath.

But the terrified face that peeped around the door frame
was Alysha's.

'Hey!' he called to her, quickly dropping his arm so she
didn't see the gun. 'It's Jason. Come in, sweetheart, quickly,
and close the door. Check no one can see you first.'

She was shaking.

'Are you OK?'

'I thought you'd gone,' she said.

'I did, but when I heard what happened I came back to help
you.' He moved closer to her and put his hand on her shoulder.

'I'm running from the Brotherhood,' she said. 'They came
round and beat up Luanne and Chantelle. I just ran. I came
over here, but now this estate is crawling with Feds too.
Someone's been shot.'

He edged the gun round behind him, hoping she wouldn't
see it. 'I heard,' he said. 'Luanne belled me, she told me what
happened. She's OK – just a bad arm and a smacked face.
Are you hurt?'

Alysha shook her head.

'Luanne went to the hospital to get patched up. Chantelle's
there too. She's worrying about you.' He handed her his mobile.
'Call her and tell her where you are. She needs to know you're
OK.'

Alysha's lip curled. 'They were hurting Chantelle and they
twisted Luanne's arm and hit her in the face. She was
screaming, they hurt her so bad. I was scared, so I ran.'

Jason nodded. 'You did the right thing, babe. Chantelle's
in a bad way.'

Alysha slid to the ground next to him, her eyes dark with
fear. He joined her on the shed floor and slipped his arm
around her. 'It's OK, darling. I'm gonna take care of it. They
won't hurt any of you again. I promise. Who was it hurt
Chantelle and Luanne? I need to know. Was it Boot?'

'You got a gun there?' she asked him.

'Yes.'

'Did you just shoot someone? Someone got shot, that's why
the Feds came.'

He shook his head. 'Not me.'

'Are you going to kill those Brotherhood scum?'

'You don't need to know that.' He levered himself upright and walked to the door. 'Stay here where you're safe. If you hear anyone coming, climb up there, into the roof.' He pointed to the footholds in the wall which would take her up into the rafters. 'And listen up: don't come out until either me or Luanne comes back for you.'

No one on the Romney had seen or heard anything; a few admitted to hearing the shot, but shook their heads blankly and said, 'I thought it was a just car backfiring.'

Georgia and Stephanie were inside Sally's flat, going through her things. As the ambulance siren shrilled its way out of the estate, Stephanie's phone bleeped.

It was TIU support again; they had picked up another signal. Jason Young was somewhere on the estate; they didn't have an exact location yet but they were working on it.

'Get on to CO19,' Georgia told Stephanie. 'We need their back-up. Jason Young is around here, probably with a gun. He stabs Haley Gulati then shoots his own grandmother,' Georgia sighed. 'And he's been out of the slammer less than a week.'

'I wonder if he knows Chantelle is in hospital,' Stephanie said.

'Maybe he put her there. Who knows what he's capable of?'

'Maybe he'll go to Luanne's?'

'Good thinking, sergeant. Let's go.'

House-to-house enquiries had drawn a blank. Dawes and Peacock decided to get in the car and drive around the perimeter of the estate. After only a few minutes they spotted Yo-Yo Reilly walking down the road holding two ugly dogs tugging at the end of short gilt chains.

Two boys followed close behind him: one also held a dog, and the other was very tall.

'Well, whaddya know,' Dawes said. 'Dwayne Ripley and Michael Delahaye. Boot and Mince. And big man Reilly himself.' He pulled up and wound down the window.

Reilly recognized them right away. 'Fuck me,' he said, 'this is starting to look like harassment. These dogs are legal . . .'

Dawes leaned out of the window and held his hand up to silence him. One of the dogs flew at his hand, and Dawes pulled it back quickly.

'Just doing its job,' Reilly said with a grin. 'Thought you were having a go at me.'

Dawes looked past him at the two behind. 'Ripley, Delahaye, I'd like you both to come to the station and answer a few questions regarding the murder of Haley Gulati.'

'Nothing to do with us,' Boot Ripley said dismissively.

'We have reason to believe you both had sex with her just prior to her death.'

Dawes expected them to leg it; in fact he rather hoped they would. They wouldn't get very far, and he might get in a punch or two if they resisted. Much to his surprise, neither moved.

Luanne's front door was wide open. Georgia knocked and called the girl's name. No one answered.

Luanne was sitting on the sofa, her arm in a clean, white sling, with only her long mauve fingernails visible. Her other hand cradled her forearm, and her mobile lay on the table in front of her.

Georgia sat down beside her, noticing the purpled swelling below her left eye. 'I am so sorry.'

'See the damage caused by talking to you lot,' Luanne snapped. 'Chantelle's in intensive care, I'm like this and my sister's disappeared. If anything happens to Alysha, I don't know what I'll do.' She dropped her head into her unbandaged hand. 'Chantelle's bad. She's not even conscious. You could see inside her head as they took her away. They're operating on her now.' She took a deep breath. 'What have we started here?'

'Was it Reilly?' Georgia asked.

Luanne pressed her lips together.

Stephanie tried. 'If you give us a statement . . .'

Luanne's eyes flared. 'I didn't see their faces, OK?'

'Just tell me how many there were?'

She shrugged. 'Two.'

'Could it have been Jason Young? Has he got anything on you?' Georgia asked.

Luanne spun round. 'Not Jason. No.'

'It's since his release that all this has kicked off,' Georgia pointed out. 'He's involved somehow, and we need to find him.'

'I don't know nothing about that,' Luanne snapped. 'I just want Alysha safe. She's twelve-years-old. Can you just go, please, before anyone knows I've talked to you again. My sister is in danger.'

'Your father should be here,' said Stephanie.

'Yeah, right.'

'When is he likely to come home?'

'I told you before, he comes and goes. Lysha and I look after each other.' She turned a piercing gaze on Georgia. 'This estate lives by its own rules and we know what they are. We need you to leave us be.'

Stephanie's phone buzzed and she walked outside to take the call. She returned after a few moments. 'Dawes has picked up Dwayne Ripley and Michael Delahaye.'

Georgia stood up. 'I'm putting a police guard outside your door,' she said to Luanne.

'No!'

'Just for the time being. They'll stay put this time.'

'You'll make it worse!' Her voice moved up a notch. 'Please! Just leave us alone.'

'OK.' Georgia put her hands in the air. 'As long as you promise to stay in and not answer the door. We'll circulate Alysha's description, and see if we can pick her up for you. What is she wearing?'

Luanne tapped the fresh bruise on her cheek. 'I got this for talking to the Feds. I don't want Alysha to get hurt.'

'That's why we are going to find her and pick her up.'

'You don't get it, do you?' Her voice had an edge of hysteria. 'No one on this estate talks to Feds. It's not safe.'

'I thought you said you were tough,' Georgia reminded her.

Luanne gave her an appraising look. 'I'm scared for Alysha. You don't make the law around here, the Brotherhood do.'

TWELVE

Dwayne 'Boot' Ripley was as thin as a rat. His narrow, mud-coloured eyes slid from Georgia to Stephanie, and his long face remained motionless. His lank, mouse-coloured hair, pointed features and large ears made Georgia think he would look at home among the vermin that prowled the overflowing bins on the Aviary Estate. All he needed was a few whiskers.

He even smelt as if he had slept in garbage. Georgia took shallow breaths and watched with disgust as he prodded at one of his white-headed pimples with a dirty fingernail.

The solicitor who was unfortunate enough to be on duty was a middle-aged woman in a well-pressed grey pinstriped suit and clean white blouse. She sat as far from him as the small room allowed, and held a tissue in the palm of her hand.

Ripley started scratching his thigh through the white nylon forensic suit he had been given to wear while his own clothes were tested. After a few moments he hunched over the table and started finger-walking like a bored child. He seemed incapable of remaining still.

As yet they had no evidence to charge him with anything. He had admitted having sex with Haley Gulati prior to her death, but claimed it was with her permission. Even his dogs had been declared legal.

But he was here, and she was going to make the most of the opportunity.

'Why this upsurge of violence on the estate?' she asked him with steel in her voice.

'No idea.' His gaze never left the table, and the finger-walking started again.

He was violent, but he wasn't very bright, and like many of the Brotherhood he felt protected by Reilly, and did exactly as the bully told him. He'd learned that if you lived where he lived, the best way to survive was to join the strongest army.

Georgia pushed a photo of Haley Gulati across the table. He glanced at it and shrugged. 'Nothing to do with me.'

'You had sex with her.'

He shrugged again. 'She put it about.'

'Where did you have sex with her?'

'At the party.'

'What party?'

'In the empty flats. We set up some music and we were hanging out, and she came in.'

'She was thirty-six years old, a churchgoing woman with a niece who is older than you,' Georgia snapped.

'She was gagging for it.' He looked up and met Georgia's eyes. 'She liked shagging. Some bints do.'

Stephanie leaned towards him. 'I think Yo-Yo Reilly forced her to have sex, and you went with the flow.'

'No.' He tipped his chair back. 'She was up for it.'

The duty solicitor blew her nose.

Ripley dug his nail into a pimple on his cheek. His eyes flicked from Georgia to Stephanie, then to the duty solicitor. 'Plenty of women like gang-banging, but no one wants to admit it.' His eyes travelled up and down her body, then over Stephanie's, and he licked his lips slowly.

'Pack it in and answer the questions,' Georgia snapped.

He raised his hands. 'I answered. You asked if I had sex with Haley Gulati and I told you. She liked rough sex. Older women do.' His eyes pierced into Georgia's, and the tip of his tongue appeared between his lips. 'Unless you're a tight-arse, of course. Some women are.'

The female brief threw him a warning glance.

Stephanie sensed that Georgia was seconds away from landing him a well-deserved smack in the mouth. 'Why did you stab her?' she asked. 'Did she turn you down?'

'She was into gang-banging, I'm telling you.'

'Where did you have sex with her?' Georgia pushed.

'Told you that too. In the derelict flat, at the party.'

'Well, you see, we've got a problem with that,' Stephanie said calmly. 'Your DNA was also found on the wall outside the empty flat.'

There was a second's pause. 'I took her outside.'

'You just said you had her at the party.' Georgia again.

She was getting to him; he began to tap the table with his knuckles.

'It was at the party,' he repeated. 'The party went outside. Some of us were having a drink outside. By the window, so we could hear the sounds.'

'It was raining,' Stephanie said. Ripley made no reply. 'Where was she stabbed?' she added casually.

'Watch my lips. I. Do. Not. Know. I wasn't there.'

'I'll tell you. It was outside the empty flat. By the window. Where the party was.' Stephanie spoke clearly as if he was a child. 'She was stabbed *where you say you had sex with her.*'

He blinked rapidly and raked a cluster of pimples with a fingernail. 'Well, not while I was giving her one.' He peered at the finger and wiped it on his jeans. 'She was a slag. I fucked her. I didn't stab her. End of.'

'What time was it when you fucked her?' Georgia was growing bored with this.

'Don't know, mate. I'd had a drink and a couple of pills. I just fucked her.'

'I'm not your mate. What did you do afterwards? Did you go back into the party?'

'No. I was tired. I went back to my place. You've got my clothes. I ain't had time to change them since yesterday, what with being harassed by the Feds. You won't find no blood on them.' He mimicked Stephanie's tone. 'I never fucking stabbed the slag. Got it? I just fucked her.' He turned to face his solicitor. 'They've got nothing on me. Can I go now?'

'You admitted having sex with the victim just prior to her death, so we need to eliminate you from our murder enquiry,' Stephanie answered. 'Your clothes have been sent for forensic testing, and I'm afraid we can't release you until we have clearance on them. That may take up to twenty-four hours.'

He spun around to the duty solicitor again. 'I ain't done nothing,' he protested. 'They can't lock me up for having a fuck.'

'It's not for having a . . . fuck,' the woman told him quietly, her eyes firmly on the papers in front of her. 'You're a suspect in a murder case, and until they prove your innocence I'm afraid you have to stay here.'

'You're no fucking help,' he told her. 'You're supposed to be on my side. I didn't do nothing.'

'In that case you'll be out as soon as forensics can corroborate that,' Stephanie told him.

'Who attacked Chantelle Gulati?' Georgia asked him casually, leaning back in her chair.

His eyes slid from her to Stephanie again. 'What's happened to Chantelle, then?'

'She's been badly beaten. As I think you know.'

The eyes moved to one side, checking the solicitor's reaction. 'I didn't know.'

He was a bad liar. He also wasn't very bright; if he had stabbed Haley or beaten Chantelle, it would have been on Reilly's orders. Even if they could prove he had done it, Reilly would find other suckers to groom and take the rap for him.

The problem was like the pimple he kept picking, Georgia thought. There was no point getting rid of the surface, you had to get the root, and the root was Yo-Yo Reilly. Or Jason Young.

Now Young was back, more trouble was brewing and more killings were likely. The only way to prevent this was to get both Young and Reilly behind bars, and to do that she needed to win over one of the gang.

It was quite possible Boot had stabbed Haley. With or without her consent he had had sex with her, and her death followed shortly after. Reilly was clever enough to have ensured that his own clothes would be burnt or buried by now, and they hadn't found the weapon which Georgia felt sure would point to Jason Young as the murderer. They were at stalemate.

'Sally Young.' Georgia looked straight into the shifty eyes. They went on the move again.

'What about her?'

'She's been shot.'

'Nothing to do with me.'

'I didn't say it was.'

'Why say it then?'

'I wondered if you had any idea who might want to shoot her.'

'I don't have nothing to do with guns,' he said, folding his arms and leaning back. 'Try her grandson for that one. I heard he's just out.'

'You're a knife man, are you?' Stephanie examined her fingernails.

'Everyone has to carry a shank to survive around ours. We're the Brotherhood, man.'

Jason slid on his belly like a snake through a hole in the fence at the back of the Aviary estate, at the other end from the derelicts. The whole area was swarming with Feds, even the armed squad, and sirens wailed continuously as more approached. If he was caught with the gun, he'd be back inside for seven years if he was lucky, and the dream of becoming a hip-hop dancer would be history.

But whatever the price, Chantelle was his girl, and Reilly was going to pay for what he'd done to her. South London would be better off without the Brotherhood running the streets. Everyone knew the law would never get Reilly; he was too clever for them. So it was up to Jason. A minute ago he had lost his best chance of taking out Boot and Mince. He'd had the gun in his hand, cocked and aimed, then, just as he was about to fire, the Feds had turned up and arrested both of them. They went off in a van, totally unaware that Jason was lying behind the hole in the fence with a gun pointed at Boot's groin.

There was too much going on around here. He decided his best plan of action was to hide again until everything died down. When the coast was clear he'd surface again, and with Ripley and Delahaye in custody, Yo-Yo would be without his lieutenants; taking him out then would be a doddle. He was actually looking forward to blowing his balls off and spreading his brains over the wall. The time he spent inside would be worth it.

As long as Chantelle was there when he came out.

Stephanie Green was dunking a Bourbon biscuit in a large mug of tea when Georgia walked into the investigation room.

'Did forensics come back with anything on the five different shoe prints around the scene of Haley Gulati's stabbing?' she asked, perching on the edge of the sergeant's desk.

Stephanie pushed the rest of the biscuit in her mouth and clicked on the screen in front of her. She found the forensics report to date. 'The rain didn't help; they can only tell us there were five different shoes.' She looked up. 'We've identified three of the assailants. We also know Jason Young was there too, so there's only one more we need to identify. It's not impossible it just belongs to some random passer-by.'

Georgia peered at the screen. Stephanie continued, 'Reilly, Ripley, Delahaye, Young, and one footprint from someone not as tall at Michael Delahayc.'

'Delahaye is six and a half foot tall,' Georgia retorted. This was going nowhere. 'I still think Young stabbed her,' she went on, 'regardless of those prison reports. I think he made the call from the phone booth too, to send us in the wrong direction. His DNA's there, after all. And if he didn't do it, why did Chantelle lie? It's not hard to work out, is it? She wanted to buy Young time to get away. So Reilly has her and Luanne beaten for it. Any news yet on Alysha's whereabouts?'

Stephanie shook her head.

'OK. So, next bit of the puzzle – who shot Sally Young and why?'

Stephanie swallowed her mouthful of biscuit. 'If only we could find the gun, or at least the bullet casing. And the knife that stabbed Haley, and whatever they used to crack Chantelle's head open.'

There was a burst of rap music and Stephanie reached for her phone. She had changed her ringtone again; that's what having teenage kids did for you, Georgia reflected. She didn't have a clue how to change a ringtone.

Stephanie ended her call. 'That was TIU. They've got an exact location for Jason Young. He's on the corner of Tupton Lanc.'

'Let Dawes and Peacock know; they can pick him up,' Georgia said. 'Is the CO19 unit still down there?'

'Yes.'

'Better let them know too. Young's likely to be armed and dangerous.'

The rap music trilled again. It was forensics.

'No gun or blood residue on either boy's clothing,' Stephanie said, snapping the phone shut. 'They both said they were wearing the same trousers last night. No semen stains either. Interesting, that.'

'So we can't hold them.' Georgia clicked her tongue against her teeth. 'Just when you don't want forensics to move their arses, they do.'

'There's still Jason Young,' Stephanie said. 'He's got a motive, and form for gun violence.' She wiped sugary hands on her trousers and clicked on her keyboard. 'He was done seven times for GBH to his grandmother between 2002 and 2005.'

Georgia sighed. 'When he was between ten and thirteen.'

'He broke her finger once. Another time he knocked her out and put her in hospital for three days.'

'And Dawes says guns are his thing.'

'As well as knives.'

'There was blood on that sweatshirt, and I don't think it was Sally Young's. We still need those forensics results, and we need to pick up Jason Young. Nothing else we can do.'

'We can pray both Sally and Chantelle will come round soon.' Stephanie wiped her empty mug with a tissue and put it in the desk drawer. 'That will be the best result.'

'We're not doing too well at the moment,' Georgia said. 'One woman dead and two more from the same estate fighting for their lives, and no one, *no one* saw a thing.' She put her fingers to her temples.

'That estate has been gang-run for ten years now. The residents are terrified of talking to us. It's an uphill battle, but we'll get there. Think of King Alfred and the spider.'

'Don't you mean Robert the Bruce and the spider? King Alfred was the one who burnt the cakes. You obviously flunked history at school.'

Stephanie grinned. 'I was better at biology. Let's just hope Dawes brings Young in.'

Apart from his height, Michael Delahaye looked like any ordinary black teenager. He wasn't even particularly unattractive. But

Georgia had a strong urge to knock his drug-inhaling head into another planet. He had raped a woman old enough to be his mother, and didn't seem in the least concerned that he was sitting in an interview room in the murder unit, possibly in serious trouble.

He must have the IQ of a pea, she thought. His accent was such a hybrid that she had to concentrate to be sure she was getting what he said. The recording of the interview would be very difficult to understand.

But Georgia and Stephanie both agreed that out of all Reilly's sidekicks, Delahaye was the one more likely to crack.

'Michael—' Stephanie began in a friendly tone. They had agreed that she would take a softer line.

'Mince,' he cut in. 'This is Brotherhood business, and my Brotherhood name is Mince. I don't answer to nothin' else, innit.'

Stephanie nodded. 'Mince. That's fine by me.'

Alan Oakwood had taken the place of the nervous woman solicitor, clearly on Reilly's orders and with the promise of a fat fee. Delahaye looked at him for approval.

Oakwood's eyes were on Georgia.

Georgia leaned back in her chair and studied Delahaye, doing her best to make the boy feel uncomfortable. He had an innocent face, and it took people by surprise when he turned violent. He was handy with a knife, quick and precise at inflicting harm, and had twice done time in Feltham Young Offenders' Institution, but until now he had never been linked with a fatal stabbing.

There was a first time for everything.

'I hear you shared Haley Gulati in a gang-bang?' she said conversationally.

'That's not a question,' Oakwood chipped in.

Mince's tapping toes betrayed his agitation. He appeared to give the matter some thought, then, 'Yeah,' he replied. 'We're like family, my tribe. Families share things. Food, drink, girl-friends and stuff, innit.'

'Can you be specific? Did you have sex with Haley Gulati just before she was murdered?'

'You don't have to answer that,' Oakwood said quickly.

'You don't know when Haley Gulati was murdered. How would you know if you had sex just prior to her death?'

Delahaye's eyebrows moved closer together. 'She was wanting it. That ain't no crime.'

'Which one of you stabbed her?' Georgia asked quickly.

'Hey, you don't lay that one on me. No one stabbed Haley.' He put his hand to his crotch and started to rub himself. 'We just gave her a good time, innit.'

Georgia felt a strong urge to slap him. 'Where did you gang-bang her?' she asked, pressing her hands together.

'I don't know.'

'Of course you do. Where were you when you had sex with Haley?'

'I don't remember.'

'I'll ask you again. Where were you when . . . ?'

'Outside, by the derelicts.'

'So you do remember.' Georgia inhaled deeply. 'Something else for you to remember. Lying in an interview is an offence. It's called obstructing an enquiry, and carries a custodial sentence of up to two years, depending on your past record. And yours is a long way from clean.'

'I don't think my client meant to lie,' Alan Oakwood butted in. 'You're making him nervous. He forgot, that's all.'

She ignored him and sat back. Stephanie took over, her tone gentler. 'Tell us about having sex with Haley. How did it come about?'

His face broke into a wide grin. 'She couldn't wait. Our tribe were having a good time in the derelicts. Some of the guys were doing music and some smoke down there. She came in, gasping for it, and we all had a turn.'

'Where did you do it?'

'Come again?'

'In the derelicts or outside?'

His eyebrows moved again. 'Both,' he said after a moment. 'Inside and out.'

'What time was this?' Georgia asked.

'Around ten, I'd say.'

'Then what did you do?'

'I went and had a smoke, then I went home, innit.'

'What time was this?'

He became thoughtful and cautious, and his gaze flicked around the room. 'Well now, that's a bit hard to say,' he said casually. 'The weed chills me, do you hear what I'm saying? I lose track of time.'

'And of what you're doing?' Georgia suggested.

He raised his hands. 'I ain't done no knife, you hear me now. Ain't no knife nowhere says I held it and dug her.' He blew out a breath. 'You ain't pinning that on me. I ain't stabbed no one, you hear what I'm saying?'

He laid his hands on the table and glared at her. Georgia sat back and folded her arms. For a few seconds there was silence, then Stephanie said softly, 'Brotherhood of Blades.' There was admiration in her voice. 'They don't call you that for nothing.'

Delahaye was still tense. 'You taking the piss or something, lady?'

'Why did Haley Gulati get stabbed?' Stephanie asked gently. 'What did she do?'

He slammed the table with the flat of his hand. 'I didn't dig her.'

'Then who did?'

'How would I know? Just cos I know how to use a blade, don't mean I ain't never killed no one.'

'You did rape her, though.'

Alan Oakwood motioned to Mince to keep quiet. 'My client has already told you he did not rape the victim.'

'But he hasn't told us which one of his tribe stabbed her,' Georgia snapped. She turned back to Delahaye. 'You say you're a family, and you share things. Does that include blame? You can all go down for murder if you like.'

'We came here because we didn't dig her. You said you could eliminate us.'

'Not me, sunshine. OK, let's try something else. Why did you shoot Sally Young? She's got a big mouth, was that it?'

'Nothing to do with us.'

'But Chantelle Gulati was to do with you. You all work for Yo-Yo Reilly, don't you?'

'We're his tribe.'

'Chantelle was beaten so badly she's fighting for her life,' Georgia pushed. 'Her friends say it was because she talked to us. Did you do that?'

'She's a slag. Anyone could have done her. Haley lost something Chantelle was looking after. Chantelle should have been more careful.'

Georgia and Stephanie exchanged a glance. Now they were getting somewhere. 'Haley lost Reilly's drugs, and Chantelle was punished?'

'I didn't say that, man. She was fine when we left her.' He turned to Alan Oakwood. 'Can they do this to me? I told them I didn't do it, you hear me now.'

'No, they can't.' Oakwood sat up and leaned across the table. 'My client has come here of his own accord. He has admitted having consensual sex with the murder victim shortly before her death. He has told you he knows nothing about the stabbing, or any of these other accusations you've been throwing at him. If you have no evidence to prove otherwise, I'm going to insist that you to release him.'

'Interview terminated three oh five p.m.' Georgia clicked off the tape.

David Dawes sat in the CO19 van with Jim Blake, the commanding officer. They were following the team's progress on the monitor. The CO19 armed police had moved in and surrounded the shed the phone trace had pinpointed. The occupants of the flats near the shed had been evacuated in case of gunfire.

Hank Peacock was outside under the trees alongside the pathway. Another dozen armed officers were ready to move in as back-up if Young started firing.

Dawes's phone rang. Young had just made another call.

'We're on,' Dawes told Jim Blake.

The CO19 commander opened the van door, put his loudhailer to his mouth and spoke slowly and clearly. 'Drop your weapons. Put your hands in the air and walk out slowly. You are surrounded. I repeat, drop your weapons, and walk out with your hands in the air.'

A tense silence lasted a few seconds, but there was no sound from inside the shed.

Jim Blake spoke again. 'You have ten seconds to give yourself up and come out, or we are coming in. Ten. Nine.'

David Dawes picked up a second loudhailer and stepped out of the van.

'Eight. Seven. Six.'

Dawes took over. 'You've less than five seconds. We are coming in. Throw the gun down and come out.'

'Four. Three.'

A scream ripped through the air. Luanne was a hundred yards away, hurrying towards them, her bandaged arm bobbing up and down against her body. 'My sister! My little sister's in there,' she screamed.

'Hold it! Hold it!' Dawes shouted urgently throwing his hand in the air to halt the team.

Luanne was still yelling. 'She's only twelve! Alysha! Alysha, it's OK. I'm here, babe.'

Dawes hurried over to her, wincing as he saw her bruised face. He loathed the thought of these young girls being used and knocked about.

'Jason Young's in there,' Dawes told her. 'We believe he's armed.'

'No, he's not! Alysha is. She's just rung me. She's on her own.' She pushed him aside and hurried toward the shed.

Hank Peacock quickly moved in to stop her, but Dawes motioned him to stand back.

As Luanne approached, the shed door opened an inch, then another, then Alysha's terrified face peeped out. In her raised hand she was holding a phone.

THIRTEEN

'Hold fire!' David Dawes and Jim Blake shouted in unison.

'That's my sister,' Luanne screamed. 'You nearly shot my sister.'

Dawes ran towards the terrified girl, put a protective arm around her and kicked the shed door open. Blake gave his men the signal, and they moved into the shed calling, 'Police! Throw down your weapon.'

A woman constable restrained Luanne, who was still yelling. Dawes looked down at Alysha, still cradled in his arm. 'Where did you find that phone?'

'Jason gave it to me,' she told him. 'I ran away when Luanne and Chantelle got a beating. I met Jason and told him what happened. He gave me his phone and told me to ring Luanne and tell her where I was.'

'When was this?'

'Not long ago. Maybe an hour? I've been hiding. I don't know how much time has passed.'

'Do you know where Jason is?'

'He's not in there,' she said. 'He's gone.'

Luanne was still shrieking her sister's name.

'Let her through,' Dawes said to Blake, releasing his hold on Alysha.

Luanne ran towards Alysha and pulled her into a tight hug with her good arm. 'Thank God you're safe, darlin'. No one's gonna shoot you, I won't let them . . .'

'He didn't hurt you?' Dawes asked Alysha.

'Of course not. Jason wouldn't hurt us,' said Luanne.

'Or hold you against your will?'

'He wouldn't do that. Not to us.'

'Do you know where he's gone?'

Alysha looked at Luanne, her large brown eyes bulbous with fear.

'It's all right, babe, you ain't in any trouble. Go ahead and tell them,' Luanne urged.

'He's got a gun and he's gone after Yo-Yo Reilly. He said to phone Luanne, cos there was a shooting on the estate and she'd be worrying about me.'

Dawes dragged his fingers through his hair. 'Any idea where he was heading?'

Alysha looked at Luanne again.

'It's OK, babe. If you know, tell them.'

'He's gone over to the Aviary. Said he's going to kill . . .'

Dawes didn't wait for her to finish. 'Peacock! Back-up to the Aviary, now.'

Jim Blake was barking orders to his team. 'All units – Aviary estate. Armed gunman in the Aviary estate.'

A small crowd had gathered just outside the police cordon, determined to find out what was going on. As the police vehicles drew away, David Dawes spoke to the onlookers through the loudhailer.

'There is an armed gunman on the loose,' he told them. 'He is extremely dangerous, and must not be approached. If you think you spot him, please call 999. We have armed police units in the area. For your own safety, please, all of you, go home.'

David Dawes placed Luanne and Alysha in the care of a female sergeant. 'Make sure they get home,' he told her, 'and keep an eye on them till this is over.'

He hurried away towards the car where Hank Peacock was waiting. Alysha pulled free of the sergeant and scurried after him. 'I'm coming with you,' she shouted.

'Lysha!' Luanne shouted. 'You come back here!'

Dawes turned to face Alysha. She was good at playing tough, but the truth was she was a terrified twelve-year-old child.

'No,' he said gently. 'You've done really well, but now your sister needs you to look after her. You go home with her. I'll send a couple of my officers to keep you safe.'

Luanne caught up with her sister. 'We don't want you to do that,' she told Dawes. 'It ain't safe for us to have uniformed Feds guarding us.'

'They don't have to be in uniform. I'd like to make sure no one hurts you again.'

Luanne shook her head vigorously. 'How many times do I have to spell it out? If you hang around us we're even less safe. I have to look out for my sister.'

'It's my job to keep you safe,' Dawes told her.

'It doesn't work like that round here. We look out for ourselves.'

Peacock appeared from behind the car. 'What about Alysha? You want her to be safe?'

'You don't get it, do you? The best way to keep us safe is to stay away. We don't want no Feds at our house.'

Alysha shook her hair extensions. They sounded like beaded curtains. 'I can look out for myself,' she said defiantly.

'You could have been shot just now,' Dawes told her. 'If not by Jason Young, then by CO19.'

'But I didn't.'

'No Feds at our house,' Luanne repeated.

Dawes was aching with frustration. The girls were too afraid to accept his help and that made them more vulnerable. He turned his back on them and climbed into the car.

The drive to the edge of the Aviary Estate took only a couple of minutes. Dawes sat in silence, unable to trust himself to speak. Alysha and Luanne reminded him of his sister: not physically, but in other ways. They were all vulnerable, victims of the drug pushers who ran the estate. Alysha was still a child, and Luanne was devoted to her, but she was too afraid to accept police protection.

'You all right, sir?' Peacock asked him. 'It's those girls, isn't it?'

This lad was growing on Dawes. He was green, and he lacked tact, but he was young and new to all this. He was also loyal, likeable, and keen, and unlike a lot of them at this South London nick, he listened. Today was a baptism of fire for a trainee detective.

'They need someone to keep an eye on them,' he answered.

'They'll have it.' Hank winked. 'I spoke to uniform, told them to keep a look-out, but from a distance.'

Dawes opened his mouth to tell him he had done well, but he suddenly caught sight of Alysha in the side mirror. She was running down the middle of the road, dashing in and out of the hooting traffic, beaded plaits bouncing around her face.

'Jesus Christ. Where's she going?' Hank wound down the window.

Dawes put out his hand across to stop Peacock tooting the horn and shouting to her. 'To find Jason Young, I'll bet. She's going to tip him off that we're on to him.'

Hank Peacock gave a bark of laughter. 'Like he won't know.' He was still laughing as Dawes picked up his radio and told all units to keep the young black girl with sequined jeans and chin-length plaits in sight. She would lead them straight to their target.

Georgia tidied the papers she had been reading back into the file and checked her wristwatch. It was five p.m. Her team had hardly slept last night, and it looked highly likely that tonight would be the same.

Stephanie clicked her phone shut. 'DI Dawes,' she told Georgia. 'They think they know where Young is.'

'Again.'

'He'll call us when they're sure. Unless you want us to go over anyway.'

'No. We'll wait it out. If Young gets to Reilly it will save us a lot of paperwork.'

'Isn't that exactly what Dawes said last night. And didn't you read him the riot act?' Stephanie asked, amused.

'Yes, all right, I was wrong.' Lack of sleep was beginning to creep up on her. Stephanie emptied the change from her pocket on to her desk, 'Black coffee?' she said, and headed to the drinks machine without waiting for a reply.

As Stephanie fed coins into the machine a thought occurred to Georgia. 'Are Ripley and Delahaye still in custody or have they been released?'

'I'll check with the duty sergeant.'

'We'll tail them.' Georgia looked pleased with herself. 'They'll go straight to Reilly, and Young will be just a breath away.'

Steph handed her a steaming paper cup, waiting only to pick up the chocolate bars she had paid for, before heading off in the direction of the cells.

Georgia picked up her bleeping mobile. It was the crime scene manager from Sally Young's flat. The news was good; they had found a bullet shell in the walkway close to where Sally was shot. It was on its way to ballistics, and they should get some information about both bullet and gun within hours.

She rang the uniformed sergeant on the Romney Estate to check on progress, but he had little to report. They had had no luck finding the gun, and no one had seen or heard anything; most wouldn't even open the door. Some officers had had water poured over them; another had been hit by a used nappy, which had been tossed over the balcony.

Her next call was to the officer on standby at the hospital. Both Sally Young and Chantelle Gulati were still in intensive care. Chantelle was slipping in and out of consciousness but unable to speak. Sally was about to be operated on to remove a blockage they believed was caused by a bullet; the operation would be long and delicate, and it was touch and go if she would survive. Georgia reminded the officer that she needed the bullet if it was in there.

She swallowed the last of her coffee, slipped her arms into her leather coat and was waiting with Stephanie's car keys when the sergeant came back into the investigation room.

'Ripley and Delahaye are both giving the custody sergeant grief,' Stephanie said. 'They refused a lift in a squad car back to the estate, but he didn't give them a choice. I told him not to put them in a car until we're out there.'

'Good,' Georgia said. She shook her head. 'No, nothing's good. Only one thing will make three attacks in one day good. If we can get both Reilly and Young behind bars before I kill them myself.'

'Patience,' Stephanie said.

'I've run out.'

'KitKat helps.' Steph handed her a stick of chocolate.

It hadn't been easy getting into the old tunnel. Jason had crawled over to it on his belly, over the used nappies, around the dirtied needles and stale condoms, turning his head away as rats scampered across his path. The entrance was through a half-rotted discarded door; he could tell it hadn't been used in a while because spiders, maggots and more rats scattered around him as he pulled it open. He'd dragged himself in among them and closed the door behind him. There was no light; the large black hole felt like a rehearsal for death. But sure as hell he was going to get Reilly first.

He could hear Fed cars approaching the estate like wailing banshees. He had the upper hand; he knew the geography of the estate like his own hand, and he also knew the residents wouldn't help the Feds. A lot of them were old enough to remember when Jason ran the estate; he was good to them, rewarded them well when they covered for him during Fed raids. He had taken the trouble to find out what they needed, and he made sure they got it: CD player, sofa, even a wide screen television, the Buzzards would provide it. Jason cared for the welfare of the estate, and they knew it. He used to think of himself as a Robin Hood.

The young kids, or tinies as they were now called, had always liked him too. Remembering his own childhood, he made sure none of them went hungry. A lot of those tinies grew up to be his Youngers. Some of them were dead already; others followed Reilly now.

Jason understood that. It was all about survival; you did what you had to, and if you joined a gang, the gang protected you. Reilly terrified everyone with his dogs, and ruled the estate by fear. The residents wouldn't give him up to the Feds either, not because they liked him, but because they were afraid of the consequences. Reilly even stabbed his Youngers if they made mistakes. In the old Buzzard days you never hurt your own crew. You looked out for each other, like family.

Jason couldn't wait to shoot the fat bastard and rid the estate of him, no matter what the cost to himself. Reilly was going to pay for what he did to Chantelle and Luanne, and the estate would be a better place for it.

For an estate boy there were two choices: die young, or spend your life in and out of the slammer. What a fool he had been to think he could be different. He dashed away a few tears with a dirty hand, and groped for the gun.

It felt good.

*　　*　　*

Dawes spoke into his radio. 'All units eyeball on young black girl, braided hair, sequined jeans and trainers, running toward the Aviary estate. Do not approach, repeat do not approach. Maintain eyeball.'

A reply came from Georgia. 'Approaching Aviary estate in an unmarked car. We have eyeball on Alysha. She is heading around the back of the dustbins by the derelicts. I am pursuing on foot. Sergeant Green will follow in the car.'

Dawes updated her on his position.

'Back-up moving in to estate perimeter.' This was Jim Blake, the CO19 unit coordinator.

'Take it slow,' Dawes told him. 'We don't want to frighten Alysha off. We believe she is leading us to Jason Young.'

'Alysha is on her stomach scraping at the ground,' Georgia said. 'There must be some kind of hideout hidden behind those dustbins.'

'I'm parked by the kerb, ma'am.' Stephanie Green. 'Right by the derelicts. If anyone tries to run I have this edge of the estate blocked off.'

Georgia kept her eyes pinned on Alysha. The girl's legs suddenly disappeared.

'OK, all units, go, go go,' Georgia shouted.

The CO19 team jumped from the vans, guns at the ready, and moved in behind Georgia to surround the area.

'It looks like a door, under the ground,' Georgia said, kicking it hard with her boot. 'Alysha, can you hear me?'

There was no answer. She tried again. 'Alysha, are you in there?'

Dawes sighed. It felt like Groundhog Day; less than thirty minutes ago he had stood with a CO19 team, expecting Jason Young to be on the other side of a shed door.

One thing was certain: Alysha was around here somewhere, and if Jason was with her, there was no way CO19 could shoot.

Dawes nodded to Jim Blake, who fired a warning shot into the air. A few nosy residents appeared, including Stuart Reilly, who stood watching with a wide grin.

'Alysha!' Dawes called into the loudhailer, moving closer together with Hank Peacock and a team of uniforms.

He pushed at the corner of the door, which was balanced

against a pile of dirt. The door gave way and slid to one side. Behind it Jason Young lay on his belly, a gun in one hand and Alysha beside him.

'Throw that gun out!' Dawes shouted, stepping in front of Georgia. 'And let Alysha go. Now! Do it.'

'This isn't what it looks like,' Young said loudly. 'I wouldn't hurt Alysha.'

'Prove it,' Georgia shouted. 'Let her go.'

No one moved.

'Let her go,' Georgia repeated. 'Then throw the gun out, and we'll listen to what you have to say.' She stretched out an arm. 'It's OK, Alysha,' she said calmly. 'Climb out, and walk towards me.'

Alysha let out a loud wail.

'It's OK,' Georgia assured her. 'Just climb out. Your sister's waiting.'

Young threw his gun on to the ground and slid it toward David Dawes. 'She doesn't like the Feds,' he said. 'She won't go near you. She knows the Brotherhood will punish her if she does.'

Alysha looked terrified. Her eyes flickered from Jason to Georgia, and then to David Dawes. Suddenly she leapt past Georgia and was over the grass and heading for the stairs to Sparrow tower block in a matter of seconds.

Dawes picked up Jason's gun, and two burly uniformed officers moved in quickly to pull Young out of the old tunnel. They turned him, frisked him, grasped his hands behind his back and clicked handcuffs on him as Dawes read him his rights.

Hank Peacock set off across the grass after Alysha.

'Leave her,' Georgia called. 'She's only going home. She's scared stiff. I'll send Steph up there in a while, to take her statement.'

'No wonder so many estate kids turn to crime,' Hank said. 'I wish we could . . .'

'Better concentrate on getting through your training before you try to change things . . .' The sentence trailed away. One of the uniformed officers who had been searching Jason Young's clothing stood up.

'This was in his sock, ma'am,' he said, holding up a short knife.

Hank Peacock moved in with an evidence bag. Georgia had rarely seen anyone look as bleakly despondent as Young did at that moment.

'That's it, then,' he said. 'My scholarship's fucked. I should've known it was too good to be true.'

'Shoot your own grandmother too, did you?' Peacock said.

Jason visibly paled. 'Gran Sals has been shot?'

'Don't pretend you didn't know,' Hank Peacock scoffed. 'Where did you get the knife?'

'It's for protection.'

Dawes silenced Peacock with a little shake of the head. 'A knife and a gun,' he said to Jason. 'That will put you straight back inside. And that's just for starters.'

Two constables led him to the waiting police van, as Stephanie Green approached with her phone in her hand and a grim expression on her face.

'Ma'am, a word. The hospital's just phoned. Sally Young died on the operating theatre, and Chantelle Gulati has been rushed back into surgery with complications.'

Jason let out a deafening howl. One of the officers put one hand on his head and pushed him into the back of the police van. He closed the door, but Jason's shouts could still be heard.

'No-o-o-o! Tell me it's not happening!'

Alysha had grown up a lot, Yo-Yo Reilly noticed as she approached the stairs of the Sparrow. She was tall for her age, no bad thing, and like her mother she had long, slender limbs. Blokes liked long legs. She looked cute too, which was another plus when someone wanted a young thing. He'd have her out on the streets earning before long.

It hadn't taken him long to work out she was sweet on Mince Delahaye. Reilly made it his business to know other people's weaknesses.

He blocked her path as she hurried toward the stairs. She fixed frightened eyes on him.

'You've done well today,' he said.

The hideous dog he was holding snarled and pulled at the end of its chain.

'Sally Young's dead,' she said flatly.

'Where did you hear that?'

'Feds are talking over there. They're all over her walkway, looking for a bullet.'

'Did they find one?'

She shook her head and raised her head defiantly. 'Mince said I should ask if you'd let me have some of your good grass.' She stopped to watch his reaction, and he gave her a tight smile. She carried on. 'Cos Luanne got a beating today.'

Reilly's face broke into a wide grin. She was so like her sister – a greedy little cow. 'You want some, you can have it, darling, but it's for you, not Luanne. I'll even throw in a bit of crack for your added enjoyment. And as you've had a tough day, I'm gonna tell Mince to give you a go-o-o-od time.'

Mince and Boot were sitting on a low wall a little way off, listening.

'I ain't giving this one a good time,' Mince said, taking a step forward. 'No way, little princess. You are way too young, innit?'

Reilly wondered why he'd never noticed how alike these two were. They both had long, gangly limbs they couldn't quite control, and both had oval faces. Only their eyes were different: Alysha's large and round, Mince's almond-shaped.

'This little princess wants some gear and a good time,' he told Mince. 'If that's what she wants, that's what she gets, after the day she's had.'

Mince's tongue moved nervously over his full lips. 'No,' he said. 'There are some things I won't do, Yo. The kid's too young.' He looked at Boot and Scrap for support.

Boot Ripley pushed himself off the wall, all ears. Scrap Mitchell, who had been standing a few yards away, moved closer. Nobody said no to YoYo, not even his Elders.

'I don't give a monkey's fuck what you think,' Reilly said to Mince with an edge of threat. 'That tattoo on your arm says you are my Brotherhood. That means you do as I say. Got that, Mince?'

Mince stared at him for a second, then said quietly, 'She's still a child.'

'I ain't no child, Mince,' Alysha said. 'Please. Let's do some skunk and have sex.'

'You heard the lady.' A triumphant grin spread across Reilly's face.

Mince looked at Alysha. 'We will, Princess. When you're a bit older, d'you hear me now.'

'She wants some charlie and a good fuck, now,' Reilly said.

'I won't do that.'

Reilly looked across at Boot and Scrap. 'What d'you think, boys?' he asked, not expecting an answer. His mouth twisted and his voice became a growl. 'You'll do as you're told, Mince, like all Brotherhood do. You know the rules.' He turned back to Boot and Scrap. 'Ain't that right, bros?'

Georgia was tidying around Stephanie, who was at her desk writing up reports. She brushed crumbs into a pile with a piece of paper, then fetched the bin and swept them in.

'I'm all in,' she said.

Stephanie nodded. 'Nothing more to do here tonight. Jason Young is locked up, and hasn't called anyone. The gun's at ballistics, and the knife's gone to forensics with his clothes. And my report is finished.' Stephanie threw her pen down.

Georgia picked up her coat.

'I haven't had time to shop for days. I was going to pick something up on the way home,' Stephanie said. 'Fancy coming back to mine for pizza? I don't even know if the kids are stopping in. Lucy's in charge, but she's been staying out till two in the morning some nights. I'd like to be there when she gets in tonight, to ask her what's keeping her out all hours.'

'She's probably fallen in love,' Georgia said. 'Sixteen is an impressionable age for a girl.' Georgia didn't have a clue if it was, but it sounded good. 'Pizza would be great. And I'd like to see Lucy and Ben again. If they're in.'

'Fat chance. It's Saturday.'

'My new Black Eyed Peas CD's in the car. Lucy can borrow it if she likes.'

'Give me Robbie Williams any day.'

Stephanie's maisonette was in darkness when they arrived. She opened the door, and before she had a chance to reach for the light switch Georgia tripped over a pair of wellingtons in the middle of the hallway.

'Sorry,' said Stephanie as the hall filled with light.

'Not a problem. At least it's not that motorbike you were rebuilding. It took four washes to get the grease off my jeans.'

There was no sign of either Ben or Lucy. Stephanie left a message on Lucy's mobile. 'Peaceful night for us,' she said reaching into the cupboard for plates as Georgia unloaded the beers from the off licence bag and looked around for glasses.

Stephanie tossed her a bottle opener. 'We don't need glasses. Saves on the washing up.'

They settled on Stephanie's lumpy sofa, pizza boxes on their laps, beer on the table in front of them, vying for space with old newspapers.

'Two murders on that estate in twenty-four hours, and another balancing on the edge,' Georgia sighed. 'DCI Banham is asking for a lot of paperwork. I just hope we can wrap it up quickly.'

'You reckon on Jason Young for both?' Stephanie asked her. 'I do.'

Georgia pulled at her bottom lip. 'He has a strong motive for stabbing Haley. She grassed him up.' She bit into a pizza slice and pushed a strand of sticky cheese into the side of her mouth with her finger. 'But why shoot his own gran?' She shrugged. 'Dawes believes Reilly is involved.' She wiped her mouth on a sheet of kitchen roll. 'They won't be in it together, so which one is it? I'd go for Young. But there's something that doesn't add up.' She swigged some beer down. 'We need to get the ballistic tests back to know more.'

'Young's prison reports say he was attacked on a daily basis towards the end of his stretch, but he never retaliated.' Stephanie lifted the beer bottle to her mouth and took a long slug. 'Maybe he's just clever, and planned to get Haley all along, and then his gran found out.'

'Possibly. But Haley was a police informant. Anyone who knew that would want her dead.' She shrugged. 'It's not cut and dried, that's for sure.'

'The faint bloodstain on the sweatshirt we picked up at Sally Young's was too weak to give us anything, which is a shame.' Stephanie licked tomato sauce from her fingers, reminding Georgia of a cat she had seen in a television advert.

'Young will go down again anyway, for carrying a firearm and a knife, and with his record he'll be off the streets again, for a good few years this time.'

Georgia carefully laid down the remains of the pizza slice. 'That's not enough,' she said fiercely. 'If he killed Haley Gulati, I want him for murder. I want justice for that woman.'

Stephanie cracked open another bottle and handed it to Georgia. She took another bite of pizza and chewed thoughtfully for few moments. 'David Dawes wants Reilly for this. He seems to know everything about the Brotherhood. I really do wonder why he is so interested. It doesn't seem healthy.'

'It'll be personal.' Georgia lifted her eyebrows. 'We'd all like to know more about him. I thought you were going to find out.'

Stephanie nodded. 'I wouldn't mind shagging him anyway. I don't need a reason. He's kind of hot, don't you think?'

Georgia smiled. 'Not my type.'

'Who is your type? You're so fussy!'

'Certainly am.' Georgia made an effort to relax her shoulders. 'Anyway, with you around there's never enough for two.'

'I wish.'

'I'll happily pay up if you do shag him, but you have to get some info on him too,' Georgia told her. 'Find out why he's got such a thing about gang crime.'

'I'll do my best.' Stephanie gave a burst of laughter. 'But I'll wear him out first.'

Georgia laughed too. 'Have you never heard the expression, *leave 'em wanting more*?'

Stephanie grinned. 'That's for comics, not nymphos.'

Georgia laughed. 'Tell me what's going on with Ben and Lucy. Is Lucy still planning a career in the force?'

'So she says.'

'And Ben?'

Steph shook her head. 'No way. He says we live and breathe the police. All he wants is to get away and travel.' The smile left Stephanie's face. 'I'm not sure I'm a good influence on them. I'm never here.' She sighed. 'Perhaps it wasn't such a good idea to keep them away from their father.'

Georgia took a long swig of beer and swallowed hard. 'You've given them everything you can, including a lot of love,' she told her friend. 'They're teenagers, and they're good kids.' She pulled the end off another slice of pizza and put it in her mouth. The soft cheese and tomato stuck to the roof of her mouth and she rounded it up with her tongue. 'Think about those estates kids. Most don't even know who their father is, and most of their mothers neither know nor care where they go. A lot are too busy using their benefit money to feed their drug habit. What chance do the kids have? We can't blame them for turning out the way they do. It's the system that's wrong, not the kids. In their own way they're victims too.'

'Yo-Yo Reilly doesn't fall into that category,' Stephanie said. 'I've got no sympathy whatsoever for that son of a bitch.' She tapped her forehead. 'He's clever and evil. He didn't even grow up on the estate. He had two parents, and was sent to school and given a chance. He finds out who's vulnerable, feeds them drugs and puts them on the streets. Or if they're blokes, he pretends he'll be their family, and he'll take care of them. He buys them top of the range trainers and phones, and they sell his drugs for him, and beat up a few people who don't pay, cos he tells them they're his brothers. I even feel sorry for those vicious dogs. He is one evil bastard. Dawes is right to want him behind bars.'

Georgia smiled. 'You are keen on DI Dawes, aren't you?'

'He's cute.'

'Well, you'd better make your move quickly. He's only on attachment for this case. Forensics will be back tomorrow or the next day, then Jason Young is going down for a very long time. We'll be old and grey by the time he comes out; you don't want to wait till then to get Dawes into bed. Besides, you'll have lost your bet.'

'I have no such intention, ma'am.' Stephanie gave a mock salute.

'Then I'll raise the bet to thirty quid – but only if you find out why he is so interested in the gangs on our side of the water.'

'Make it thirty-five. You'll get your information.'

FOURTEEN

Luanne took a drag on the spliff she was holding between the fingers of her right hand. The path outside Mince's flat was deserted, but the estate was still crawling with Feds. None of them seemed to be showing any interest in her smoking. Alysha had been inside with Mince since yesterday.

Yo-Yo appeared further down the path, flanked by Boot Ripley and Scrap Mitchell. Two of Yo-Yo's dogs strained against their spiked collars and throat leads; Scrap was hauling one of his behind him too.

Yo-Yo did not look happy. Luanne lowered her hand to hide the joint.

'What's going up?' he asked her.

'I'm just waiting for Alysha.' She was painfully aware what could happen to you if you disobeyed Yo-Yo, no matter how many Feds might be around. It made her nervous but she thought she was doing a good job of hiding it. 'She's well up for it, but what I hear is that Mince don't wanna know.' The spliff was making her talkative.

Yo-Yo's eyes flared.

'Alysha wants to lose her virginity,' she rabbitted, hoping she could talk Yo-Yo out of blaming Alysha and giving her a hiding. 'It's Mince. He thinks she's too young.'

'Ain't up to him to think,' Yo-Yo snapped. One of the dogs leapt at Luanne, and she had to jump a couple of feet back to avoid getting bitten. She felt a hot trickle of urine between her thighs.

Yo-Yo jerked his head at her bandaged arm. 'That tells you who's running this gaff.' He took a step closer. 'Got it?' The dogs growled.

She gave a quick nod and took a careful step backwards.

'That sister of yours wants to earn, and sure as fuck she's gonna make me some money. She was begging Mince to give her one yesterday.' He moved in on her again, and she smelled stale sweat and yesterday's alcohol. 'You should be thanking me. I've let Mince to do the honours. I usually take care of the pretty ones myself.' He stroked her braided hair. 'We want her to like it, see.' His hands tightened around her braids and tugged them spitefully, pulling her head back. She was used to being hurt, and had learned not to show pain or fear. Bitter experience had taught her that was Yo-Yo's weakness; fear and pain in a woman's eyes made him wild with sexual desire.

'There's a lot of bastards out there with big wads of money,' he said. 'Those that like 'em young. *Very* young.'

'Yeah,' she said turning her head away and dragging hard on the spliff.

Yo-Yo snatched it from her and passed it to Boot. He pushed Luanne aside, yanked his dogs by their choke chains and went to hammer on Mince's door.

'Just give them a bit more time,' Luanne pleaded.

The clout seemed to come from nowhere. The side of her head jolted against the wall and pain exploded inside it.

'Fucking don't tell me what to do!' he spat at her, turning back and aiming a kick at the door. The dogs burst into a terrifying chorus of ferocious barking. Luanne again felt warm urine run down the inside of her leg.

A couple of seconds later Mince's face appeared around the door. 'What's up?' he asked.

Yo-Yo pushed past him, followed by Boot and then Scrap. Luanne was left on the path, her good hand nursing her newly swollen lip. She thought of Chantelle, and almost started to cry, but she took hold of herself. Her sister needed her. She followed them into the flat.

Jason Young sat bolt upright in his chair, opposite Georgia and David Dawes. Beside him was Clive Bury, the duty solicitor. Bury suffered from dust allergies, a problem which irritated the hell out of all the detectives he worked with. Interview recordings were often ruined because his incessant sneezing or nose blowing obscured vital evidence. Georgia used his presence on the duty roster as a way to ensure the custody suite was properly cleaned, but Stephanie had no patience with him. This morning he sat next to his client with a large maroon and white handkerchief protruding from his cuff and the usual jaded expression across his face.

David Dawes placed the transparent evidence bag containing the handgun on the table in front of Jason, next to another containing the knife found in his sock. Both had undergone intensive forensic testing, and the police were only waiting on the results before charging him.

Those results could take another day or more. During the morning meeting Georgia had suggested they push for a confession from Jason. Dawes had still insisted that Reilly was behind it all, which to Georgia seemed irritatingly pointless. They had caught Jason Young red-handed with the weapon; what they needed was for him to tell them why he killed his gran.

She had asked Dawes in front of the full murder squad if his vendetta against Reilly was personal. Dawes had looked furious, but refused to be beaten down. Everything that happened on that estate, he maintained, had Yo-Yo Reilly behind it; no one dared cross him. He studied this gang and knew everything about them. Georgia pointed out that before Jason Young went down he had been the one who ruled the estate; now he was out, it was highly possible he was going to claim back his turf.

Their job, she reminded Dawes, wasn't to clean up the streets of South London, but to solve a fatal stabbing, a cold-blooded shooting, and an attack, which looked as if it was about to turn into yet another murder. And though she whole-heartedly agreed that getting Reilly off the streets would prevent further crime, their current energies should be focused on these murders. She suggested that Dawes ask himself whether his determination to take Reilly down might be clouding his judgement.

Dawes had come straight back at her. He had been called in to give them the benefit of his expertise about the gangs, and that was what he was doing. His instinct still told him Reilly was behind all the recent trouble. Maybe he had even done it to set Young up.

That was when Georgia had given up. 'OK,' she'd told him.

'Let's try for a confession from Young, and see where that leads us.'

Dawes leaned back in his chair and studied Jason. The boy certainly had motive for stabbing Haley Gulati, and there was no doubt that he was capable of shooting anyone, including his grandma; he had just finished a stretch for armed robbery. But *why*? Why would he shoot his own gran?

Jason claimed that the first he knew about the attack on Sally Young was when he was arrested. He had a gun, and had been planning to use it, but he hadn't fired it. He admitted that he had fully intended to shoot Reilly, because the Brotherhood had put Chantelle in hospital. But he would rather kill himself than his gran.

He hadn't had a chance to shave, yet the stubble around his cheeks was faint; but his eyes looked as if they had seen the beginning of time. It was hard to believe he was only nineteen-years-old. The whites of his eyes were clear: evidence that though he had dealt drugs, he wasn't a user. Dawes thought of his own sister Philly; her hollowed cheeks and sunken eyes had made her look twenty-years-older than her age. It wasn't until after she died that Dawes discovered she had been using for four years. A whole family of police officers and no one had noticed; they were all too busy helping other people to hear one of their own cry out for help.

Her premature death had broken his parents. His father had taken early retirement and now spent his days growing vegetables, and his mother barely spoke. Dawes couldn't remember seeing either of them smile since before Philly died.

He had traced the heroin that killed her to the Aviary estate. Jason Young was about to go down when it happened; so it was possible he had sold her the heroin that killed her, but it was more likely to be Yo-Yo Reilly who by then had taken over Young's patch.

Sitting opposite Jason Young, Dawes realized he might never know for sure which of the two sold his sister her death sentence.

The boy clenched his fingers into a fist and placed them on the table in front of him, his whole body tense.

'Do you want to tell us why you shot your gran?' Dawes asked him.

'I've been set up. I didn't shoot my gran.' He looked up. 'Why would I shoot my gran?'

'You tell us,' Georgia said.

Jason's fingers splayed, stiff and wide as if they had been spray-starched. His hand cradled his cheek again. He looked at Dawes, then at Georgia, and spoke quietly.

'I've done a lot of bad things, but believe it or not, I had given up all that. I was trying to move on.' He leaned forward. 'I had a chance to move on. I had a dance scholarship. But I've screwed up.' He took two quick breaths. 'It's not a crime to love someone.' He looked Georgia in the eye. 'I love Chantelle. I gave up my chance to get away because of what Reilly did to her. I came back to kill him for it. But that's what he wanted me to do, I see it now. He set me up. Believe me. Please.'

'Give me one good reason to believe you,' Georgia said. 'You had a knife and a gun when we picked you up. Why would we believe it's a coincidence that we've been looking for a knife of that size and a .38 pistol? The weapons that killed Haley Gulati and your gran?'

Dawes interrupted. 'Why would Reilly set you up?'

Jason didn't answer.

'Then you'll go down for them both,' Dawes said matter-of-factly. 'With your record, you're looking at two lifes, with no parole.'

There were tears in Jason's eyes. 'I had a chance. I had a scholarship to a dance school. Why would I give that up to kill Chantelle's aunt? And why would I kill my gran?'

'You tell us,' said Georgia.

Jason looked at Clive Bury. The lawyer's face remained as blank as ever.

'I might have known it was too good to come true.' His voice cracked. 'If you come from down there, no one lets you go straight. No one ever gives you a chance.' He looked Georgia in the eye again. 'We were going to give it a go, me and Chantelle, give up all the shit and move on.'

Georgia stared at him for several seconds. 'Where did you get the gun?' she asked.

He chewed the inside of his cheek nervously. 'I found it in the bin by the shed.'

'Convenient,' Dawes said, raising his eyebrows.

Jason lowered his head. 'Reilly set me up.'

'What about the knife you had in your sock?' Georgia asked. 'The same size as the one that killed Haley Gulati?'

'I didn't kill her.'

'Your DNA was found in the blood on Chantelle's door,' Georgia reminded him.

'I found Haley's body. I touched her, so I knew I'd left a trace and that you'd pull me for it, so I went to tell Chantelle and then I legged it. I called you guys too, from the phone box by the alleyway.'

Georgia let out an exasperated sigh. 'So where did you get the knife?' she repeated.

He pressed his lips into a thin line. 'Someone gave it to me. That's all I'm saying.'

Dawes was losing his patience. 'You'll have to do better than that. Who gave it to you? And if you'd decided to go straight, why did you need a knife at all?'

'I was on my way up west. I was going to keep my head down till I started at dance school.' He looked at Georgia and Dawes. 'Have you ever slept rough on the streets?' They didn't answer. 'I didn't think so. It's tough out there. Street gangs patrol their patches. I was walking through their territories. I needed a shank for protection.'

'It's an offence to carry a weapon,' Dawes reminded him.

'Where did you get the knife?' Georgia again.

He scratched his neck. 'I had to have protection . . .'

'Where did you get it?' Dawes almost shouted.

'OK, OK! I found it, right?'

'Found it where?'

'At the side of the alleyway.'

Dawes leaned back, breathing hard. Georgia tried to catch his eye. This was hard; she and Dawes weren't in tune the way she was with Stephanie. He tipped his head to one side; she took it as a signal to take over while he collected himself.

'Jason, you've told us you were there when Haley was killed, and when we arrested you, you had the knife,' she said. 'Why don't you make it easier for yourself? Admit you killed Haley Gulati.'

'I didn't.'

'And your gran found out, so you killed her too. That's what happened, isn't it?"

'No!' Jason half rose from his chair, and sank back when the solicitor put out a restraining hand. 'I didn't even know my gran was dead till your man told me. I'm telling you, I've been set-up.'

Georgia pushed on. 'So how did you get Haley's blood on your hands?'

'He stabbed her because she grassed him up and got him sent to Wandsworth,' Dawes said wearily. 'He found out she was a grass while he was inside, and decided to get even.' A curl of scorn crept in. 'Before he left to go up west. To be a dancer.'

Jason's fist thumped on the table. 'No! I didn't like Haley, but she was Chantelle's aunt.' He swallowed hard. 'I've been set-up. I have. Only way out of that estate is in a box.'

'How?' David Dawes's eyes bored into Jason's. 'How did Reilly set you up?'

Desperate words began to pour out of Jason's mouth. 'I've been bad. I know I have. I ran the estate, I dealt drugs, I took all the profits. Everything that went down was on my say-so.'

Dawes held his breath.

'But I've learned my lesson. Prison ain't no place to be. I was never going back. Me and Chantelle, we were going away together. My probation officer helped me. We were going to start over, live clean and good like ordinary folks. But if you're an estate kid that ain't going to happen. I'm telling you the truth here, man.'

Now even Clive Bury was listening.

'We were so young when it all started, we just wanted what other kids had. DVDs, trainers, phones. We did bad things to get them.' He blinked. 'We've paid the price for it. Joker, one of my tribe, got shot in the eyes. Pots had his balls – sorry, miss, testicles – cut off by a North London gang when he went over that way to see a girl he'd met. That's how it is out there. It's a jungle. That's why I took a shank when I went up west. To stay alive. I swear to you.' His eyes fixed on Georgia. 'Don't put me back inside for that. Please.'

Georgia held his eyes. 'Chantelle is in hospital, unconscious, fighting for her life.'

He covered his face with his hands. 'And I couldn't get to see her because the hospital is surrounded by Feds. Then I heard Alysha was missing.' His hands dropped into his lap. 'I was going to kill Reilly. I would have shot him for what he's done to her.'

'Who got you the gun?' David Dawes asked quickly.

He shook his head. 'I ain't a grass.'

'Not even to prove your innocence?' said Georgia.

His head moved more vigorously. 'You know as well as I do, I'd be killed if I told you.'

'If you'd kill Reilly for her, surely you'd grass him up for her?' Dawes argued. 'If he killed Haley and your gran, you can help us send him down. If you found Haley then I think you saw who killed her.'

Jason chewed his lip.

'It was Reilly, wasn't it?'

There was no reply, and Dawes went on, 'If you're innocent, prove it by telling us what you saw. And we'll see if the CPS will go easy on the firearm charge.' He paused and held Jason's eyes. 'That carries a five year custodial for starters.'

'But if you lie to us,' Georgia chipped in, 'I'll make sure you go down for a very, very long time.'

'You just said it yourself,' Dawes pressed. 'It's hard if you grow up somewhere like the Aviary. This scholarship you talk about is a chance to move on. If you really are innocent, and you help us, we'll help you in return. You have my word.'

'Things aren't looking good for you,' Georgia told him. 'If you saw who stabbed Haley, you need to help us put them away.'

Jason looked away and bit down hard on his bottom lip.

'You said you love Chantelle,' Georgia added. 'Do this for her.'

Jason rubbed his mouth. 'I can't. I ain't a grass.'

'Yes, you can. Then you can get away, and start over.'

Jason flicked his eyes up. 'Where I come from no one gets away.'

* * *

'What do you think?' Dawes asked Georgia as they walked back along the corridor to the investigation room.

'I think he could be lying,' Georgia said, 'but if he is, he's good at it. If they find a bullet at the post-mortem this morning, and it matches his gun, we can charge him with murder. His DNA in the blood on Chantelle's wall will put him in the frame for Haley's murder too, but it isn't sound. That could go either way.' She looked at Dawes uncertainly. 'But what if he is telling the truth. What if has been set-up?'

'We'll keep pushing him,' Dawes said. 'He may give us Reilly.'

Georgia stopped walking. 'He may also be lying,' she reminded him. 'We'll know more when we get ballistics report.'

'That will only confirm the bullet and the gun. We're nearly sure the bullet came from the gun we took from Young, but it's possible that he did find it by the shed after someone else had shot Sally Young. The shed is next to Sally's block. But if Young doesn't tell us what he saw, he'll go down for Haley Gulati. And those girls are too afraid to give evidence against Yo-Yo Reilly. All we can do is keep pushing Young. Offer to speak up for him with the CPS and he might even give us Reilly's drug supplier too.'

'This isn't about drugs. For the moment let's concentrate on getting the right murderer,' Georgia retorted.

'Agreed,' Dawes said, a little too quickly.

'You really want Reilly, don't you? Is there something you aren't telling me?'

Dawes looked at her speculatively. 'You don't know the story?'

'What story?'

'I'll tell you over a celebration drink, just the two of us, when we've got him.'

Georgia was stunned. Was Dawes making a pass at her? She never went on dates with colleagues, but this time she actually felt tempted.

Not enough to create bad feeling with Stephanie, though. She didn't reply.

Yo-Yo stormed into Mince's living room shouting, 'What's going down?'

Alysha jumped up from the sofa, a can of Red Bull in her hand. Mince was sitting on the floor. 'Nothing, man, nothing's going down. How ya doing?' he answered, scrambling to his feet. He read the expression on Yo-Yo's face and terror crept into his eyes.

Luanne stood in the hallway trying to keep her distance from the snarling dogs. 'I've told him the truth,' she shouted over Yo-Yo's shoulder.

Yo-Yo took a drag on the spliff he was holding. It was common knowledge that Yo-Yo always smoked a joint before he hurt someone. And Mince had disobeyed his leader's order.

Mince swallowed hard.

Luanne felt a kind of respect for Mince, though she couldn't see why taking Alysha's virginity was such a big deal. The sooner Alysha lost her cherry and got out and started earning, the easier life would be for the two of them. Hers had gone when she was ten; everything you had was an asset to earn with. It was like Jason always used to say: you did what you could to survive round here, and the only way out was in a box. Jason was just dreaming if he'd started to think any different.

'I couldn't do it,' Mince said in a pathetic voice. His almond-shaped brown eyes threw an appeal to Luanne. 'She's twelve years old, you hear what I'm saying?'

'You heard what Yo-Yo said, innit?' came the angry reply from Scrap.

'I heard, I heard, but she's a kid, man. She's a good Younger, and a good look-out when the Feds come, but she ain't ready for the streets.'

Luanne watched Yo-Yo raise his hand and wipe his sausage-like fingers across his mouth. Everyone knew those signs. No one in the Brotherhood was allowed an opinion of their own. Anyone that had one got hurt. Usually Yo-Yo would make one of the other Brotherhood damage the offender. That was his way of reminding them who ran things.

Mince bravely continued to argue his case.

'Let her do the running and the Fed alerts, bro, just for a bit longer. But no punters. Not yet.'

Yo-Yo fixed his hard eyes on Mince. After a few

uncomfortable seconds Michael's gaze dropped. 'I can't do it to her, that's the truth. I see her as a child still, you hear what I'm saying?'

Everyone waited. Each of them secretly admired Mince for refusing to take the virginity of a twelve-year-old, even though Alysha looked and acted as if she was twenty-five.

Yo-Yo dropped the spliff and ground it into the carpet. The flat belonged to Mince's mother. She was still out after working all night in a North London massage parlour; she often wasn't seen for days. All the same, Mince knew she would go mad when she saw the burn hole. He dug his front teeth into his bottom lip, but said nothing.

Yo-Yo slowly unbuckled his belt, and Luanne's glance shifted to Boot, who was trying to look cool, then to Scrap, whose eyes sparked like fireworks from the cocktail of drugs he had swallowed over the last hour. Finally she looked at the dogs, who sensed something was brewing and stood flat-eared and waiting. Just for a moment she wished she hadn't given Jason the gun. She could have used it herself, to shoot Yo-Yo and then the dogs. As it was, she had no choice but to remain quiet.

'She's going to earn some money for me,' Yo-Yo said, flicking angry eyes at Luanne. 'You've had your orders, Mince, and you'll be punished for disobeying, but right now . . .' He dropped his trousers, allowing the expanse of white flab that hung over his black boxers to wobble freely. He grabbed Alysha and pulled her toward him. Her round brown eyes widened. 'You and I are going in the bedroom,' he told her. 'And I'm going to show you exactly what you do to earn money from punters.'

Alysha looked past him at Luanne, and her mouth broadened into a wide grin. 'OK,' she shrugged. 'Fine by me.'

By the time Georgia arrived at the post-mortem, Hank Peacock and Stephanie Green were already gowned up in green overalls. Georgia quickly pulled on a gown and a white mouth mask. In her hand was the report she had made on the gun they had taken from Jason Young.

Stephanie was explaining to the exhibits officer exactly how they wanted Sally Young's skull to be photographed: how to get the exact angle of the victim's neck where the bullet had entered and lodged in the back of the lower cranium. If they were lucky enough to find the bullet, she told him, they would need a close-up of its resting spot.

The sound of a zip being drawn back took their attention. Sam, Phoebe Aston's assistant, opened the body bag and revealed the corpse. Sam picked up the cutting knife and handed it to Phoebe.

Phoebe traced a clean cut in the waxy skin from the base of the throat down to the groin. She used the same knife to slice open the base of Sally's neck. Then lifting the greying skin she peeled back the chest area, almost like opening a book.

The removal of the heart and lungs took only seconds, and while Sam took them away to be weighed, Phoebe opened the top of the head with an electric saw and removed the brain. Sam took it away, and the exhibits officer moved in to photograph the inside of the skull. Sam returned, and shone a torch inside the open head.

'There,' he said, flicking his eyes towards Phoebe. The camera flashed busily, and Phoebe picked up a pair of tweezers. With great care she lifted out a bullet, which dropped with a chink into a dish which Sam lifted like an offering for the photographer.

It reminded Georgia of childhood Christmases; she thought she was the luckiest child in the world when she found a sixpence in a Christmas pudding and made a wish over it. Now she reached into her overall pocket for the peppermints she had brought to keep her stomach in check.

Stephanie took the bullet into the light to examine it. Georgia took the opportunity to lift her mask and pop a peppermint discreetly into her mouth. She sucked hard until the cool scent flooded her nose and the rancid taste of bile slid back down her throat.

'It's a .38,' Stephanie said, wiping her soiled rubber glove on the side of her overall. The woman had a constitution stronger than a rhinoceros, Georgia thought, half admiring, half envious.

'We've got him,' Stephanie said. 'It's a match to the .38 handgun. This'll put Young away for a long time.'

'It was trapped in the cerebral nerves and blocked the blood to the brain,' Phoebe told them. 'That was what killed her.'

Georgia had the gun with her. She carefully lifted it from its plastic bag, and held it out for Stephanie to match the bullet to it.

The sounds and smells as the mortuary assistants sluiced away the blood and debris threatened Georgia's composure again. Another peppermint came to the rescue, and as she crunched, she silently cursed the dentist's bill that was surely on its way.

Stephanie had finished examining the gun. She nodded and grinned. 'The scoring matches,' she said with conviction. 'That's the gun that killed Sally Young.'

Back in the interview room, Dawes and Georgia faced Jason Young again.

'It's been confirmed that the bullet that killed your gran came from the gun we found in your possession,' Dawes told him.

Jason visibly paled.

'Are you still saying you've been set up?' Georgia asked, studying him carefully.

He nodded slowly.

'If you love your gran and Chantelle, as you say,' Dawes said to him, 'surely you'll want the right people to pay for their crime. Help us nail them and we'll help you.'

Jason said nothing.

Georgia let out a long breath. 'Jason, you're nineteen. At the moment you're looking at a very long stretch. When you come out this time you'll be too old to dance!'

That hit a spot. He lifted his eyebrows and swallowed hard, but still said nothing.

Dawes held up the report from the forensic lab, hot off the fax machine. 'We can also prove that the knife we found in your possession was the one that killed Haley Gulati. So if this was a set-up, talk to us. We're all ears.'

Jason leaned towards him. 'You don't get it, do you? If I

grass up Reilly, and he comes after me, fine.' He held Dawes' eyes. 'But he won't, he'll hurt Chantelle again.'

'He won't get a chance. We'll lock him away.'

'What about the carrying charge? I'll go down for that anyway.'

'We'll talk to the CPS on your behalf. Especially if you help us put the rest of the Brotherhood away too. Then you can get away and prove it's possible for an estate kid to go straight.'

Jason closed his eyes. He was thinking about it. Georgia looked at Dawes.

There was a knock on the door and a blonde WPC put her head around it. 'Sorry to disturb you, ma'am,' she said. 'It's very important.'

Georgia was back in less than a minute. 'Jason,' she said. 'I'm sorry to tell you Chantelle has just died.'

The colour seemed to drain out of his light brown skin before her eyes. His forehead crumpled and his head slowly shook from side to side. Then tears welled and tumbled. He wiped them away on the ragged grey cuff of his grubby sweat-shirt, but they kept on pouring down his face.

'No!' he said softly. Then, 'No! No! No!' His voice rose to a scream and he banged his fists on the table over and over again.

'Talk to us,' David Dawes said.

'She was my girl.'

'So tell us who killed her.'

Suddenly words flooded from his mouth, through tears and rage. 'I'm gonna tear that bastard limb from fucking limb. He set me up with that gun. But you know what?' His curled fist crashed down on the table and snot flew from his nose. 'It don't matter. Nothing matters no more.' He looked Georgia in the face and was suddenly still. 'You know what? It'll be me next. But he can bring it on. I don't care about nothin' no more.'

Clive Bury turned his face away in embarrassment. Georgia and Dawes waited patiently for Jason to cry himself out.

After several minutes the storm of tears abated and Jason spoke. 'Is Luanne OK? And Alysha? Are they all right?'

'Luanne's got a broken arm and a swollen face, but she'll be OK,' Georgia told him. 'Alysha's just fine.'

'For now,' Dawes added. 'Help us, Jason. Help us to put Reilly away.'

Jason's nod was barely perceptible.

'OK. Tell us everything you know.'

Georgia took a clean tissue out of her trouser pocket and handed it to Jason. He wiped his face and blew his nose, then began hesitantly, 'Reilly's known as Yo-Yo. He runs the Brotherhood. His lieutenants are Michael Delahaye, known as Mince, Dwayne Ripley, known as Boot, and Winston Mitchell, known as Scrap.'

'We know all that,' Dawes said irritably. 'We need to know what you know about the killings.'

'Like what?' Jason asked, a note of desperation in his voice.

'We need a witness who will tell us he killed Haley and Chantelle, and your gran – or at least that he authorized it,' Georgia told him.

'I saw them stab Haley,' Jason said uncertainly.

Georgia tensed, and glanced at the recording machine to check it was still running. 'Go on,' she said quietly.

'They were raping her.' He lowered his eyes. 'I didn't like her, but I . . .' His breath whistled between his teeth. 'It was wrong, disgusting, and there was nothing I could do. There were four of them.'

'Four?' Georgia asked. 'Who?'

'I can't say for sure, except for Yo-Yo. The others all had their hoods up.' He shrugged. 'But Reilly didn't dig Haley. He never does the business himself, he keeps his own hands clean. I saw him give the word to one of them to do it. I watched it all, and I watched one of them shank her.' His eyebrows almost met. 'I couldn't do nothing. They'd have done me.'

He fell silent. 'Go on,' Georgia persuaded.

'Suddenly she was on the ground. I had to put my hand over my mouth to stop myself crying out. I knew they'd dug her, but she was making a noise, so it didn't look too bad. They all legged it. I stood there, trying to think what to do, then one of them came back, and dug her again, then again.' He looked at Georgia. 'I had to listen to her scream. I couldn't do nothing to help her. I waited again, a bit longer, until I knew it was safe. I was praying, that they hadn't done Chantelle first, that Chantelle was alive.' He looked Georgia in the eye. 'I hated Haley, but I wouldn't kill her.' He gave a shuddering sigh. 'When it was safe, I ran over to her. She had no pulse, and there was blood all around and some still coming out of her belly where they'd shanked her. I was going to give her that mouth-to-mouth, that's how I got her blood all over me, then her body started jerking. I took my sweatshirt off and held it over the wound, really tight like, but there was too much blood and I knew she wasn't going to make it. No one was around, and I didn't want to use my own phone, so I ran to the phone box and called 999. I asked for an ambulance and the police, then I ran up to tell Chantelle. We both went down to her, but she was dead.'

Tears began to run down his face again, but he swallowed them back and continued. 'Chantelle told me to leg it, and she'd take care of it. I told her I saw Yo-Yo give the word on it. That's why she told you it was his handprint in the blood on her door. It wasn't him that shanked her, but he did order it.' He wiped his face with the back of his hand again. 'I told Chantelle about the scholarship, that I'd come to get her and take her away with me. She said she'd sort all this first, then come and find me.' He gulped and dashed his hand across his eyes. 'I shouldn't have left her. I should have made her come with me.'

He fell silent again, and sat with his hands clenched in his lap, staring into space.

'What about the knife?' Georgia asked him.

He raised his eyes and looked at her as if he'd forgotten who she was. 'I found it near Haley's body.'

'And the gun,' she added.

'The gun? Oh yeah. I asked someone to get me a gun. So I could go after Yo-Yo. He had Chantelle beaten and I was going to kill him.' He took a deep breath and seemed to collect himself. 'That was how he set me up. The gun I picked up was the one that was used to kill Gran Sals.'

'Who did you ask to get the gun for you?' Georgia asked him.

He shook his head, and for a moment she thought he

wouldn't answer. Then, 'Luanne. She'd taken a beating too and wanted Yo-Yo paid back. It wasn't her fault; she didn't even know. She's terrified of him. I told her to leave it in the shed.' He looked up. 'I'd never hurt my gran, I swear to you.'

The silence when Jason stopped speaking was almost tangible. Georgia reached across to the recording machine. 'Interview terminated at three twenty-five p.m. Jason, we're going to give you some time with your solicitor.' She looked at Dawes and jerked her head towards the door. 'Thank you for your cooperation.'

She stood up and left the interview room, with Dawes close behind.

He struggled to keep up as she walked rapidly up the corridor. She said nothing until they reached her office; as the door swung shut behind them she turned to face him.

'He's giving us Stuart Reilly. Do we believe him?' she asked Dawes.

'I do,' Dawes said. 'But let's make absolutely sure.'

'How?'

'Send Young into the lion's den.'

'OK,' Dawes said, back in the interview room half an hour later. 'This is the deal. You're going back to the estate, as if we couldn't find anything to hold you on. You're going to find Reilly, and you're going to make him talk. You'll be wired, and we'll be close by. We need him to tell you which of his gang stabbed Haley Gulati and who shot your gran, and who gave Chantelle that beating, and we need to hear him admit he was behind it. No need to tell him Chantelle's died; we'll keep that until we have him in custody.'

Jason gasped and screwed his eyes shut. Dawes gave him a moment before continuing.

'If we get what we need on tape, we'll tell the CPS it was all down to you, explain why you were carrying and push hard for a suspended sentence. Then you can leave the estate, and take up your scholarship. We can even put you under witness protection and change your identity. But you have to help us put Reilly away first.'

'Everyone says it's impossible,' Georgia told him. 'You said so yourself. But it's within sight, Jason. You can get away and start fresh.'

Jason shook his head and looked at the floor.

'Do it for Chantelle,' Georgia urged. 'Don't let her die in vain.'

'Think what you'd be doing for the estate. The Brotherhood will be locked up. The residents can live without fear in their own homes, and you'll be a hero. At least Chantelle and your gran won't have died for nothing.'

Jason lifted his hands in the air. 'Where are you living, man? Are you in Wonderland or something? If you put the Elders away, their Youngers will take over. You ain't never gonna stop gang rule. The gangs are bigger than the Feds.'

'No gang is bigger than the Feds,' David Dawes snapped.

'Man, I wouldn't take your money on that!'

'All right,' Georgia said, trying to keep things calm. 'For Chantelle and your gran, then. Help us get their killers.'

Jason raised his hands again, palms outward. 'OK. Makes no odds now, they'll get me anyway.' His eyes looked old and sad. 'It's how it goes in my world – a bullet, a blade or drugs, or the nick. No one grows old.'

'Be the exception.' Georgia said. 'Give the young ones some hope for their future. Be a role model.'

Jason narrowed his eyes. She waited for him to speak, but he said nothing.

FIFTEEN

Jason stepped out of the unmarked police car a few hundred yards from the Aviary estate. He put his hand up to check the tiny mike in his ear. Georgia's voice came through it loud and clear, making him jump. 'Keep your hand away from your ear.'

'Can you hear me?' he muttered.

'We're watching your every move.'

Jason nodded.

'No, don't nod. Don't do anything someone might notice. Just walk on down the road and on to the estate, and don't talk to us again. If you so much as fart we'll hear you.'

Jason began to walk. He would have preferred to blow Yo-Yo's brains out himself, then piss on them as they spilled on the ground. He wouldn't even mind doing the lump for it, after what Reilly had done to Chantelle. This way the Feds would get Reilly, and the bastard wouldn't die. With luck, he'd get his face slashed a few times, or his head plunged into boiling water in the slammer. Best of all, he wouldn't be top dog and he wouldn't call any shots. In a way that was more satisfying. And the Aviary would be way better off without him.

Sure, a new gang leader would come up and take over, but maybe it would be someone who looked out for the kids and the older residents, not another who used and abused them.

Jason himself would be free to take up his scholarship and pursue his dream. What was left of the Brotherhood would never find him, not with the new name the Feds had promised him. And if the CPS agreed on a deal for the carrying charge, his story would be told over and over for years to come, as proof to the estate kids that drugs and weapons weren't the only way. Maybe sometime he could come back and teach the Youngers to dance.

But without Chantelle. He swallowed the lump in his throat.

He looked down at the needles and used condoms, discarded among polystyrene food containers and empty drink cans strewn around the rundown garages. As a kid he used to ferret through those containers for bits of food. No wonder he started thieving. His mum never meant him to go hungry; it was just what happened when drugs took a hold. He remembered the way the dealers banged on the front door when she owed them money. They would hide, shaking, under the table as the heavies kicked the door in and dragged her out to beat her senseless. He used to wet himself with fear.

One memory still haunted him: his mother's screams when they dropped a lighted cigarette down her cleavage. When her trembling hands couldn't locate it, Jason had rushed out from hiding and poured a jug of water over her. The dealers repaid him by smashing his seven-year-old head into the door before they left.

He and his mum had spent the next hour cooling her burnt flesh with cold water. The only thing that relieved the pain was an injection of heroin. It was dodgy – another punishment from her dealer – and she fell into a deep coma. Jason called Gran Sals at work and she told him to ring 999. The ambulance got hijacked on its way into the estate, the paramedics were tied up and robbed, and by the time the emergency service sent a replacement, his mum was dead.

That night taught Jason that the man with the money and the gun makes the rules. He determined then that it would be him. And as he grew up, and one friend after another got shot or bled to death from stab wounds for disrespecting another gang, he learned another lesson: you have to make your own luck; no one gives you a chance. The only thing that made his life worthwhile was Chantelle and their dream of becoming dancers. How he regretted not taking her with him on Friday. Luanne and Alysha too, before Alysha went bad.

'Jason?' Georgia's voice again. 'What's going on? Why are you dawdling? Is something wrong?'

'No.' It came out numbly. 'I'm on my way.'

The place was still crawling with Feds; for the moment he was safe. He heard Dawes's voice in his ear. 'We're not coming any closer at the moment. When you locate Stuart Reilly we'll move in. The police inside the estate are watching out for you. You're safe, and we can hear you breathe.'

People were beginning to notice him. The jungle drums were starting to bang: *Expect trouble, Jason Young is back.*

'I'm going to Luanne's first,' he said quietly. 'I'm going to warn her and Alysha to stay indoors.'

'Tell them to lock themselves in,' Georgia said.

As Jason walked on toward the Sparrow block he became aware that the groups of two and three people watching him walk brazenly through their estate were growing into sixes and sevens. Uniformed police also began to gather in groups.

'Jungle drums,' Jason said quietly.

'We can be with you in seconds,' Dawes assured him. 'But we need Reilly to say he gave the word on the murders; we need three confessions. Got it?'

'Yeah.'

But Jason had stopped listening. He was weighing up the possibility of getting a gun and taking Yo-Yo out himself, and to hell with the consequences. He could knock at Luanne's, and write down that he needed a gun or a shank. She knew where to go; she'd get it in minutes for him. Then he could take the bastard by surprise. He liked the idea of Yo-Yo rotting in prison, but the truth was he didn't trust the Feds not to cock up. What did they know about estates and gang life?

He walked toward the stairwell at the back of Sparrow block, heading toward Luanne's flat on the thirteenth floor. His stomach churned as he reached the walkway and saw the cordons around the door. This was where Chantelle met her fate.

Alysha answered his knock. She looked terrible. Her eyes were swollen and some of her hair extensions were loose at the root. Her dark skin was uneven and blotchy with reddish welts across it, as if it had been scrubbed with a stiff brush. Her legs wobbled, and she put out a hand to support herself on the door frame. He said nothing. He wasn't giving the Feds more than he had to.

Luanne's voice sounded from inside. 'Alysha, I told you not to open the . . .' Her voice trailed off as she appeared in the hallway. She threw her good arm around Jason and hugged him hard.

'We thought you'd been arrested,' she said.

'I got bail. How's your arm?'

She lifted her bandage. 'It hurts like hell, but I got off lightly.' Her eyes filled with tears. 'I can't believe Chantelle's never coming home.'

Her cheekbone was distorted and swollen, and the shiny mauve bruise under her right eye was new. Alysha too was in worse shape than when he had last seen her, but she hadn't lost the attitude.

'Can I come in?' he asked, stepping over the threshold without waiting for a reply. 'You look rough,' he said as Alysha pushed the door closed. 'Did they hurt you too?'

'Why are you here?' she asked warily. 'Yo-Yo will have you killed if he sees you.'

'Alysha, tell me. Did they hurt you?'

'Yo-Yo's just had sex with her,' Luanne said in an offhand tone. 'It hurts for a bit the first time. She needs to rest.'

Jason blinked. Alysha was twelve. That was it; the Feds could go whistle, he was taking that bastard out himself.

'Come on, Jason, you know the score,' Luanne said wearily. 'Chantelle and I lost the stash of drugs we were holding for him, so we owe three times their value. He's decided he wants Alysha earning for him on the streets. It's either that, or more beatings until I pay the debt.'

'Luanne, she's a kid!'

Luanne put her good hand to her forehead. 'I can't take this no more. We're shitting ourselves. He's killed Chantelle, and he'll be back for us. We owe him big time.' She turned away. 'We are way in his debt, man, and it's all down to Haley. She flushed the stash.'

'Is that why he had Haley killed?' he asked quickly.

'I want to do it,' Alysha butted in, flicking her plaits like a thirty-year-old diva. 'I want to go on the street and earn. I wanted to lose my cherry. I wanted Mince to do it, but he wouldn't.' She pouted. 'But Yo-Yo stuck it up me, and it bloody hurt.'

Jason felt an urge to cry. She actually sounded pleased with herself. She was going wrong in a big way, and there was no one to stop her.

'Did he hurt you?' he asked her. 'Apart from . . . you know?'

She shrugged bravely. 'Yeah, a bit.'

'But that's Yo-Yo,' Luanne added.

Jason looked Luanne in the eye. For the first time he was delighted that he was wearing the wire. 'She's twelve years old,' he said. 'They call it statutory rape. Where I've just been, guys get cut up for that.'

Luanne pulled a face. 'Like anyone cares.'

'I care. Where is the bastard?'

'He's sorting Mince out, for disobeying him and not doing Alysha.'

'I wanted to do it,' Alysha protested. 'I can go and earn money for us now. And it's none of your business.'

Jason ignored her. 'Where? Where is he sorting Mince out?'

'In his mum's flat, ground floor of Eagle block. Why? Are you going to take them all on single-handed?' Luanne asked. 'Face it, man, Yo-Yo rules around here. Don't get yourself killed over something you can't do nothing about.'

Jason put his hand on Luanne's good arm. 'Chantelle's dead,' he said quietly. 'I don't really care if I get myself killed. But he ain't getting away with this, and he ain't gonna hurt you two no more. When we're done with this you're both coming away with me.' He looked across at Alysha. 'Where did you get the shank you gave me on Saturday?'

'Mince gave it me. I'm his Younger, and I've done good.'

'And the gun? Where did you get the gun you put in the shed?'

Luanne shrugged. 'I got it from them.'

'Who?'

'What's got into you?' Luanne demanded. 'You know who.'

Jason sighed softly. 'I need you to say it.'

Alysha's chocolate-coloured eyes widened. 'Hey, are you in with the Feds or something?' She blinked, and he knew she had him sussed. 'He's wearing a wire,' she said to her sister. 'He didn't get bail. He's got no money.'

Alysha was the brightest and most streetwise of them all, Jason reflected ruefully. He nodded. 'You're right.'

'Careful,' said Georgia's voice in his ear.

'Is that why they let you out, so you'd grass for them?' Luanne asked.

'I'm gonna bring the Brotherhood down,' he told her. 'You'll never have to be scared again.'

'I ain't scared,' Alysha said. 'I'm going on the streets, and when I've got my own money I'll run the drug business and really earn. I'll be running this estate one day, and I'll be rich. Tell that into your wire.'

'I'm taking you away from here,' Jason told her. 'We're gonna find a better life.'

'You're really scaring me now,' Luanne said, pushing him towards the door. 'Get out of here, will you? I ain't gonna take the rap for you being a grass.'

'Drugs ain't good news,' he said to Alysha. 'They catch up with you, and take you down. Either that or you get sent down. Let me tell you, prison is not fun. It's cold and lonely and scary.' He looked at them, aware his words were falling on deaf ears. He tried to lighten his tone. 'You don't deserve to end up there, but if you carry on working the streets and selling crack for Yo-Yo, that's what will happen.' He hesitated. 'That's if Yo-Yo don't get you first.'

Luanne was looking nervously at Alysha. She was getting the message. He carried on.

'Look at what he's done to you – your arm and your face.'

He could see Luanne was trying to hide her fear.

'I've lost my mum, my gran, and now Chantelle. You're all I've got left. I'm not going to lose you.'

Luanne raised her voice. 'Will you get outa here!'

'Yo-Yo's not in a good mood,' Alysha said as he opened the door and came face to face with the cordons that marked the place Chantelle died. 'He's got his dogs down there to sort Mince out.'

'You're doing well,' Georgia said as Jason walked back down the stairs. 'We can already arrest Reilly for sex with a minor. But you still have to get him to hold his hands up to the three murders. We've moved on to the estate. You won't see us, but we're within eyeball of the Eagle block.'

'There are dogs in there,' Dawes said. 'Be careful.'

'The dogs scare me more than Yo-Yo,' Jason said, heading

for the rubbish-strewn pathway that led to the Eagle block.
As he turned up the hood of his sweatshirt against the piercing
wind, the sound of barking halted him. There were voices too,
raised and angry.

'That's Yo-Yo,' Jason said quietly.

'Second flat along. No lights on, but they're in there. Knock
on the door.'

Jason hesitated. How he wished he was holding a gun.

'We're right here,' Georgia assured him. 'And CO19 are on
standby. We just need to hear him say that he authorized the
killings, and we'll come straight in. End of.'

'Yeah, end of my life.'

Jason took a deep breath and walked down the path.

The front door opened before he had time to knock. Yo-Yo
stood in the doorway. His dark T-shirt was stained with
perspiration, and other stains marked the front of his jeans.

'So. The snake crawls back.' Yo-Yo crossed his tattooed
arms. 'I heard you were around.' His dark, cropped hair stood
erect, making the veins in his temples look more prominent.
His eyes bored into Jason's.

If Jason had had a knife, he would have stabbed him right
there. He wanted to shoot him between the eyes and kick him
in the bollocks as he lay bleeding on the ground. But with
neither knife nor gun, he had no choice but to play it out as
he'd been told.

'You've got front, I'll give you that,' Reilly said. 'You're
on my territory. What d'you want?'

'You put my girl on the streets, after you gave her a taste
for the brown. And you beat her to death this morning.'

'Your girl?' Yo-Yo said. One side of his cruel mouth slid
into a humourless smile. 'She wanted drugs.' He gave a
dismissive shrug. 'A habit has to be paid for, and she was
fuckable. I tried her out to be sure, then I sent her out to
earn.'

Jason's eyes searched around for weapon: a stick or a piece
of broken glass, anything. He was going to give this bastard
a beating, no matter what the consequences. There was a piece
of concrete like a small rock within his reach; he took a step
toward it.

'Steady.' Georgia's voice in his ear halted him. 'Don't lose it. You're doing well.'

A crowd had started to gather. Word had gone round that two rival gang leaders were facing up, and everyone wanted to see who would come out alive.

That half-smile still played on Reilly's face and his hand stroked his pocket. He was tooled.

'You had my gran shot too. Why d'you do that?'

Yo-Yo raised a hand. 'Don't pin that one on me, sonny. You did it yourself.'

Jason swallowed hard. Yo-Yo pushed open the door of the flat. 'If you got a bone to pick, come inside. And leave the stone where it is. My dogs don't like no one having a pop at me.'

The snarling and barking grew louder as Jason approached. He stopped. 'I ain't going in there.'

'If they bother you I'll lock them up.'

'I don't trust you. I ain't going in there.'

'Like you got a choice. You wanna talk to me, you come inside. Out here there's too many ears.'

Jason hesitated.

'Go ahead,' said David Dawes's voice. 'We're within yards of you.'

'You get a five-minute truce,' Yo-Yo said, turning towards the building. 'After that, you're off my territory, or you leave in a box.'

Jason followed him inside.

Yo-Yo kicked the door shut and pulled out a revolver. 'In there!' He pushed Jason into the kitchen. Jason stumbled over Mince Delahaye, who lay bleeding and barely conscious on the floor.

Jason knelt down beside him. 'You need to call someone,' he said. 'You've shanked him and he's bleeding hard. He could be dying.'

'That ain't none of your fuckin' business,' came the reply. A kick from Yo-Yo's steel-capped boot knocked him to one side.

Jason looked cautiously round to check for an escape route. There was none. Winston 'Scrap' Mitchell stood in the doorway with two Rottweilers, which looked ready to tear into

someone as soon as he gave the word. In the hallway another
Brotherhood member held a flat-headed dog, which was trying
to pick a fight with Scrap's two. He kicked it in the balls until
its eyes moved so far into its head that only the whites were
visible.

Terror suddenly seized Jason. If these dogs attacked him,
his dancing career would be over before it began.

Yo-Yo's menacing smile had spread.

'He needs an ambulance,' Jason repeated, jerking his head
at Mince.

Yo-Yo folded his arms. 'Now see, you're like your gran.
She wouldn't have it that I make the fucking rules.' The smile
disappeared as fast as it had come. 'I say who gets punished,
and I say who gets an ambulance. Got it? Mince has been
punished, and you're gonna be next. But you know all that,
don't you, Buzzboy?'

The dogs were still spoiling for a fight. One word from
Yo-Yo and his throat would be torn out. Question was, would
the Feds realize how much danger he was in, or would they
only go in when he got them their evidence? Was this the end
of the line for him?

'I ain't a Buzzboy,' he said quietly. 'I ain't running the
Buzzards no more.'

'None of them to run, my old son.' Yo-Yo cocked the gun
and pointed it at Jason's face. 'Those that ain't been shot are
serving time. Ain't that the truth, Buzzboy?'

'You gave me your word,' Jason said. 'A five-minute truce.'
He dropped his head a little closer to the mike inside his vest.
'You don't need to point a gun at me.'

'He's got a firearm,' he heard Georgia's voice. 'Make the
CO19 call. I want the building surrounded.'

Dawes's voice spoke in his ear. 'Hold it together. Push him
on the murders.'

The dogs had started fighting, and hair and flesh was flying.
The gun bothered Jason less than the snarling animals; they
were seriously unnerving him.

Yo-Yo kicked out at one of them. 'Shut your fucking noise.'
The dog leaned on his front paws and whimpered, then eased
itself down on to the carpet and became quiet.

Jason leaned over Mince again to check his wound. 'This is bad, man,' he said. 'What did he do to deserve it?'

'None of your fucking business,' came the reply.

Jason persisted. 'Why did you stab Haley?'

Yo-Yo opened his mouth to speak, but closed it again as Mince struggled to raise himself to a sitting position. His hand clutched the bleeding wound in his stomach and he spoke with difficulty. 'I want my mum, you hear what I say now?'

Jason had seen more knife wounds in his time than he wanted to remember: enough to know that this one was serious. Mince might have been a rival gang member, but right now he was a vulnerable boy who needed help.

'Man, that needs seeing to,' he urged Yo-Yo.

'What the fuck's it got to do with you?' Yo-Yo shouted, moving toward him with the gun pointing at his belly. 'What are you, some sort of reformed freak?' He grabbed the front of Jason's sweatshirt and hauled him to his feet. Then he froze as the penny dropped.

Yo-Yo slowly raised his eyes and looked Jason in the eye. After a second that seemed like an eternity, he said quietly to Boot Ripley, 'Hold his hands. He's wired.'

He laid the gun on the kitchen table and pulled a knife from his pocket, holding Jason's eyes with his own. Jason waited, still as a statue.

Yo-Yo used the edge of the knife to lift the hem of Jason's sweatshirt and the T-shirt underneath. The cold steel prickled against Jason's bare skin and Jason fought not to flinch. Yo-Yo's lips widened into an ugly sneer. He turned the knife so the sharp edge touched Jason's chest, then pressed it against his heart, where the wire was secured with duct tape. Jason closed his eyes, counting the seconds of life he had left.

The pressure eased and there was a sound like a zip opening. He opened his eyes to see Yo-Yo slowly run the knife from the tail of his T-shirt right up to his neck. The thick black tape was now in full view.

The knife cut into the wire and a warm dribble of blood rolled down Jason's stomach. His life was in Yo-Yo Reilly's hands.

*   *   *

'He's found the mike,' Dawes whispered to Georgia.

'How near are CO19?' Georgia asked Stephanie.

'A few minutes away,' came the reply from Jim Blake.

Jason's chest felt as if half a dozen wasps had landed on it. Yo-Yo's heel ground the remains of the wire into the green lino beneath them.

'So, you're an arse-licking grass,' he said, poking the knife under Jason's balls. 'I had you down as cleverer than that.'

Everyone knew Yo-Yo Reilly was half mental when he was sane. When he lost it, no one knew what he was capable of.

He bent his head towards Jason's until their noses almost touched. 'Penalty for grasses is death and looks like I've got the pleasure.' He hacked the knife into Jason's shoulder as if he was testing a joint of meat for tenderness. Jason tried not to scream.

'You think I'm stupid or something?' Yo-Yo yelled. 'You come in here bleating about your gran and that slag Chantelle. They got what was coming to them.' He ran the knife across Jason's chest. A trickle of blood rolled out. It stung like hell and his legs were growing weak. This was going to be a slow and painful death. He wondered if the Feds would save him.

Boot, Scrap and three dogs moved in behind Yo-Yo. Jason's vision was bleary, but he heard those dogs, spoiling for someone's blood.

Yo-Yo smashed a fist into his head, once, twice, three times. Then he butted him, and blood spurted from Jason's nose. He was pinned against the wall, and all he could see was a galaxy of stars, but still the noise of snarling dogs was crystal clear. He wondered if Chantelle felt this bad as she prepared to meet her maker.

A hard kick in his balls buckled his legs, and he toppled to the ground.

A blurred hand waved in front of his face, and he heard Yo-Yo say, 'I'm having this bastard myself.'

Not the dogs then. He saw a glint as the knife caught the single shaft of light from the window. It was a long blade with jagged edges. The edges would catch on his skin as it entered his body.

*　　*　　*

Police surrounded the flat. Stephanie Green stood at one side with David Dawes; Georgia Johnson and Hank Peacock were at the other. A couple of uniforms struggled to keep the swelling crowd back. Chants of 'Feds, Feds, out the Feds,' warned the Brotherhood members inside the flat.

'That's enough,' Georgia shouted. 'Keep your distance, or we'll arrest you for obstruction.'

The crowd didn't move. 'Let's move in,' she said to Dawes. He shook his head. 'Wait for CO19.'

'We can't wait. There's someone in there with a serious knife wound. And we don't know what's happened to Young. We gave him our word we'd look after him.'

'It's not safe,' Dawes pointed out. 'Someone in there has a gun.'

Stephanie caught Georgia's eye. 'Surround the building,' she told the waiting uniformed officers.

A dozen or more police spread out across the entrance and round the side of the flats.

'There's no back entrance, only a tiny window,' one shouted.

'The last thing we heard was Jason saying a knife wound needed urgent attention,' Georgia repeated. 'We haven't time to wait for CO19.'

SIXTEEN

A round the estate, the usual array of missiles and foul-smelling liquids were raining down from the high-rises. Stephanie Green tried to make herself heard over the clamour of dustbin lids and shouts of, 'Out, Feds, out!'

'Keep everyone back. Try to keep this area clear,' she shouted to a uniformed sergeant who was trying to control a gang of youths.

Georgia picked up the loudhailer and turned to the flat. 'Listen up inside,' she shouted. 'This is DI Johnson. Everyone in flat number three walk out slowly, keeping your hands in the air.'

There was no reply.

'We know you have an injured man in there. We have para-medics waiting to help.' A rotten apple landed on her back and she shrugged it off. 'An ambulance is ready. You need to release him, and come out with your hands up.'

A stick landed on the ground close by, and the uniformed sergeant shouted up into nowhere, 'Pack that up!'

'We have the building surrounded,' Georgia continued. 'We know you are in possession of a firearm.'

No answer.

'For your own good, throw out any weapons, and come out with your hands above your head, or we will come in.'

Still silence from inside the flat.

Dawes moved up beside her. 'Wait for CO19,' he said. 'We can't risk any officers getting hurt. We already have three murders to account for.'

Georgia was too angry with herself to look at him. This was her responsibility; she should never have agreed to this pantomime. It had turned into a mess, and she was going to carry the can. DCI Banham had made it quite clear that no risks were to be taken, and they had disobeyed that direct order. It was clear Dawes was only interested in bringing in

Yo-Yo Reilly; the man was completely blinkered. He wasn't even thinking of her officers' safety; all he cared about was losing Reilly. She had never been a hundred per cent sold on Jason Young's innocence, or Reilly's guilt for that matter, but right now lives were at stake, and their job was to make sure they saved them.

Shc lifted the loudhailer again. 'Reilly, every moment you hesitate is a threat to your friend's life. Throw your weapons down and come out.'

No reply.

Stephanie approached, breathing hard. 'It's getting to crisis point, ma'am. We need to stop threatening or go in. Someone has just thrown custard over two uniforms and called them yellow bellies.'

'They'll live.' A bubble of hysteria almost escaped Georgia's mouth.

'There's at least one gun in there,' Dawes argued. 'Maybe more. We have to wait for CO19.'

'And while we're waiting, what if Reilly shoots Young and Michael Delahaye bleeds to death?' Georgia snapped. 'How many deaths do you want on your hands?'

Stephanie instructed Hank Peacock to get uniform to cover both sides of the flat. As they moved around the building, Reilly shouted through the window. 'We ain't got no gun in here. That's Young, lying as fucking usual. And I ain't done nothing neither. The dogs ain't dangerous, and Mince was cut when he came in here. He says 'e don't want no ambulance.'

A takeaway carton of curry landed not far from Georgia's feet. 'Then let the paramedics check him out,' she shouted, kicking at it angrily.

A filled nappy landed on the ground next to a group of uniformed police. It was impossible to see which balcony it came from; they had no choice but to ignore it.

'At the moment you are suspected of possessing a firearm with intent to cause harm,' Georgia shouted, keeping her temper with an effort. 'Unless you let us in to see for ourselves, we will continue to believe you are holding a gun. If you have no firearm, why not come out? Delahaye can be checked out by a paramedic, and if all is well, we will leave you alone.'

A brief silence followed, broken by a few youths from the crowd, who made gun shapes with their fingers and shouted, 'Bang!'

'Pack it up,' the uniformed sergeant warned them.

'Reilly, if anything happens to Delahaye, or to the other hostage you are holding, the charge will be very severe. Open the door, and let us in. Now.'

'No one's being held hostage. And Mince says he don't want no ambulance. That ain't a crime, is it?'

Dawes was staring at her. She changed tactics. 'He's a suspect in a murder enquiry. Lock the dogs away and let us in, or let Michael Delahaye come out.'

'You don't seem too interested in Young, your grass. You think he's innocent, is that it? My, lady, you are so wrong about so many things. Listen. We ain't got no gun. It's only Young that says we have. He's lying, like he lied and wound you up about his gran and the other woman he killed. If I let you in you'll take my dogs again, and I ain't letting that happen.' Yo-Yo was getting angrier. 'What, you think I'm stupid or something?' he shouted. 'You lot have set us up and it's backfired on you. You've got it fucking wrong again.' His voice rose. 'The dogs ain't done nothing, and neither have I, and Mince don't want to go to hospital. So can you just fuck off.'

'Last chance,' Georgia shouted. 'Come out or we're coming in.'

'Why would I trust you? You've just sent a murderer in here to set me up. He's killed three people and you think he's innocent. What kind of a Fed are you?'

A couple of flying sticks narrowly missed Georgia. She had been working flat out for nearly two days without sleep, and her nerves were jangling. And it looked as if she had allowed Dawes to persuade her into a wrong judgement. It was still on the cards that Young had killed both Chantelle's aunt and his own gran; they'd found the knife and the gun on him, and DNA evidence placed him at Haley's murder. They only had his word that he hadn't committed both murders.

Had he played them? Or was this Reilly turning the tables? At this moment she really didn't know. If anything happened to Jason Young, she was responsible. When the wire was active they had all heard him tell Reilly to put the gun away. But what she didn't know was who was playing who.

A bin full of rubbish came flying in their direction. David Dawes ducked, but some of the garbage landed on Georgia and Stephanie. Dawes flicked some mouldering vegetable from her shoulders. 'Not a great perfume for you,' he said softly.

She brushed the remains of the rotten food from her leather coat, flipping his hand away with the same swift move. He irritated the hell out of her, he was so sure he knew how these gangs thought. He wanted Reilly so badly he was past seeing anything else, and she had agreed to put lives at risk by going along with his plan. Even if Jason Young was guilty of murder, she wanted him to be brought to justice, not out in a box.

She had been ready to believe Reilly had set Young up, because Dawes told her that was how he worked, but it was perfectly feasible that it was the other way round. Young was a dangerous, manipulative criminal with a long history of violence. It was more than possible he was lying, and they would look very foolish when CO19 turned up if they found no firearm in the flat. But she still wasn't prepared to risk anyone getting hurt.

'Check on CO19,' she said to Stephanie.

In the few seconds it took Stephanie to make the call, a couple of youths were arrested, making the other troublemakers around them even more aggressive. Uniform were now struggling hard to keep the ever-growing crowd behind the cordon.

Stephanie clicked her phone shut. 'A few more minutes,' she told Georgia.

'Decision time,' she said to Dawes.

At that moment the door of the flat opened and Yo-Yo Reilly stood holding two angry, red-eyed dogs straining at their spiked leads. He looked around at the mob, which was shoving and jeering the police. His mouth curled in an approving half-smile.

'Seems Mince don't wanna come out,' he said, flicking his nose with a finger. 'Says he's feeling better. And I ain't got

no shooter in there.' He shook his head. 'All this fuss. I'm
flattered, but no need. We ain't got no drugs here, neither, by
the way. This place is clean. See, Young is a bit . . .' He
tapped the side of his head. 'He tells porkies, like he's gonna
be a dancer and all shit like that.' He tightened his grip on
the dog leads. 'I would invite you in, to check for yourself,
but, see, my dogs are a bit protective. They don't like
strangers . . .'

'You've got three seconds to lock those animals away, or
we'll stun-gun them,' Georgia snapped. 'We're coming in, like
it or not.'

Yo-Yo pushed the dogs behind the door and kicked it shut
behind him.

'You don't fucking touch my dogs,' he shouted angrily from
inside. 'They're guarding my property. Ain't no law against
that. This is harassment.'

A voice came from the back of the flats: one of the uniformed
officers. 'There's a child climbing in the back window.'

Georgia and Stephanie dashed around the back just in time
to see Alysha's glittery trainers disappear.

'Oh shit,' Stephanie yelled. 'Alysha, please don't! Come
back!'

Georgia opened her mouth wide to let her frustration out.
Alysha must have heard them saying that Michael Delahaye
was injured, then waited her opportunity. When Reilly came
out and all attention was on him, the kid must have run from
the stairwell and in through that small window before any of
them noticed.

Georgia ran her fingers through her tousled hair, pulling
some of it from its ponytail so it hung loose around her shoulders. She rubbed the back of her neck to ease the tension.

David Dawes was staring at her. She dropped her hands,
embarrassed.

'The girl's got a crush on Delahaye,' he said. 'If anyone
can help us get him out it's her.'

Georgia closed her eyes. 'So now we've got a minor in
there, as well as a man with a gun. And a knife. How can a
twelve-year-old girl possibly make the situation any better?'

'CO19 will be here any minute,' Stephanie soothed. Another

stone landed inches away forcing her to jump back. She swore under her breath.

'We have to protect that child,' Georgia said. 'Reilly isn't sane. We all heard her say he had sex with her.'

'He has a gun and four dogs,' Dawes reminded her.

'No. We *think* he has a gun.'

Jason watched Alysha creep past the growling dogs. That kid really was something. He was pinned against the open lounge door with Dwayne Ripley on one side of him with the gun in his hand, and Yo-Yo on the other with the serrated knife glinting in his hand. Jason was wearing only his beige combat jeans, spattered with his own blood. The few small knife wounds on his bare chest were only bleeding a little, but they stung furiously as perspiration broke out all over his body. A small cut on his forehead smarted too, the wound in his shoulder was bleeding, and his face was swollen and aching.

'What's going on?' Alysha said, not waiting for a reply. She hurried over to Michael, who still lay on the floor, his hand clutching his stomach, where blood had seeped through the cut in his black T-shirt and on to his light-skinned palm. It dripped towards the brown carpet, reminding Jason of jam being squeezed over a chocolate cake.

Alysha knelt down and cradled Michael in her arms.

'Good timing,' Yo-Yo replied. 'We need you to get rid of this gun.'

'Don't do it,' Jason warned.

'You've got to let them take him to hospital,' Alysha told Reilly in a tone no one else would dare to adopt. 'This is worse than you think.'

'Dump the gun and they can have him,' Yo-Yo said to her. 'But get a fucking move on. It's all going up any second.'

Yo-Yo turned his attention to Jason. He rubbed the jagged blade of the knife across the end of one of his own fingers. Dark blood appeared, and he licked at it as if it was a rare delicacy. 'Shame,' he said to Jason. 'Too many Feds around. I'll have to catch up with you another time. Get dressed and fuck off.'

As Jason leaned over to pick up his sweatshirt, Yo-Yo's boot connected with his balls, sending a pain like a bolt of electricity through him. It robbed him of both breath and balance, and as he steadied himself another kick followed. He toppled to the floor, and as he hauled himself up he made a quick decision. He was well outnumbered in here, but the Feds were about to burst in, which had to put them at a strong disadvantage. This bastard had killed Chantelle and raped Alysha. He wasn't getting away with it.

He tugged his sweatshirt over his head, and sudden and fast as a bull charging he landed a punch in Yo-Yo's temple; then, before anyone registered what had happened, he head-butted him.

A click of metal froze him to the spot. Dwayne had released Yo-Yo's dog.

The beast flew at Jason, and he rolled in a heap as the animal sunk its malicious teeth in his leg.

'Stop that!' Alysha screamed. 'Don't let him bite, or they'll have your dog destroyed.'

Yo-Yo hauled the animal off Jason and held him back. 'You and me have got unfinished business,' he spat, clicking the chain back on the dog one-handed. The other hand pressed his cracked nose in a vain attempt to stop the pumping blood. 'You're a cunt of the first degree and I am gonna kill you. But not now.'

'I'll sort the gun,' Alysha said to Yo-Yo. 'I'm taking Michael out to the ambulance?'

Jason ignored his smarting cuts and bitten leg. Alysha's quick thinking had just saved him from a savaging; if he did get away, which at this moment looked very unlikely, he was taking Luanne and Alysha with him. He wanted to take good care of them. Alysha was completely out of her depth and didn't realize it. She reminded him of himself when he was younger; she'd had no kind of childhood either, and learning to fend for herself had made her believe money was the way to happiness.

He had made a big mistake turning grass; all he'd done was swap being banged up for a terrible death, which would surely come as soon as the Feds were out of the picture. He would be remembered as a Fed informant, if anyone remembered him at all. The police had used him to get to Reilly, and he had failed; they wouldn't care what happened to him now. And he had been stupid enough to think he could get away, change his name, and take up a dance scholarship. An estate boy like him? How stupid was that?

So now the police would raid the flat, and he'd get arrested again. They had enough to send him down for murder, and in prison the penalty for being a grass was death.

Yo-Yo, one hand still cradling his bleeding nose, was staring at him. The others were running around, clearing and hiding things, and the police were still shouting outside.

'I can't fucking wait till next time,' Yo-Yo said.

'You'll have to hope there'll be a next time,' Jason replied.

'Oh there'll be a next time. You're the worst kind of toerag – a fucking grass. Next time I'll hurt you a lot, then I'll tie you up and leave you for my dogs.'

Jason believed every word. Torture was Yo-Yo's speciality. He said nothing.

Michael was on his feet, leaning heavily on Alysha. They made their way towards the door so slowly it hurt to watch.

'Get rid of the gun and the knife, and tell the Feds someone attacked him in the street,' Yo-Yo told her.

Alysha barely reached Yo-Yo's chest. Her plaited braids bounced as she turned her head and looked at him, her eyes hard, sad and determined. 'You had sex with me. I'm twelve years old. If I told the Feds, it wouldn't look good for you. Seems to me I make the terms around here.'

Yo-Yo grabbed her braids and tugged them hard. 'You don't make no terms, missy, not if you don't want a taste of what Mince's had. You say he was shanked by someone in the street, got it? And you hide the gun. And you need to remember the penalty for grassing.' He gave her hair another vicious tug.

'She's cool,' Michael said quickly. 'She'll do it, bro.'

Stephanie Green clicked her phone shut. 'CO19 are at the end of the road,' she told Georgia.

'We're going in.' Dawes gave Georgia a thumbs-up.

*   *   *

Dwayne Ripley didn't seem concerned that Yo-Yo had shanked another Brotherhood member or that Mince was now struggling to breathe. Winston Mitchell cared even less; he was only interested in his dogs.

Jason's Buzzard gang had been so different. The Buzzards were like brothers; no one had ever harmed another gang member, although more than one had lost his life defending one. Jason, as their leader, never bullied any of them. They all held together, looked out for each other, like a family. A wave of longing for his own gang washed over him. He really missed them.

Scrap was checking the windows. 'They're moving round the back,' he told Yo-Yo. 'I'm gonna lock the dogs up.'

'Leave 'em,' Yo-Yo said.

No one was paying Jason any attention; he could have walked out the door. But what was the point? They were all going to be arrested at any second.

'You do as you're fucking told,' Dwayne Ripley reminded Alysha as she opened the front door. 'They'll put you in a home if you open your mouth.'

'I'll do what I want,' she snapped back.

That set Yo-Yo off again. He grabbed her braids and dragged her backwards, leaving Michael slumped against the wall.

'I ain't scared of you!' Alysha squirmed and wriggled to free herself. 'I'm dealing with the gun and the knife for you, aren't I? I'll give you a blow job later if you like.'

Yo-Yo released his hold on her hair and burst out laughing.

The banging on the door was sudden and loud. The dogs started barking and snarling, over the top of their noise came the voice of Jim Blake, the CO19 team leader.

'Armed police. Put your hands on your head and walk out slowly. If you don't we are coming in. Muzzle your dogs, or lock them away. If they attempt to attack we will shoot to kill.'

Alysha jumped away from the door and looked at Yo-Yo.

'Lock the dogs away and walk out with your hands in the air,' came the order again.

'This is fucking harassment,' Reilly shouted back. 'We ain't done nothing. I ain't got no hostages, and I ain't got no firearm and my dogs ain't illegal. So what is your fucking problem?'

The lower floor balconies grew busier and busier as more people arrived to watch this battle of wits. Georgia looked at Stephanie; they were thinking the same thing. If they stormed the building, and found no firearm, people could get hurt and the responsibility would lie at their door.

'Oh no. Look.' Stephanie suddenly noticed and pointed at Luanne, who was hurrying towards them, her arm bobbing about in its sling.

'Have you seen Alysha?' Luanne yelled. 'I can't find her. Please tell me she's not around here.'

A uniformed officer put out a hand to block her way.

'Let her through,' Georgia said. David Dawes raised his arm to put the CO19 team on hold.

Georgia sprinted to meet Luanne. 'Alysha's in there,' she told her. 'You have to leave this to us, for your own safety. Go back to your flat. I'll send someone with you. We'll look out for Alysha.'

'Alysha!' Luanne screamed. 'Where's Jase?' she asked Georgia.

'Luanne, please, stay back.' Georgia nodded to a female officer who came over and put a careful arm around the girl, steering her away from the flat.

Luanne couldn't put up much of a struggle, but she did her best. 'She's my sister. I ain't going nowhere. Don't make me, please,' she pleaded.

Georgia lifted the loudhailer to tell the residents who were inching forward to move back, but Yo-Yo's voice cut across hers.

'Alysha's in here, Luanne,' he shouted. 'She's with Mince. He's been hurt.'

'Reilly . . .' warned David Dawes.

Yo-Yo cut him short. 'Fuck off. I ain't talking to you.'

Dawes persisted. 'You'd better listen up Reilly, cos I'm talking to you. You're wanted for questioning in connection with three murders, and . . .'

Reilly cut him off again. 'I'm telling you, this is

harassment,' he shouted. 'You're having a laugh ain't ya? You've got me down for three murders. Well, you've got the wrong bloke. I didn't kill them. I'm holding the cunt that did, but he's trying to blame me. Why would you believe a yellow-bellied grass?'

Georgia held her breath, praying he wasn't telling the truth. 'If that's the case, you've nothing to fear,' she said. 'Send Delahaye and Alysha out first, then follow yourself.'

'Young's having a laugh on you. He's your killer. Ain't that right, Luanne?'

Luanne scowled at Georgia. 'How the fuck do I know?' She looked towards the window Yo-Yo was behind. 'Yo-Yo, you let Alysha out of there, or I swear I'll come in and kill you myself.'

'Luanne, please!' Georgia put a hand on the girl's shoulder. 'Leave this to us.'

Yo-Yo shouted again. 'Tell them the truth, Luanne, then I'll send Alysha and Michael out.'

'What truth?'

'Tell them who stabbed Aunt Haley, and who shot old lady Young.'

'He's flipped,' Luanne told Georgia. 'OK,' she shouted back. 'Whatever it takes. Jason killed Aunt Haley because she grassed 'im up. We helped him get away. When he found out his gran knew he'd stabbed Haley, he shot her to shut her up.'

Georgia looked at David Dawes. All their forensic proof backed this up, but they had dismissed it. She turned to face Luanne. 'Is that the truth?'

Luanne nodded her head slowly.

'Would you go into the box and say it in court?'

Luanne lowered her eyes and nodded again. 'He was covered in blood, Haley's blood, when he knocked at Chantelle's on Friday. He had the knife in his hand. I helped him get away because Chantelle was my mate and she loved him. She thought it was Yo-Yo done it, because we lost some drugs we were hiding for him. It would have broken Chantelle if she'd known the real truth.'

'Who beat up you and Chantelle?'

'I don't know,' she said. 'They were wearing masks.'

David Dawes lifted the loudhailer again. 'OK, Reilly,' he said. 'Listen up. We have a witness who will put Jason Young in the frame for all three murders. At the moment all you're looking at is possession of a firearm and carrying a knife.'

'Will you listen to me? I ain't got no fucking firearm. There are kitchen knives in here. Are you going to do me for having a vegetable knife in my mate's mum's kitchen?'

A moment later the front door opened and Michael staggered out, supported by Alysha. The waiting paramedics ran to help. Alysha climbed into the ambulance with Michael, and Georgia sent Luanne with her. Within minutes the siren was screaming and the ambulance was on its way.

Dwayne and Yo-Yo came out, followed by Jason and Scrap. Uniformed police searched and handcuffed all five of them, finding no gun, while Stephanie Green read them their rights.

David Dawes walked up to Yo-Yo and looked at him appraisingly. 'I forgot to mention – unlawful intercourse with a minor,' he said. 'That's an imprisonable offence.'

Yo-Yo grinned broadly. 'Who's that? Alysha?' He laughed. 'Christ, she don't 'alf tell porkies. Course I ain't had *intercourse with a minor*. If she says I did she's fucking winding you up.'

Dawes gritted his teeth. 'Get him out of my sight.'

Yo-Yo began to protest again. 'I ain't killed anyone, and I ain't fucked no minor. You're setting me up. My dogs need me. They don't deserve to suffer.'

'And living with you isn't suffering?' Dawes shoved him hard towards a uniformed officer, who steered him in the direction of the waiting police van.

SEVENTEEN

Alan Oakwood had arrived at the station and was demanding that his client be released. Dawes had already interviewed Reilly, and told the solicitor he was being held pending further enquiries.

Back in Georgia's office, Dawes took the chair opposite her, while Stephanie made herself comfortable on the wide window ledge with a view of parkland behind her.

'We've got practically nothing on Reilly,' Georgia said. 'All we have is the recording of Young saying, "No need to point that gun." And who's to say there really was a gun? Uniform and forensics have turned the flat upside down, and so far there's no sign of a firearm. No drugs either, and the dogs have been proved legal. DCI Banham says there is nothing to hold him on and Alan Oakwood is smiling from ear to ear again.'

'They're still searching,' Dawes said, but for the first time a note of despondency crept in.

Georgia tried to feel just a little triumphant; it was looking increasingly as if she'd been right all along. But she surprised herself; when she looked at Dawes, all she could see was how good looking he was. A thought took her unawares: was he as dominant in bed as he was at work? No doubt Stephanie would fill her in, in the very near future.

He was still a pain in the arse, though. She pulled herself together and rubbed the tension out of her forehead.

She had re-interviewed Young herself, and the need for sleep was threatening to overtake her. She flicked through the new pile of forensic results on her desk. 'Forensics have now found very faint traces of Young's and Haley's DNA on the sweatshirt we confiscated from Sally Young's flat.' Dawes opened his mouth to speak, and she put her hand up. 'Yes, I know,' she continued. 'Young said he bent over Haley to try to stop the bleeding. There's the ballistics report too; there's no doubt that the bullet that killed Sally Young was fired from the revolver that was in Jason's hand when we picked him up. He had firearm residue on his clothes and hands, and the knife we found on him fits the fatal stab wounds to Haley Gulati.' She looked at Dawes. 'That's one hell of a lot of coincidences.'

'Reilly is a clever bastard,' Dawes shrugged.

'So Young tells us,' Stephanie chimed in. 'He said he saw four youths who were all involved in Haley's rape. We know Ripley and Delahaye had sex with her, and Reilly's semen was in her mouth. All three of them claim she consented.' She rolled her eyes. 'That's highly unlikely for starters. And we know there were five sets of footprints around her body. That tells us there was a fifth person; so was someone else there when Haley was murdered. Are we missing something here?'

'It could just have been someone walking through that part of the estate shortly before the stabbing,' he said. 'There was a party going on there, after all.'

'Young said Reilly was the only one he recognized,' Georgia reminded them.

'Reilly never does his own dirty work,' Dawes pointed out.

'Young says he found the gun near the shed,' Georgia said. 'He says it was dumped in the bin.' She picked up a forensic report. 'Forensics confirm gun residue around and in that same bin.'

'Young could have dumped it himself, then changed his mind and retrieved it when he knew the Brotherhood were lurking,' Stephanie said.

'Or when he heard police sirens,' Georgia agreed.

'He says Alysha gave him the knife.'

'What does Alysha say about that?'

'Luanne and Alysha are both testifying against him,' Georgia told him.

'And what does Young say about that?' asked Dawes.

'That they're frightened,' Georgia said. 'And under pressure.'

'Which is true.' Dawes pressed his thumbs against his mouth thoughtfully. He turned to Stephanie. 'Have you taken written statements from them?'

She nodded. 'I took them at the hospital while they waited for Delahaye.'

Dawes looked from Stephanie to Georgia, and tapped the desk with his knuckles. 'I still believe Jason Young,' he said. 'Reilly is terrorizing those girls into lying for him.'

Stephanie butted in. 'If you don't mind my saying, sir, it strikes me you've got a bee in your bonnet over Reilly. We have nothing to link him to any of the murders, and everything we need to convict Jason Young.'

Dawes looked directly at Stephanie. 'I was seconded to this case because I study the gangs in South London and I know how they operate. The Met regards me as something of an expert.' He turned back to Georgia. 'This is your territory and I respect that, but I still believe Reilly is our killer. It's his turf, and the whole chain of events started when Haley Gulati handed over his stash of drugs to us. OK, Jason Young may have decided to get even with Haley the same day Reilly gave her a punishment beating, but that would be a big coincidence. Reilly has strong motive for killing Haley, and I think when he found Young was trespassing on his territory, he set him up. Two birds and all that.'

'What about Sally Young?' Georgia asked him. 'Why kill her?'

'Collateral damage. She got in the way.'

'Jason Young has served time for gun, blade, and drug crime.'

'Only because he got caught. Reilly's guilty of all of those. He's a lot smarter, that's all.'

There was a knock at the door and Hank Peacock walked in carrying a tray of coffee. They each took a mug; Hank chose a white one decorated with pink matchstick figures adopting different sexual positions.

Dawes sipped his coffee, oblivious to the expressions on Georgia's and Stephanie's faces. Stephanie went scarlet. Georgia had to bite her lip to stop herself laughing.

'Is that mug new?' she asked Hank.

Stephanie's face still glowed like a stop light. The young trainee was leaning nonchalantly against the wall. He nodded. 'It was left for me at reception, in a brown paper bag addressed to the new detective. Looks like I've got a fan.'

Georgia looked down at the desk, unable to meet her friend's eye. So Stephanie had left the mug for Dawes as a come-on, and someone had given it to Hank, another new detective. If he found out Stephanie had left it there, the twenty-two-year-old trainee would think he was in with a chance with her. Georgia bit down on her lip again to suppress her laughter.

'Can we move on?' Dawes said impatiently.

Hank held out a sheet of paper. 'Certainly can, sir,' he said confidently. 'This is from forensics – second blood tests on the handprint by the door of Chantelle Gulati's flat. Jason Young's DNA is in there.'

Dawes shook his head. 'It doesn't help. He's already admitted he was there.'

'We've got enough evidence to charge Young,' Georgia persisted. 'Let's do it and leave it to the CPS to decide.'

'Then Reilly goes free again. No!' Dawes raised his voice. 'This isn't finished.'

'We've got Reilly for sex with a minor,' Hank reminded him. 'That's a custodial, and he won't get bail. That'll give us time to investigate further.'

'We haven't,' Stephanie said flatly. 'Alysha has withdrawn the accusation. She says she made it up.'

'This isn't about nailing Stuart Reilly,' Georgia pointed out sharply. 'I agree it would be good to get him locked up, but our job is to solve three murders. I'm sorry, David, but I have to charge Young. After that it's up to the CPS.'

Dawes pushed his chair back and stood up. 'I was given this case to help clean the estate up. That won't happen until we disperse the Brotherhood of Blades gang and put Reilly away.'

Georgia raised a hand. 'We'd all like that to happen. But please, let's do the job in hand. All the evidence points to Young.'

'I'm trying to do the job in hand,' Dawes said. 'Our job is to keep law and order; putting Reilly away will take a dangerous drug dealer off the streets.'

'Right now our job is to find a cold-blooded killer.'

'Er . . . ma'am . . .'

'What is it, Hank?' Georgia combed her fingers through her hair to keep the loose strands from falling on her forehead.

'I believe Jason Young is innocent too,' Peacock said.

They all turned to look at him. He put his coffee mug down on the desk and stood up straight, facing Georgia. 'I was reading up his prison report from Wandsworth,' he said. 'All he talked about was turning his back on crime and becoming a dancer. He's just won a scholarship. I don't think he'd risk losing it.'

Georgia sighed. 'We know all about that,' she said. 'People like him learn to be smart. They'll say anything to get out of prison, and as soon as they're back on the street it's dealing and thieving and goodness knows what. We were nearly taken in by that too. I'm sorry, Hank. Give it a couple of years. You'll see.'

'The FME told him his stab wounds would heal, and he'd still be able to dance,' Stephanie said thoughtfully. 'And you know what? He cried.'

But Georgia had stopped listening. 'When did Alysha tell Jason that Reilly had sex with her?'

'This morning,' Stephanie said.

'Jason went round there late this morning. We heard him on the wire. He said she looked a mess. Her clothes were dirty.'

Stephanie jumped up. 'And she's still at the hospital with Michael Delahaye.'

'So she probably hasn't changed out of those clothes. If we can get them to forensics, we've got Reilly for sex with a minor whether she admits it or not. Come on, let's go.'

'Where are the two girls who came with him?' Georgia asked the uniformed officer guarding Michael Delahaye.

'The doctor told them to go home. He's going to be OK, and they looked pretty exhausted. They said they'd come back in the morning.'

Georgia threw Stephanie a desperate look.

'How were they getting home?' the sergeant demanded.

'They didn't say.'

'They must have taken the night bus. They probably haven't got there yet. We're still in with a chance.'

It was one in the morning when Georgia and Stephanie raced into the Aviary estate. Lights were on all over the blocks. It had been a long and eventful day.

Stephanie drove right into the estate and parked by the back stairs to the Sparrow block. The lift wasn't working. They ran up the thirteen flights of stairs and banged on the door. A few seconds later Alysha's nervous face appeared.

'Sorry to disturb you,' Georgia said gently. 'I need to talk to you again. Can we come in?'

Alysha hesitated, but opened the door. Georgia and Stephanie exchanged a glance. Alysha was wearing grey pyjamas and slippers, and for once she looked her age.

Georgia said a silent prayer that she hadn't had a bath or washed her clothes.

'We need to ask you some more questions,' Georgia said.

Alysha rolled her eyes, and the kid with attitude was back. 'I already told you all I know.'

'Stuart Reilly is in custody,' Stephanie coaxed. 'If we have our way he won't get bail. He can't hurt you. And if you're honest with us we can make sure he goes to prison.'

'What for?' Suddenly she was terrified again. 'He ain't done nothing. I told you, I was winding you up when I said he stuffed me.'

They needed an adult present before they could use anything Alysha said. 'Is Luanne around?' Georgia asked.

'She's in the shower,' Alysha said with a bored sigh.

They could hear the water running. 'Alysha, have you had a shower?' Stephanie asked.

'Course I have. I was mingin' after all that stuff before.'

'Where are the clothes you were wearing today?' Georgia asked quickly.

There was a pause, and Alysha looked at them speculatively. 'In the washing machine. They were covered in Michael's blood.'

Georgia closed her eyes. Too many TV cop shows, that was the trouble. The kid clearly wasn't going to cooperate.

'What about your underwear?' Stephanie asked.

'That too.'

The door opened at the end of the hall and Luanne appeared wrapped in a towel. The bruises on her face were subsiding, and the bandage was gone from her arm. Her forearm was red and swollen, but not because someone had beaten her up.

On the angry red skin was a new tattoo – a knife with the letters BB written across it. There was a new cut beside it, from the blood ritual. To be accepted into the Brotherhood of Blades as a member of the gang meant the newcomer had to mix their blood with the blood of the other gang members.

Luanne's fearful face spoke volumes.

As Stephanie stepped forward to grab her, she darted past them quick as lightning, out of the door, around the next flat and on to the fire escape. Alysha was right behind her, through the door before Stephanie could catch her. Georgia gave chase as Steph called for back-up.

Georgia followed them up the stairs. She dashed up the last flight and found herself on the roof of the high-rise. Luanne was standing there, with Alysha beside her.

Footsteps thudded behind Georgia. A team of uniformed officers from the grounds below had arrived at the top of the staircase.

'Stay back,' Georgia shouted to them, taking two steps towards Luanne.

Luanne moved nearer the edge of the roof. 'Tell them to get away from me, or we're going over,' she yelled.

A gust of wind made Georgia sway. Luanne had no shoes; all she had on was the towel. Alysha, in her pyjamas, huddled about a foot away from her, terrified.

One of the uniforms stepped forward and Georgia quickly ordered them all to stay back. They retreated to the stairs.

Stephanie moved across the roof and stood in the middle, leaning against the chimney stack. Georgia edged a little closer to the girls. The wind whipped around them, strong enough to knock any of them off balance.

Alysha and Luanne were now dangerously close to the edge.

'Talk to me, Luanne,' Georgia spoke over the gusting wind. 'Why have you joined Reilly's gang?'

Luanne reached out and pulled Alysha to her. Alysha shrieked. The tough, streetwise girl had disappeared, leaving in her place a frightened child.

'Come one step nearer and I'll jump and take her with me,' Luanne shouted.

'Don't!' she pleaded to Luanne. 'Please, Luanne.'

'Mince'll look after you,' Luanne shouted to Alysha. She released her hold on her sister and inched toward the edge of the roof.

'Luanne, please don't do anything silly!' Georgia had to shout very loudly over the noise of the wind.

'What is it they say?' Luanne said, her voice now trembling. 'Either you die from drugs or the Feds get you, but you never get out of this crumby estate. Well, I'm getting out.'

Forensics had run more tests on the gun and it was now found to be the one that had been used for an armed robbery – the armed robbery that had put Jason Young in Wandsworth. The gun hadn't surfaced until now; it looked as if Young had hidden it, and retrieved it when he got out.

Dawes decided to interview Jason Young.

Once Jason began to talk it was as if he couldn't stop. Yo-Yo had been his rival Elder on the estate, he said. Every time Jason landed a prison sentence, Yo-Yo took over his drug business, but when Jason came out his customers came back to him, because he was fair to them and didn't sell dodgy gear – something Yo-Yo was famous for.

Dawes's ears pricked up.

In prison this last time, Jason told him, he had heard about a girl who died from Yo-Yo's dodgy heroin. It turned out the girl's name was Philippa, and her older brother was a Fed.

Dawes felt as if he had been hit by a train.

'That girl . . .' Jason said to him, 'she got to me, man. Not because she was a Fed's sister but because of what had happened to her. Yo had fed her a bad hit, and killed her.' He shook his head. 'That started me thinking 'bout what I was doing. I wasn't up for killing innocent kids. That decided me I wasn't never gonna sell again. I talked to this probation officer, and I told him I didn't want no more to do with drugs and that. I told him about the dancing, and how it made me feel. That when I danced, I came alive and it was all different, I was in another world and I wanted to be there and not do any of the bad stuff any more. He got me this, what you call it, an audition for a dance school. The place was called the Sylvia Young Stage School. I told them I didn't have no money to pay for lessons, but I musta done good at that audition thing, cos they said I could have a scholarship, and that would pay for everything.'

'You know this for certain, do you?' Dawes put his hands on the table and gazed intensely into Jason's eyes. 'This is really important, Jason. Are you absolutely certain that Reilly fed dodgy heroin to this Philippa.'

Jason nodded. 'That's the word around the estate. But no one would ever say nothing. Everyone is frightened of him.'

'You know Luanne and Alysha are giving evidence against you.'

Jason shook his head. 'Even them, eh? Everyone's scared of him. I told you, he gave the word on Haley, and I know he killed my gran.'

'What about the gun? Tell me about the gun. We know it's the one you used in the armed robbery, the one you went down for.'

Jason's face told him he hadn't known that.

'The Feds never found that gun,' he said.

'So where was it? You must know what you did with it.'

He looked at the floor and shifted in his seat. 'I expect it stayed somewhere around the estate.'

'Jason, I need to know. Where did you hide it. Who could have found it?'

For a few moments Jason said nothing. Then, 'I buried it. See, that's what I don't understand. Only people who knew where it was were Chantelle and Luanne.' He shook his head. 'I asked Luanne to get me a gun when I heard what he'd done to them. She must have got that one, but she said—' He looked puzzled. 'What I can't work out is how Yo got it first and shot my gran with it.' He looked at Dawes. 'I've been fitted up, I swear, but he's fitted me up good.'

He rubbed his eyes and looked across the table. Dawes thought he had never seen such desolation in a suspect's eyes.

'I was up for it, you know,' Jason continued, his tone dull and lifeless. 'I was gonna help you put him away. But I couldn't even get that right. So I'm going down for a murder I didn't do, aren't I? He's got me well fitted up.' He put his head in his hands. 'And they'll get me in there for grassing.'

His voice trailed away as someone hammered on the door of the interview room. Dawes stood up and strode to open it.

'Peacock! What the f . . . ?'

'I'm sorry, sir.' The young DC didn't sound sorry at all; he sounded full of importance. 'There's been a development.'

Dawes returned to the table, recorded an Interview Suspended message, and hurried out into the corridor, closing the door carefully behind him. Hank quickly updated him on the situation with Luanne and Alysha.

Dawes went back into the interview room.

'Luanne's broken arm isn't a broken arm, it seems,' he told Jason. 'She was wearing the sling to hide her new tattoo.'

Jason looked puzzled.

'A Brotherhood of Blades gang induction tattoo.'

Jason's chin nearly hit the floor. 'Jesus. Now it fits,' he said. 'That's how Reilly made sure I got the blade that stabbed Haley. Alysha gave it to me. She's Mince Delahaye's Younger, and she said he gave it to her, and Luanne gave it to me. And I told you Luanne knew where I'd hidden the gun.' The desolation was back in his eyes. 'I thought of them as family.' His hands flew to cover his face, then he took them away and said quietly, 'Please don't tell me they had anything to do with Chantelle's murder.' He shook his head. 'Or my gran's.'

'I don't know,' Dawes said. 'What I do know is Luanne's on the roof of the Sparrow with Alysha, and she's threatening to jump. I've got to get over there. Will you come with me? Maybe help talk them down? We need her to tell us all this herself, if we're going to prove Stuart Reilly fitted you up.'

There was a pause. Jason shrugged. 'I'll try.'

'And when we do I'll make sure you get witness protection and a new identity.'

'And my scholarship?'

Dawes hesitated. That was hardly in his gift. Jason looked at him steadily.

He nodded. 'I'll do my best.'

What did they call it in the movies? Last Chance Saloon, that was it.

That's what this was, Jason thought. Climbing the fourteen

flights, he had never felt so wretched, so alone and let down. The only girl he ever wanted was dead before her life had begun; his gran was gone, murdered by the scum who now ran the place he used to call his home. Even Aunt Haley, who he'd hated because she nagged them all senseless: she was gone too, and now he saw that all she'd been trying to do was keep them from going wrong.

The Buzzards as well, all gone, mostly dead, just a couple still inside. And now Luanne and Alysha, who he had risked everything to protect, were members of the Brotherhood. That really hurt. He wanted to believe it was because they were afraid and desperate, but deep down he knew there was no one you could trust around here. It was every man for himself. Apart from Chantelle. He just hoped Luanne wasn't responsible for her murder, or for his gran's.

Whatever happened now, he had to do this last thing. He had to find out the truth, not for the Feds but so he could sleep at night. Maybe, just maybe, he'd still have a chance to move on and start his life again. Or maybe he'd end up inside. Or dead. He didn't know which, and at this minute he wasn't sure he cared any more.

Sparrow block had never been livelier than these past two days. It seemed like all the residents had forgotten how to sleep. People were standing around, some down on the ground, others on their balconies, determined to get a good view of the drama on the roof.

As he emerged on to the roof he saw the woman Fed, the dark-skinned one with the ponytail, by the big chimney. And that wind was really going it. Luanne was very close to the edge, too close for her comfort or his. She looked like she had just come out of the shower; her hair lay in damp strands around her shoulders, and just a towel wrapped round her body leaving her legs and shoulders bare. As he watched, a gust of wind buffeted her and she struggled to stay upright. Je-sus, he thought, anything could happen here. Alysha was sobbing, close to her and to the edge. One strong gust, he thought, and they would both go over.

'Luanne. What's going on?' he said trying to sound calm.
'Stay away!' Luanne shrieked.

He tried again. 'Hey Alysha! Can I come over there with you, babe?'

Alysha sobbed louder.

'What you doin'? It ain't safe up here, babe. Come over here, come over to me.'

'This is all your fault,' Luanne screamed at him. 'You shoulda never come back.'

Jason stretched our a hand to Alysha. 'You told me to come,' he reminded Luanne. 'You rang me and told me what happened to Chantelle. To all of you. I wanted to help you. Because I care about you. All of you.'

Luanne took another step.

He took a deep breath. This could all go up any second, and he had to find out what she knew. 'Was Chantelle one of Yo-Yo's gang too?' he shouted at her. 'Did Chantelle go over to the Brotherhood with you?'

'No.'

'Why Luanne, why d'you join them? Why that bastard?'

Luanne teetered as another gust of wind caught her. 'He helped us escape. He gave us stuff that made this stinking life bearable.'

'And he made you work to pay for it,' Jason shouted back. 'I wanted to take you away from here. I'm moving on. I've got a chance of a new life. I wanted you and Alysha to come too.'

'Dream on, boy.'

The wind whipped up and she fought to steady herself. Alysha yelped in terror.

'Alysha, come away from the edge.' Jason raised his voice and stretched out his hand. 'You too, Lu. There's nothing to be frightened of. It's over. They've got Yo-Yo.'

'Jason Young, the Buzzards boy, turned Fed grass,' Luanne yelled at him. 'No one trusts a grass.' She staggered, and Jason closed his eyes, unable to watch. When he opened them again she had steadied herself, but she was even closer to the edge than before. She was half-turned towards him.

'No one wants you around here no more. You're as unwelcome as the Feds,' she shouted. 'They'll get you for what you done.'

A fire engine roared into the estate and pulled up below Sparrow block. A team of fire officers descended from the truck and started unloading equipment.

'Give it up,' Luanne shouted down to them. 'There's only one way I'm coming down from here.'

Jason took the opportunity to get a step closer. 'Luanne, I need to know what happened to Chantelle,' he said. 'Did you hurt her? Please tell me the truth.'

'We didn't know she was gonna get a brain clot,' Alysha shouted defensively.

'Alysha, don't go there,' Luanne warned.

The warning fell on deaf ears. 'It was only a set-up,' Alysha continued, 'So Luanne could wear the bandage to cover her tattoo. Lu didn't mean her to be hurt that bad. They were only pretending to jump us. Lu was supposed to get a black eye and I was to make a run for it. Chantelle fought back.' Alysha's voice rose. 'She shouldn't have fought back. they hit her too hard. We were only . . .'

'Shut it!' Luanne yelled.

Jason took another step. 'My gran, Lysh, who shot my gran?'

An edge of hysteria had come into Alysha's voice. 'She had a big mouth. Lu didn't have no choice . . .'

'She wasn't supposed to die,' Luanne wailed. 'I didn't mean to kill any of them, Jason. I didn't.' She wailed again into the air. 'I didn't know Haley would die. I was only gonna stick her.'

Behind him, Jason was aware that the three detectives were creeping closer. He struggled to take in what the two girls had just told him, and stared as the woman Fed shouted, 'Luanne, did you kill them all?'

Luanne raised one bare foot and dangled it over the edge of the roof. Alysha shouted something incomprehensible and then screamed to Luanne. Luanne drew her foot back and put it on the roof.

'Did Reilly make you do it?' That was Dawes.

Luanne shook her head and faced outwards again.

'Don't, Luanne!' Jason pleaded. 'Think of Alysha.'

'I stabbed Aunt Haley. It was for my induction into the Brotherhood. But I didn't mean to kill her.'

'Were you there when she was raped?' he asked desperately. 'With the crowd that gang-raped her. Were you there?'

'Yup. I stuck her after that. But she wasn't supposed . . .'

'Did Yo-Yo Reilly tell you to?' Dawes shouted.

He wasn't helping. Jason wanted to tell him to shut up. A hot anger began to rise inside him.

'Let me get this right. You shot my gran? And you knew they were going to beat up Chantelle?' Jason felt his own anger bubbling.

Luanne inched forward.

'OK, Jason,' the woman Fed shouted. 'Cool it now. Luanne, we can talk about this.'

'Luanne, I need to know.' Jason fought down the anger, determined not to let it get the better of him. Bad things happened when he got riled.

He was only a few steps from Alysha now, and not much further from Luanne. The wind punched him sideways and lifted the edge of Luanne's towel. It seemed to be getting stronger. All three of them could end up over the edge, and it could happen any second.

He risked a glance over the edge at the ground. The fire brigade were rushing around, but he couldn't see what they were doing. Were they coming up, or putting something in place to give them a soft landing if they fell? And how long would it take?

Suddenly he was afraid and he knew he didn't want to die. He stretched out one hand to Alysha and the other to Luanne. 'Come away from the edge. Please.'

Luanne looked at him sadly. 'Don't feel sorry for me, Jase. I set you up. I killed your gran too, and Haley, but I swear I didn't mean for them to die.'

Suddenly Alysha stepped closer to Luanne and grabbed her hand.

'Let go, Alysha.' Jason heard the woman Fed echo his words.

Alysha ignored them, clinging to Luanne's wrist.

'What did Sals do wrong?' Jason asked, partly to distract Luanne.

'She told Yo-Yo she'd go to the Feds. He broke her fucking stall up, and she still wouldn't back down.' He was close enough to see her legs trembling. She was inches from the edge of the roof. 'I wasn't supposed to kill her. The bullet was just meant to graze her, give her a scare, you know?'

Out of the corner of his eye Jason saw movement at the other side of the roof. He turned his head slightly; two firemen had come to join the Feds. The woman put a finger to her lips to keep them quiet, and her arm out in front of her to keep them from moving any closer. She herself began to inch very slowly towards the three of them.

Jason was growing desperate, his anger swallowed up by fear now for all their lives. He reached Alysha and put out a hand. She took it, and he tugged her towards him. But Luanne didn't let go of her other hand.

'Let go of Alysha, Lu,' he shouted. 'And move away from the edge.'

'They told me to hit her in the shoulder.' Luanne was growing hysterical. 'But I killed her. I don't want to go to prison. I'd rather die.'

A shout came from behind them: Dawes. 'Who told you to hit her in the shoulder?'

The wind whipped up again and snatched Luanne's towel. She dropped Alysha's hand and tried to grab it. It danced almost like a kite in the wind, flapping and balancing, before tumbling over and over and heading for the ground. Luanne stood completely naked.

Jason looked behind him. The woman Fed was taking her coat off. 'Here, Luanne, take this.' She held it out and took a step closer. 'Don't catch hypothermia on top of everything else. Alysha needs you. You can explain everything to us.'

She took careful steps forward and held her coat out at arm's length.

'You stay away,' Luanne shouted at the Fed.

'Take my hand,' Jason pleaded stretching his arm to her.

'Stay back, Jason.'

Alysha started to panic and reached out for Luanne's hand again.

'Don't,' Jason shouted. 'Let go, Alysha!'

The female Fed took another step nearer.

The wind suddenly picked up, and everything seemed to

happen at once. Luanne pushed Alysha away. Alysha stumbled towards Jason and he caught her and shoved her towards the woman Fed.

There was a beat. He looked back at Luanne and Luanne looked at him and lifted her hand, and for that moment he thought she was going to take his. Then the wind rose again, and in the second it took him to regain his balance it was over. A desperate chorus of 'Luanne! No!' was followed by a moment's silence before the sickening thud as she hit the ground.

EIGHTEEN

Five days later, Georgia sat upright in the round-backed wooden armchair in Dawes's temporary office. Dawes himself was gathering papers and stacking files and his few personal belongings into a box.

Stephanie had perched herself on the side of the desk. A black file balanced precariously on her lap, and she was chewing a piece of gum. Georgia was familiar with the chewing gum phase; it was part of Steph's diet regime. The only thing that made her diet was being turned down by someone she had been trying to get into bed.

Georgia had wanted Stephanie to win their bet; she wanted to find out why Dawes had such a keen interest in the street gangs. Stephanie would have delivered too; the detective in her never switched off, no matter how good the sex was.

But it wasn't to be. They were in the gum chewing phase, which Georgia loathed. In a day or two she would find stale, concrete-hard gum-balls in her office and her car, as if they were bugged. But she was too conscious of Steph's bruised feelings to say anything. At least both car and office would be free of crumbs and chocolate wrappers for a while. Not that Stephanie's diets ever lasted more than a few days.

Dawes's briefcase and laptop lay open on the desk, and his jacket hung on the back of his chair, but everything else had been packed up. Georgia had seen the files as they went into the box; they were all named for a street gang: The Brotherhood, Big Cs, FDB, Buzzards, At Your Perils. There was a large stack of them; the problem was clearly growing.

Dawes checked a few last papers, deciding which ones to take and which to dump. He had already made it clear that he wasn't satisfied with the result, even though they had put the case to bed. He was incensed that no charges were being brought against Stuart Reilly, and Georgia couldn't really quarrel with that. Even though Luanne had admitted killing both Haley and Sally Young in front of witnesses, Reilly, they knew, was ultimately responsible.

'One of these days he'll trip up,' Stephanie said, as Dawes took a final glance inside the Brotherhood file. 'And when he does, we'll be there.' She gave him an encouraging smile and popped her gum. The broken bubble stuck to her top lip.

Dawes managed a small smile, but said nothing.

'We know he's behind everything that goes down on that estate,' Georgia assured him. 'We're not giving up.'

Dawes shrugged. 'My remit was to bring him in.'

'We did solve the case,' Georgia reasoned. 'Luanne Akhter killed both those women, she admitted it in front of witnesses. And there's the new DNA evidence too. So there's no doubting she did it.'

Dawes said nothing.

'We won't get an accessory charge to stick,' Georgia added. 'Reilly's brief would make mincemeat of us.'

'And no one will give evidence against him,' Stephanie added. 'Look what happened to Chantelle when she tried.'

'He raped a child of twelve,' Dawes snapped.

'Yes,' Georgia agreed. 'But there's no DNA, and Alysha swears she made it up to shock Jason.' Georgia ran a hand through her hair. 'End of, case closed.'

'For now,' Stephanie said. 'The DCI won't give it any more man hours for the time being. But Reilly's only off the hook temporarily; a hint of trouble and we'll be down on him like a ton of garbage.'

Dawes's computer whirred and flashed as it closed down. 'You can't blame me for not being thrilled,' he said. 'I was sent here because it was gang-related crime. And Chantelle Gulati's murder isn't really solved.'

Georgia was as disappointed as Dawes with the result, but she dared not show it. 'Alysha has given us a written statement. It says she recognized Sally Young at her door wearing a black balaclava, and it was Sals who attacked Chantelle. She reckons she heard Sally's voice accusing Chantelle of breaking her stall up, and getting Jason mixed up in crime again. Chantelle's supposed to have lured him on to the estate so he could get the blame for a murder he had nothing to do with.

According to Alysha, Sally called Chantelle a troublemaker, and hit her with a cricket bat.'

Stephanie pulled a sheet of paper from her file and handed it to her. Georgia read, '"Don't s'pose Sals meant her to die. These things happen around here; that's the way we live. Luanne got Sally back, anyway. She didn't mean her to die either, but she did, like Chantelle. It's what happens around here."'

'And you believe that?' Dawes looked at Georgia with sad eyes.

'Not a word. But we never found any DNA on the cricket bat to prove otherwise.'

Georgia was a little annoyed with herself for noticing how attractive Dawes's wide-set grey eyes were. Normally Stephanie's taste ran to anything in trousers, but this one had something. Even though he was stubborn, and driven, and difficult to work with. She couldn't remember noticing any man's eyes before. Sex was something that she needed every now and again, to ease her tension and her migraines. She enjoyed it, but she didn't allow anyone to get close. But not for the first time, she found herself wondering what Dawes would look like without clothes, and if he was a forceful or tender lover.

'The cricket bat that forensics found in the shed behind Sally Young's flat was covered in Chantelle's blood,' she said, giving herself a mental shake. 'But there were no prints, so that took us nowhere.'

Dawes threw the last bundle of papers into his case.

'Yes, of course the attack was Reilly's payback,' she added quickly. 'And no, Sally Young didn't kill Chantelle. But Alysha's the only one who can say for sure, and she's given us this load of rubbish. Sally Young is dead, so we can't question her. We have to go with the evidence we have, however misleading it is. The DCI won't give us any more time, so – case closed.'

'And Reilly's celebrating,' Dawes said dryly.

Poor bugger, Georgia thought; he wanted Reilly so badly, it was eating him away. 'We'll keep a watching brief, and I'll keep you informed,' was all she said.

'All this has made me mindful of how little time I spend with my kids,' Stephanie said, taking the chewing gum from her mouth, rolling it into a ball and flicking it across the room. The sticky gobbet hit the black metal bin Dawes had just emptied, and clung to the outside like a snail on a wet night. Stephanie was oblivious; she was busy undoing the silver foil from her next strip. The foil followed the dead ball of gum, but landed inside the bin.

'At least Jason Young got his new life,' she said, munching on the fresh gum. 'I'm glad for him.'

'As far as you can with his kind, I quite took to him,' Dawes said.

Stephanie smiled. 'Me too. He may have form as long as my arm, but with no parents, no stability, what chance has he had?'

'There speaks a mum,' Georgia said lightly, watching the eye contact between Dawes and Stephanie.

'Oh, Young isn't fundamentally bad. Reilly is, though, and I think I hate him more for what he tried to do to Jason.'

'You do think like a mother,' Georgia teased. She looked across at Dawes for support. 'We cynical singles just see Young's scholarship as a small hope that it'll keep him out of the overcrowded prison system for a year or two.'

'Is that all sorted? Jason Young's change of identity?' Dawes asked Stephanie.

Stephanie nodded. 'He is now officially Laurence Dunning. He starts life as a scholarship student at Sylvia Young's Dance Academy in two weeks.'

'And we'll be keeping tabs on him too,' Georgia added.

Stephanie's gum cracked. The sound was as sharp as a cap in a child's gun. Georgia could feel one of her migraines brewing.

'I'll be surprised if he sees the inside of a cell again,' Stephanie said. 'He so nearly lost his chance, and he knows it. I think he'll give it a good shot.' She turned to Georgia. 'Every kid deserves a chance. You must agree with that.'

Georgia felt her insides turn, and a familiar sense of burning in her heart. Thanks to the sex predator that damp, dark evening on Clapham Common, she had been denied the chance to mother her own child. That was the reason she had joined the force in the first place – to do her bit to stop other impressionable fifteen-year-olds having their life stolen by someone who would never know the pain he caused. She wanted more from the force now though: these days she wanted to see justice done for all victims. But that was where it began, and the young ones still struck a particular chord with her.

'It's Alysha that worries me,' she said. 'She's obviously lying about having sex with Reilly. She's kept him out of jail, and she has no idea what a big mistake that is. We can't even get her into care because her father is still around. He's a drunk, and hardly ever there, but Social Services won't intervene. What kind of future does she have?'

'She'll survive,' Dawes said. He looked away. 'It's not our concern anyway, that's not what we do. Our job is to uphold the law. Social work is someone else's job.'

Georgia and Stephanie exchanged a long glance.

'With all due respect, sir,' Stephanie said, 'you've made it very clear where you stood from the first moment on this case – how much you wanted Reilly. And now you're not happy because we didn't put him away, even though we got a result. If that's not personal, I don't know what is.'

Dawes face reddened. 'Stuart Reilly thinks he's above the law,' he snapped. 'Reilly ordered Luanne Akhter to kill two women, as an initiation into his Brotherhood gang. That makes him responsible for murder, and he's walked free.'

Georgia sighed heavily. 'We're going round in circles here.'

'He runs the gang, so he says who joins it.' Dawes lifted a hand. 'OK, we can't prove it. But there's a verbal statement from Luanne, and the tattoo to back it up. It should be worth pursuing him just for that.'

'Not a chance.' Georgia shook her head. 'It wouldn't even get to court. His bent brief would claim she had the tattoo done herself, and Reilly knew nothing about it.'

'But we know different!'

The file on Stephanie's lap slid to the floor, and papers spilled everywhere. Georgia bent to help her gather them up. 'Knowing and proving are two different things,' she said.

'Without some hard evidence, the DCI won't let us take it any further.'

Dawes picked up the file. 'You better believe I want that bastard,' he said handing it back to Stephanie.

'You'll have to get past his bent brief then.'

'You know what?' Stephanie pushed her bottom back on to the edge of the desk. 'Something tells me there's more going on here than we're seeing.'

There was a second's silence, then Dawes said, 'He gives naive young girls drugs and puts them on the streets.'

'Plenty of drug pushers do that, and a lot of girls go wrong as a result,' Georgia agreed.

'Jason Young did it too,' Stephanie pointed out. 'OK, he regrets it now, but in a way, you can't blame him. They grow up on those estates, with no one to teach them right from wrong. Maybe we should be addressing that. The crime's just the result, not the cause.'

'But Reilly didn't grow up on an estate,' Dawes told her. 'He lies about that too. He had two parents – a normal family. He's a bully, plain and simple. You've seen what he's like with his animals.' He clenched his fist, and his face began to flush again. 'The serious crime unit want him behind bars, and I was brought on to this case to help to make that happen.' He paused. 'And I've failed. I've studied him for years. I really thought I had him this time. He killed his own mother, did you know that?'

Both shook their heads.

'But no one can prove it.' Dawes looked at Stephanie. 'You're right. It is personal. I want him more than I've ever wanted anyone. How much do you know about me?'

'Enough,' Georgia said. 'I know your father was a top dog at Scotland Yard.'

Stephanie looked at her in surprise. Normally they shared what they knew. She hadn't passed this on because the DCI had only told her this morning, with a warning that it wasn't for station gossip.

'But nothing about my sister?' he asked.

'No.'

'She was a model. Talented and beautiful,' he said quietly.

'She became addicted to drugs, and was put on the game to pay her debts to her dealer. We got her into rehab, and it worked for a while, but she went back on the stuff, and back on the game.' He turned away and looked unseeingly at the window. 'She died of an overdose of dodgy heroin.' He spoke as if each syllable brought acid with it. His jaw worked, and he paused for a beat before adding, 'I know she got it from Reilly, but I can't prove it.'

His voice was clear and controlled. 'So yes, it's personal. I won't rest until he's rotting somewhere very unpleasant.'

Georgia swallowed a lump in her own throat, surprised at how emotional she felt. Normally she allowed nothing to get to her, but suddenly she could smell the dirt and feel the pain from all those years ago. When the memory of that ordeal caught her unawares, she could taste the vomit as if it had happened yesterday.

She understood only too well how Dawes felt. In a way, every crime was personal when someone lurked like that, deep in your subconscious. She wouldn't recognize her attacker's face, but she'd know his voice, and certainly she would always know the smell of stale sweat and rancid fat and garlic; and she could never forget the taste of the filthy leaves and earth against her face. She liked to think he had died an agonizing death, but she would never know for sure. If he was alive, she hoped he would be in jail for the rest of his days.

But that was her secret. She would never speak of it to anyone; it was personal. It took Dawes a lot of courage to speak of his own pain, and she deeply sympathized. But she dared not show it.

'We will get him,' she said quietly. 'Be patient.'

'I've been patient for too long.'

'I'll be watching every move he makes. The slightest hint that we've got something and I'll be on the phone. That's a promise.'

'Thank you.'

Stephanie slipped off the desk. 'Keep in touch. That's my mobile on there.' She handed him her card.

Georgia caught Stephanie's eye and twinkled at her. She knew Stephanie better than she knew herself sometimes, and

Stephanie so wanted to bed David Dawes. She would look forward to the gossip.

Right now Georgia was more concerned for Alysha Akhter. The girl was only twelve, she had been raped, and her sister had just killed herself. Alysha was alone. How would she cope? Social Services wouldn't take her case up. Dawes's words echoed in her ear: *Our job is to uphold the law. Social work is someone else's job.*

Georgia hoped with all her heart that *someone else* would make Alysha their job.

Only time would tell.